LAST OF THE RAVAGERS

BRYAN SMITH

DEATH'S HEAD PRESS

an imprint of Dead Sky Publishing, LLC
Miami Beach, Florida
www.deadskypublishing.com

ISBN: 978-1-63951-077-1

First Edition

Cover Art: Justin T. Coons

The "Splatter Western" logo designed
by K. Trap Jones

Book Layout: Lori Michelle
www.TheAuthorsAlley.com

This one's for my late father, Lonnie L. Smith, who had another book dedicated to him way back at the beginning of my career.

Still miss you after all these years, Dad.

ONE

ON A LONELY night in the Arizona desert, face turned toward the sky, a man could sometimes start to feel as if he were a solitary traveler of the cosmos, standing at the edge of the universe and staring into the depths of infinity. Or like he was the only living soul left in the world. The desert, however, was alive with all sorts of things. Silent, slithering, nasty things, invisible in the darkness. Venomous pests and predators.

Gnawing on the sodden end of a stogie, Russ Harper crushed a scorpion with the heel of his boot, grinding it into the dry desert soil. As the scorpion was expiring, somewhere out there in the dark landscape a pack of coyotes started yipping and yowling at each other. Russ looked up and scanned the jagged top of the rocky outcropping near where he'd pitched camp for the night, watching for any tell-tale glint of moonlight in the eyes of hungry predators.

In his experience, coyotes weren't much to worry about for two-legged types such as himself. They tended to shy away from people in general, but he'd heard tell of the occasional vicious exception. It mostly only happened when a large and hungry pack was driven to the edge of desperation due to a scarcity of food in their territory. A big pack like that just might collectively work up the nerve to overcome the species' natural timidity around human beings, particularly when the human in question was traveling alone.

1

Like Russ was tonight.

Well, alone, if you didn't count the unfortunate fella wrapped up in burlap and strapped to a travois over by his horse. The man was an outlaw named Beauregard Conklin. Beauregard was more commonly known as "Bo" or "Boom Boom". The latter nickname derived from the sound his pistols made. He'd worn a Colt revolver on each hip and was known for his penchant for drawing and firing both at the same time, often in a showy way. For years Bo was the notorious leader of an elusive gang of bandits who committed robberies all over Arizona and Nevada. The gang was considered invincible and beyond the reach of the law for the better part of a decade, but all good things must eventually come to an end.

For Bo's gang, the end came in the form of a midnight raid on their camp by a sneaky group of hatchet-wielding redskins. Most of his men died in their sleep, their skulls cleaved open by the flashing blades. Few had any real opportunity to defend themselves. Bo was the only one to escape with his life. He wasn't heard from for a while thereafter, but eventually reemerged as a solo operator, once again robbing banks and the occasional stagecoach, albeit not quite as successfully as before. Leads on his general whereabouts and a possible home base emerged. People started saying it was only a matter of time until someone finally caught up with him.

That someone eventually turned out to be Russ Harper, and now big, bad "Boom Boom" Conklin was just an odiferous carcass with a bullet hole in the middle of his forehead. A $2,000 payday awaited Russ upon delivering the corpse to the head lawman in a town called Snakebite, a thing he hoped to accomplish within a couple hours of sunup tomorrow. Barring any unforeseen setbacks, that is, such as being set upon by a pack of ravenous beasts.

As best he could tell, however, there were no predatory creatures slinking about along the top of the outcropping.

LAST OF THE RAVAGERS

Moreover, his concerns regarding any potential danger began to abate the longer he listened to the song of the coyotes. They weren't quite as close as he'd initially imagined. The vast, wide-open desert could play tricks on a man's hearing, a phenomenon he'd encountered often in his travels. He also no longer perceived any degree of danger or lethal intent in the sound. The animals were talking to each other, laughing in their beastly way and having a grand old time in the middle of the night, like a bunch of rowdy ranch hands blowing off steam at the saloon after a long day.

Russ grunted as he took the sodden stump of the stogie from his mouth and flicked it into the campfire. "Have fun, fellas. Reckon it's time I hit the hay."

He would sleep close to the fire and not just to ward off the cool temperatures of the desert at night. The heat from the well-stoked flames would also serve to discourage encroachment by most of the landscape's creeping, slithering creatures. The horse would alert him to approach by larger things. Bedelia was well-trained in that regard and just about as reliable as any two-legged sentry.

Taking his heel off the crushed scorpion, Russ got as close to the fire as he could comfortably tolerate and stretched out beside it, lying flat on his back with his head resting on his bedroll. He opened a well-worn copy of Mary Shelley's *Frankenstein* and began to read by the light of the fire. This was his fourth time reading the book, which he'd pilfered from the belongings of an earlier quarry, another man who, like Bo Conklin, no longer had use of material possessions.

The book was an old favorite, but the actual reason for the repeated readings was more a product of carrying only a few volumes with him at any given time. Traveling light was a necessity when one's work involved the frequent transport of corpses. *Melmoth the Wanderer, Uncle Silas,* and *Varney the Vampire* were the only other tomes currently among his possessions. He liked dark and lurid stories because they spoke to truths about the world he rarely encountered in other forms of literature.

He'd read about ten pages and was getting droopy-eyed when he heard the strange sound from the vicinity of the outcropping. Sitting up with a start, he turned his head in that direction and squinted into the inky darkness. His heart was thudding because the sound was unlike anything he'd ever heard. There'd been a distinctly *unnatural* quality to it, an otherworldliness that unsettled him on a primal level. Despite the heat from the fire, his arms and legs became pebbled with gooseflesh.

Getting to his feet, he hurried over to Bedelia and withdrew his repeating rifle from its saddle scabbard. Turning again toward the outcropping, he took several steps in that direction and once again scanned the jagged tops of the rocks. Though he still saw nothing moving about up there, he was nowhere near ready to relax. The outcropping was some thirty feet distant, just far enough away in the dark that he might easily miss seeing something crouching at the edge of those rocks, particularly if the fur or hide of the creature was as dark as the desert night.

After staring at the top of the outcropping for several additional tense moments, Russ swallowed a lump in his throat and let out a breath. The strange and unsettling sound had not repeated in all the time he'd been standing there. He was just starting to relax when he was taken aback by a belated realization.

The coyotes were no longer singing.

The entire desert, in fact, seemed to have gone deathly silent and an unsettling stillness had overtaken the entire landscape. If not for the sound of his own rapid breathing, he might've believed time itself had become frozen. A wild idea, perhaps, but in those disquieting moments any crazy thing seemed possible. He was barely conscious of his grip

LAST OF THE RAVAGERS

on the rifle tightening, and when he became aware of it, he made his fingers relax. It was possible whatever had made that strange noise had moved on already. An accidental big boom might bring it back in this direction.

Some more silent moments elapsed.

Then Bedelia whinnied softly behind him.

Russ let out another big breath and nodded.

Yeah, girl. I think it's gone, too.

He yelped in sudden fright upon hearing a loud scream of pain from somewhere out in the darkness. The sound went on and on and it took another couple moments to realize it wasn't a human sound. This was one of the coyotes that'd been yipping and singing a short while ago. Its high-pitched whimpers now sang a song of purest agony The sound set Russ's teeth on edge and he was grateful when it came to an abrupt end seconds later. He was no fan of coyotes, but the sound of the animal's suffering was a terrible thing.

Something dangerous was out there in the night. Some deadly creature. A thing capable of moving about with uncommon stealth and cunning. The only logical move at this point was to hurriedly pack up camp and move on as fast as possible. He wouldn't feel safe until he'd put many a mile between himself and that unholy beast, whatever it was. He was tired as hell after a long day's trek across the desert, but sleep would have to wait.

Before he could put this plan in motion, the strange sound that'd snapped him out of his doze came again. Hearing it with a clarity unfettered by grogginess rendered it even more deeply unnerving. There was a grinding quality to it with an undertone of ululation. His initial impression of otherworldliness was enhanced immensely by this second exposure to the noise. It made his innards clench and his nuts shrivel to about half their normal size. Russ considered himself as tough as any man, but this sound unmanned him in ways no human adversary ever could.

The sound came yet again, much closer this time. His gaze went again to the top of the outcropping and this time he saw something, the outline of a dark shape crouching at the top of the highest of the jagged stones. Though he couldn't fully discern its shape and appearance in the inky blackness, he could tell the thing was smaller than he'd expected. It was short and squat, with a thick body and a large, wide head. While Russ stared at it, the thing opened its mouth and made that dreadful sound again.

Behind him, Bedelia whinnied and bucked.

Time to run, Russ. Right goddamn now.

Russ wasn't inclined to disagree.

More of the short, stout shapes began to appear at the edge of the outcropping. That grinding, ululating noise started up again, but this time it was a chorus of otherworldly gnashing and chittering rather than a single unsettling voice. The sound had him close to peeing his pants, making him feel more like a meek and sickly child than a man. Its alien quality made his guts curdle. A few of the diminutive shapes teetered precariously at the edge of the rocks, rocking back and forth a few seconds before dropping to the ground. As soon as they hit the ground, they bounced back to their feet and began rapidly waddling their way toward the campsite.

Bedelia whinnied loudly again, clearly on the verge of terrified flight. Russ hesitated a final moment longer, torn between flight and an urge to start firing at the strangle little beasts. The decision was made for him when he glanced back and saw the burlap-wrapped corpse begin to struggle against its bonds on the travois. It was sitting halfway up and making inarticulate sounds of rage as it clumsily attempted to tear its way out of the burlap. The bounty hunter's first thought upon seeing this inexplicable thing was that perhaps he'd only wounded Conklin instead of killing him. This possibility was the most obvious and logical explanation for the man's unexpected revival, for the simple reason that expired corpses were not in the habit of returning to life under ordinary circumstances. At least not in his experience.

The only problem with the logical explanation in this case was he knew it wasn't true. He'd put a bullet through the man's forehead. A good bit of Conklin's brains had leaked out of the exit wound at the back of his head. The man was deader than the proverbial doornail and stinkier than a cow pasture at high noon on a hot summer's day.

Except now he wasn't dead anymore. Somehow.

That settled it.

No way was Russ sticking around to deal with any of this madness.

He looked around again just as one of the strange creatures launched itself into the air from ten feet away. He raised the rifle and fired. Whether he hit the thing or not, he didn't know, because by then he was running.

Dropping the rifle, he vaulted himself up into Bedelia's saddle. As soon as his butt hit leather, she was off and running, galloping at high speed into the cool desert evening. There'd been no time to lash the travois to Bedelia, but this was of minor importance in the larger scheme of things. He'd lost his rifle, too. And the book. And his bedroll. All these things could be replaced. The lost income could be made up. But he only had one life and he'd been damn lucky to escape with that.

Bedelia didn't slow down for at least an hour.

The same could be said for the manic beating of Russ Harper's heart.

TWO

NOT MUCH EXCITING ever happened in Snakebite. It was a little town smack in the middle of the Arizona desert and many miles away from any other significant population center. Most new folks who wandered into town were only passing through on their way to somewhere bigger and more interesting.

After serving as Sheriff in Snakebite for going on a decade, Ned Kilmister sometimes wondered if he should pull up stakes and start over again in some new place. Either back east where he was from or some closer rowdy city like Galveston or Frisco. The notion was not without allure, especially when some pants-pissing drunk was loudly belting out raunchy saloon songs in between puking into a holding cell bucket, as was happening right now.

Riley McKay was the temporarily incarcerated man, and though it was daylight now and several hours had passed since Ned had conked him over the head and dragged him off to jail, he still sounded far from sober. Riley was a former volunteer soldier in the defeated army of the South. Though the war was more than a decade in the past, it was still a fresh wound in the minds of many. Riley was an outwardly cheery and gregarious sort in the early stages of his nightly drunkenness, but he was prone to becoming a bitter and violent malcontent as he got deeper into his cups. Such was the case once again last night. Riley became belligerent and started waving his gun around after debating a few of the usual points of contention regarding the war with some of the other regulars at the Last Chance Saloon. He fired off two rounds and was damn lucky neither had found flesh to perforate, otherwise he'd be facing some serious consequences. Being drunk as a skunk might fly as an excuse for all sorts of questionable behaviors, but not for murder.

Ned yelled at Riley to shut his damn fool mouth as his off-key warbling reached an ear-piercing volume. The prisoner ceased singing and started cackling like a madman. This was followed by a rude comment about Ned's mother, implying she was of loose character. All Ned could do was shake his head and sigh. The damn drunk couldn't possibly know itnless he'd spent time in Baltimore at some point, which seemed unlikely—but his description of Martha Kilmister wasn't far off the mark.

Ned took his pipe from his mouth and exhaled a stream of fragrant smoke, staring at the ceiling as he sat kicked back in his chair with his booted feet propped up on a corner of his desk. He was in a reflective mood as he returned the pipe to a corner of his mouth. Sure, things could get a tad dull in Snakebite, almost painfully so at times, but when you got right down to it, he preferred it that way. Life as a lawman was better when it was boring as opposed to filled with violence, noise, and chaos.

From somewhere outside Ned's office, the usual placid quiet of morning time in Snakebite was disrupted by a burst of hollering. Ned's pipe slipped from his mouth and dropped to the floor as he jumped in his chair. He just managed not to fall out of the chair, which would've been embarrassing. Because the holding cells were out of view in back, no one would've seen it happen, but *he* would know and that would've been bad enough. A man charged with upholding the law and ensuring the safety of the citizenry of his town shouldn't be so easily startled.

Riley ceased his drunken caterwauling and said, "What in tarnation is that racket?"

Ned retrieved his pipe from the floor and set it on his desk. "Damned if I know, but I mean to find out."

He got up and went to one of two windows that looked out on the street. The hollering was getting louder by the moment, but the source of the ruckus wasn't immediately obvious. A few people were standing out there in the dusty main street with their heads turned in a westerly direction. Ned looked that way and saw nothing out of the ordinary, at least not yet, but the sound did seem to be coming from that way. A few seconds later, he perceived another sound beneath the hollering—the full-tilt gallop of what sounded like a runaway horse.

THREE

DOWN IN THE cellar underneath the Last Chance Saloon, a woman lying flat on her back on a long wooden table was clinging to life. Standing over her was a man named Albert Richardson, though no one ever called him by his given name. Because he was the only man in Snakebite operating anything resembling a professional medical practice, townsfolk only ever referred to him as "Doc".

Doc Richardson maintained an office in a small two-storey building directly across the street from the saloon. His medical practice occupied the upstairs level while Eddie Horton operated a barbershop downstairs. Proximity to the saloon meant Richardson spent a lot of time treating injuries incurred during the drunken brawls that broke out there a few times a week. He wasn't rich by any means, but the preponderance of drunken dunces in the area ensured a comfortable living.

The woman on the table did not have the kind of injuries he was accustomed to treating. Nothing that could be handled with a few sutures or a simple bandage. She was missing her right arm, from just above the elbow. It had not been removed with an axe or other sharp, heavy blade. The stump was a ragged and knobby mass of charred meat, the result of a torch being applied to the bloody flesh for cauterization purposes. That was the work of Quentin Brown, proprietor of the Last Chance. Had he not taken that step, there was every chance the woman would've died within a few minutes from blood loss. Given the extent of the woman's horrid injuries, Richardson wasn't so sure that wouldn't have been for the best.

"What do you think, Doc? Can you save her?"

Quentin stood on the opposite side of the table, his rugged features twisted in an expression of deep distress. In the weak light from the gas lamp hanging directly over the table, the ridges of his forehead looked like deep canyons. His red-rimmed eyes looked on the verge of popping out of their sockets, another indicator of the intensity of his concern.

The real answer to the man's question was, *Not goddamn likely*.

Instead of telling him that, Richardson scratched his bearded chin in a thoughtful way. "Well, the lady's in rough shape. Really rough." *There's the understatement of the damn century.* "Did anyone get a look at her assailant?"

Quentin gave Richardson a puzzled look. "Assailant? Do you think a man did this?"

The doctor made a clicking sound in his throat and shook his head ruefully as he glanced again at the quivering woman's supine form. A bloody blanket folded in half covered the midsection of her body, but she was nude beneath it. Despite the extensive damage done to her flesh, on a secondary level the doctor could not help but be entranced by the sight of her long, bare legs and slender shoulders. This was obscenely inappropriate, a fact he was completely cognizant of, but he was simply unable to help himself. Not for reasons rooted in perversion, of course. Well, not *entirely*. The real reason for his fixation on her physical attributes was his own past intimacies with the woman.

He sighed. "A man? I suspect not. I suppose it's just barely possible a person possessed of unusual strength, someone like a circus strongman, could tear off a young woman's arm in a manner similar to what we see here. However, that person would have to be in a state of extreme derangement and agitation. Even then, I'd characterize it as extremely unlikely." He took a deep breath and hesitated a moment before getting to the next point. Then he swept the bloody blanket away from the woman's midsection. "There is also the matter of the wounds we see here. I can imagine no scenario in which a man might have inflicted insults to the flesh similar to these."

Quentin gasped and bit down on the knuckles of his right fist.

Richardson nodded. "Yes. Quite gruesome, I agree."

Four ragged gashes arced diagonally across the woman's flat abdomen. The wounds weren't deep, but the adjacent flesh looked sickly, tinged with a strange greenish hue that was hot to the touch. A sign of incipient infection, no doubt.

"These are the claw marks of some filthy beast," Richardson said, gesturing at the puckered wounds with a disgusted flick of his hand. "Without doubt, they are *not* the clean slices of a blade, not even a rusty one." He tipped up his hat and dabbed at his sweaty forehead with an already damp handkerchief. "What we're dealing with here is a creature of an exceedingly fearsome nature. Something that wandered in from the desert late last night, perhaps. Whatever it was, this was almost certainly a rare foray into a populous area. It's unlikely to happen again. Let us hope, at any rate."

The way Richardson saw things, hunting the rogue beast down and killing it was the best way of preventing additional maulings of Snakebite citizens. He was on the verge of saying so when someone came clattering rapidly down the stairs into the cellar. A scrawny young man employed by Quentin on a part-time basis arrived breathing heavily, his bulging eyes reflecting some unknown source of excitement and apprehension.

Brown turned a scowling look in the young man's direction. "Well, out with it, Cole. What's got you all fired up?"

Cole swallowed with some difficulty, his visible Adam's apple looking for a moment as if it might push all the way through the flesh of his long neck. "Commotion out in the street. Fella rode into town hanging half off his horse. Started raving about monsters in the desert. Bunch of crazy talk."

Brown tilted his head. "Monsters in the desert, you say?"

Cole nodded. "Yessir. The Sheriff's out there now, trying to get the man to talk sense."

Quentin Brown and Richardson exchanged a meaningful glance. The doctor could tell they were thinking along the same lines.

Brown raised an eyebrow. "Want to go talk to this man?" He directed a quick glance at the saloon girl, Angelina, who was still unconscious. "Could be relevant to what we're dealing with here."

Richardson nodded. "You go on. I'll be up momentarily. I need to finish my examination of the young lady."

Brown gave him an odd look, but shrugged and followed Cole out of the cellar.

When he was sure they were gone, Richardson let out a breath and licked his dry lips. He placed a shaky hand on an unmarred section of Angelina's abdomen and let out a low groan. After a moment, he moved the hand up to one of her breasts and cupped it, massaging the nipple with his thumb. He continued doing this a few more moments before reaching into his pants with his other hand. After the inevitable happened, he cleaned himself off with his handkerchief and put his hands to a different use. He cupped one over her mouth and with the thumb and forefinger of his other hand, he pinched shut her nostrils.

LAST OF THE RAVAGERS

It occurred to him he never directly answered the saloon keeper's question.

Angelina could not be saved.

And there was no point in prolonging her misery.

When it was finished, he covered her still form with the blanket again and walked up the stairs out of the cellar to see what the hubbub was about.

FOUR

RUSS HARPER WAS at the brink of total physical exhaustion as a galloping Bedelia carried him into Snakebite a short while after sunrise. While still out in the desert, his trusty steed had slowed to an almost lazy trot, saving up energy after pushing onward for so many miles without proper rest, but she put on a burst of impressive speed for the final desperate stretch toward town.

When they arrived, Russ was sagging in the saddle and holding on to the pommel for dear life. Upon seeing people moving about in the streets, he sat up straighter, drew hot air into his lungs, and started hollering about the strange things he'd seen. The town wasn't a big one and it wasn't long before he found his way to the main commerce street, where even more people eyed him warily as he continued hollering. The confusion on their faces wasn't hard to fathom. He realized he must sound like a gibbering madman, almost insensible. He focused for a moment on the sound of his own voice and realized even he had little sense of what he was trying to communicate by that point.

Bedelia again slowed to a trot and finally stopped as a man with a tin star pinned to his black vest walked out into the middle of the street and held up a hand, palm thrust outward. "Whoa there. Hold up and talk to me, fella. I know you, don't I?" A light seemed to dawn in his eyes as he snapped his fingers and pointed at him. "Yeah, I do.

LAST OF THE RAVAGERS

You're Russ Harper, a bounty hunter. What's all the fuss about?"

Looking down at the man, Russ swayed slightly in the saddle and felt a sense of strange surreality envelop him. He shook his head and began to list to one side again. "I'll tell you what the fuss is about, Ned Kilmister. I ran into monsters . . . out in the desert . . . " His left foot slipped free of the stirrup on that side. "Weird little things, but scary . . . and . . . strong . . . "

Someone in the street shouted, "Whoopsie daisy!"

Russ finally slid all the way out of the saddle and hit ground. The world went black for a short time.

When he came to again, someone was slapping his face and yelling at him to snap out of it. He mumbled something indecipherable as a return to consciousness stalled, his eyes remaining shut. They stayed that way until someone tossed water in his face. He gasped and abruptly sat upright, spluttering angrily and swiping moisture from his eyes. He blinked rapidly several times as the faces of several people crowded around him began to blurrily come into focus. They were watching him with a mixture of concern and morbid curiosity. As his vision sharpened, he realized one of the faces belonged to Ned Kilmister.

Russ cleared his throat. "Could one of you fellas get me a goddamn drink, please?"

A quick look around told him he was in the Last Chance Saloon. He'd been here before. Lots of times. The place wasn't quite what you could call fancy, but it was nicer than many of the shitholes masquerading as proper saloons in this part of the Arizona territory. Saloon whores, some even close to tolerably pretty, were employed here. There was a second floor with some rooms where the professional ladies conducted business with their gentleman customers. Also up there were a few rooms available to rent on an overnight basis. These rooms were more expensive than those at the only hotel in town, but that was because a man paying to spend the night at the Last Chance was more often than not also paying for the company of one of those tolerably pretty ladies.

Ned glanced at Quentin Brown, proprietor of the saloon. "You heard the man. Get him a drink."

Russ sat up straighter in his chair. "And don't give me any rotgut. I need a proper restorative. Your best goddamn bourbon."

Ned dug a coin out of a pocket and flipped it at the barkeep, who caught it smoothly in midair with the practiced precision of a professional drink slinger. "Coming right up."

As he watched Quentin mosey off toward the bar, Russ became more aware of the inherent awkwardness of his current perch at the edge of a rickety table. The cloying proximity of the people crowded around him and the strange way they were all looking at him made him feel uncomfortable. He was reminded of the human vultures who always came out to gawk at a public hanging. Come to think of it, in a town like Snakebite, odds were good every man in this room had witnessed more than his fair share of hangings. Though he was no outlaw and therefore in no immediate danger of having a noose draped around his neck, the perception made his skin crawl.

He heaved himself off the table and felt a small measure of relief as the welcoming committee backed off some. After taking a moment to slap trail dust off his clothes, he threaded his way through the gawkers and plopped himself down on one of the stools at the bar, where a glass of whiskey awaited him. He grabbed the glass and tossed back its contents in a single big gulp. Thumping the glass down on the bartop, he nodded at the barkeep and said, "Hit me again."

Quentin Brown filled the glass a second time and set the bottle down within easy grabbing distance.

Russ brought the glass to his lips again, but this time

he hesitated, brow furrowing as he thought of something. Lowering the glass, he turned toward the sheriff. "Where's my horse? She hitched up outside?"

He was seized with sudden panic at the thought of Bedelia wandering off or being stolen, a prospect that briefly had him on the edge of vaulting himself off the barstool and racing outside to check on her. Surely somewhere amongst this group of men was someone honorable enough to hitch his steed to a post outside the saloon.

Ned Kilmister held up a hand in a calming gesture. "Taken care of, friend. Your horse is at the stables down the street. I can vouch for the man who runs the place. Gary Brooks. He'll take good care of her. From the looks of her, she could use a good, long rest."

The man had a point.

Russ acknowledged this with a sigh and a nod. Some of the tension drained out of him as he settled back on the stool and again lifted the whiskey glass to his lips. He drained the glass again but this time did not immediately refill it.

The sheriff cleared his throat. "Now that we've addressed some of your immediate needs, I've got some questions for you, Russ. You mind explaining that business about monsters you were yammering about before your swoon?"

Russ grimaced, but nodded again. "I reckon you all interpreted my words as the ravings of a man delirious from too many hours of hard riding in the desert. That I only imagined seeing monsters." Now he did fill his whiskey glass again. This time he sipped from it rather than knocking it back. He sighed. "Somewhere way out west, in the middle of the night, I had an encounter with the macabre. With monsters and a resurrected dead man."

The men in the saloon crowded closer again, eager to hear his tale.

Russ drank whiskey.

And told them all of it.

FIVE

A LOUD SHRIEK from outside caused a half-clad Tom McKinley to spring out of his bed and go to one of the bedroom's two windows. The window looked out on the area behind the family home. He peeled back a curtain flap and looked outside, squinting against the bright sunlight. The shriek came again, louder and shriller this time, and for a moment he was gripped by a sense of stomach-churning dread. It'd been a good while since native savages last raided any of the outlying properties near Snakebite. The last time it happened, years ago at this point, the natives paid a heavy retaliatory price, losing many of their clan in a vicious daytime assault led by U.S. cavalry forces.

Since that time, the people of Snakebite lived under an assumption of relative safety, confident the natives would never encroach again after that act of brutal and unforgiving retribution Still, the fear of a reprise of those bloody times always lurked at the back of Tom's mind. He was a more prudent man than most and possessed a healthy dose of fatalism. Not enough to turn him into the kind of morose drunk who drowned his sorrows in a saloon every night, but enough to keep him wary and on his toes, ready to respond to threats decisively.

Turning his head this way and that, he was initially unable to identify the source of the shrieks. The door to the barn was standing open, which wasn't unusual on days when the kids weren't at school. Like today. For the kids, Saturday morning was a time for tending to their chores, but Tom was no slave-driver on that count. The kids were allowed to work at their own pace. He would frequently hear them cutting up and having fun, running around and laughing, sometimes yelling at each other. He was reasonably certain the shrieks he'd heard stemmed from similar antics and were nothing to truly worry about—and yet that sense of gut-tightening apprehension wasn't quite ready to let go of him. He'd feel a lot better if one or more of the kids would come running into view, swinging sticks at each other, the way they often did when pretending to be medieval knights engaged in sword fights.

Some more moments passed.

The shrieks he'd heard were not repeated.

A gun belt was laid out across the top of the chest of drawers to his right. Ensconced in the holster was a fully-loaded revolver. For a moment, he considered taking the weapon from the holster and heading outside for a quick look around. He was on the verge of sliding the Colt out of its holster when Eleanor called out to him from the bed.

"Come on, honey, the kids are just playing. Come here and tend to me."

Tom turned away from the window and took in the tempting sight of his wife sprawled out naked on the bed. She had a lush mane of curly blonde hair, much of which was currently gathered in pigtails hanging over her shoulders. Not wearing a scrap of clothing, she sat with her back up against the headboard and her legs spread wide. She regarded him with a look of wanton lust as she manipulated her sex with her fingers. Her state of obvious arousal triggered the usual stirring in his trousers. He ached to give her what she wanted, but the sound of those shrieks kept resonating in his mind.

The erotic gyration of her body as she shifted her bottom around on the mattress nearly swept away the last of his hesitation. There were few things he loved more in the world than seeing those tits bounce around when she was on top of him, which was the way they both liked it best.

She moaned and arched her back again. "Come get under me."

Tom grimaced as he bit down on his tongue, drawing on the pain to stifle his own lustful feelings. "Darlin', I'll be right back. I just need to see that everything's okay outside. Won't take more than a minute."

He went to the chest of drawers and took the Colt from its holster.

Eleanor sighed heavily, her face drawing down in a sour, sulky expression, a look Tom was more accustomed to seeing on the faces of his children. He wasn't at all sure what had gotten into her today. She'd woken up like this, all riled up and ready to tear into him. Normally he'd never consider that a problem. He enjoyed making love to his wife. That she enjoyed making love to him with equal enthusiasm was one of his life's great pleasures, a blessing for which he never stopped being grateful.

It was just unusual for her to come at him so aggressively when the kids were home. During daylight hours, anyway. He might already have tended to her needs, however, if not for an ill-timed knock on their bedroom door from Lottie, their youngest child and only daughter. The girl was hungry and wanting breakfast.

Tom moved to the door, but paused there with his hand on the knob as he glanced back at his unhappy wife. "Don't be mad. I love you."

Eleanor stared straight ahead with her arms folded beneath her heavy breasts, not looking at him or saying anything.

No point trying to engage with her further for the time being. It'd only make her angrier.

"Be right back."

LAST OF THE RAVAGERS

Tom hesitated a moment longer, debating whether he should take a few seconds to pull on a shirt, but ultimately he decided any additional delay wouldn't be a good idea. He opened the door and eased it gently shut behind him. Before moving away from the door, he heard Eleanor utter a shocking expletive, the likes of which had never previously crossed her lips, at least not in his presence. There was more than mere frustration in that sound. He heard a palpable anger that was unlike her. He decided he'd try talking about it with her as soon as he came back inside.

Tom went outside through the open front door of the house and took a look around. His head slowly swiveled about as he took in the wide-open landscape. Up to this point, his concern for the safety of his children had not yet encroached into the territory of genuine fear. When he'd heard the shrieks, he told himself he was just being paranoid, an easy thing to believe. He had every expectation of his worries sliding away as soon as he stepped outside, but so far the reverse was true. The kids were nowhere in sight. Not only that, but they knew he didn't like the house door being left open like that.

Something definitely didn't feel right.

An image of the open barn door appeared in his head again. Might the piercing shrieks he'd heard have come from inside the barn? He hadn't gotten a good look at the structure's interior from the bedroom window, so it was possible.

Looking up, he saw a buzzard fly into view from over the roof of the house. Clutched in its claws was a pink and glistening piece of fresh carrion. The bird flapped its enormous wings and went flying off toward the horizon, leaving Tom gaping at it in a puzzled way for a moment.

Then he felt his guts clench up again.

The kids.

He hopped off the porch and went running around the

side of the house, heart pounding as he willed his feet to move faster and faster, pushing himself far beyond normal physical limits. Soon the barn was right in front of him. He didn't begin to slow down until just before rushing through the open door. Then he came to an abrupt stop as he was confronted with a tableau so incomprehensibly horrific and grisly it overloaded his brain and temporarily rendered him incapable of coherent thought, much less action of any kind.

All three of his children were in the barn. His two boys, Luke and Caleb, and young Lottie, his only daughter.

They weren't just inside the barn.

They were *all over* the barn.

Pieces of their little bodies were strewn everywhere, along with ropy lengths of entrails ripped from their open abdominal cavities. Lottie's head was on the ground near his feet. Her eyes were looking up at him, asking a silent question—*why didn't you come sooner, papa?*

Tom screamed.

Someone had set the chickens loose from their pens, and as he stood there still dumbstruck by the carnage, the animals strutted around inside the barn, pecking and clucking with dumb innocence as they traipsed their way through the bloody remains of his offspring. His stomach rumbled as he saw one snatch up a random piece of viscera and swallow it.

Tom screamed some more.

Screamed until his throat was raw.

As soon as the sound faded away, he heard something moving about in the hayloft, a heavy clomping of feet from somewhere just behind the stacked bales of hay. And there were other sounds, a strange snuffling and a grinding noise that sounded like the tortured turning of rusted gears. Tom's whole body shook as he listened to the obscene noises grow louder, the snuffling sound becoming a wet slurping. Whatever was up there in the hayloft was enthusiastically devouring more pieces of his children.

LAST OF THE RAVAGERS

Rage now supplanted his raw vocal expression of shock and grief. He ran toward the back of the barn, barely noticing as his boots stomped through pieces of shredded intestines and organs, grinding them into the bloodstained ground. As he began rapidly climbing the ladder to the loft, one of the hidden killers let out a loud belch. The odor that wafted over the edge of the loft, a stench so powerful it made Tom gag, nearly caused him to lose his footing as he attempted to ascend the next rung of the ladder.

Following a precarious moment of barely managing to hang on, however, he got himself steadied again and resumed climbing. Nothing would stop him from trying his damnedest to avenge the deaths of his beautiful, innocent children. Arriving at the top of the ladder, he shoved aside a bale of hay and climbed up into the loft. He'd only been standing again for a fraction of a second when he finally caught sight of the killers. To say they were not what he was expecting was a hideous understatement. He'd expected human beings, for one thing. Bandits. Or savages. Something he could understand in a basic way, even if he couldn't fathom the coldness of any human heart capable of slaughtering children.

But these things were not human.

Of that there was no doubt.

They walked on two legs like humans and had stubby little arms, but any resemblance to normal men or women ended right there. These creatures were short and round, standing no more than three to four feet tall, if that, with the protruding bellies of shameless gluttons. Standing there naked and hairless, they looked like ugly dolls fashioned from some hard, clay-like substance, which had then been painted a bright shade of blue. Their oval-shaped heads looked almost too big for their bodies, with bat-like ears at the sides and bulging, lidless eyes. Most disturbing of all was their wide mouths, which displayed rows of inch-long, blood-flecked teeth.

When they saw him, they opened their mouths wider and he saw additional rows of recessed teeth beyond the ones in front. Their lips curled and twitched and from their mouths emerged a sound so unnerving that hearing it loosened his bowels to the point where he was on the brink of actually shitting himself out of raw fear. It was the grinding sound he'd heard before, but now he could see those recessed rows of teeth moving and gnashing.

The closest of the creatures came at him, moving with a swiftness that belied its gluttonous appearance. Instinct caused him to raise the Colt and squeeze the trigger. Though there was no time to draw a proper bead on the thing, the bullet found a target anyway, penetrating one of the creature's bulging eyes. The thing reeled to one side, screeching in pain as it pinwheeled its stubby arms in an effort to keep from toppling over. Its partner was down on its knees about a dozen feet to Tom's left, where it was shoveling fistfuls of ripped-up organs and flesh into its mouth. The second creature paused in its feasting as the gunshot rang out, unleashing an angry high-pitched screech of its own.

These sounds of pain and primitive rage were even more torturous to Tom's ears than that awful grinding noise, causing him to wince and take an instinctive backward step. He was within a few inches of the edge of the loft, dangerously close to taking a potentially fatal or crippling fall, but he was oblivious to the danger as the first creature abruptly righted itself and came at him a second time.

Tom squeezed the Colt's trigger two more times.

The first round took off the tip of one of those twitching triangular ears, while instinctive aim adjustment sent the next round right into the creature's wide-open mouth. The creature stopped in its tracks and clutched at its throat, making gagging sounds as it began to wobble about like a drunkard at last call. Blood leaked from the corners of its wide mouth and from between its fang-like teeth. The other creature screeched again, much louder than before, but the sound barely registered this time as rage again overtook Tom.

Here was proof that the strange, demonic-looking things could be hurt. If they could be hurt, they could be killed. Unleashing his own scream of rage, he rushed forward and jammed the barrel of the Colt into the wounded creature's mouth, angling the barrel upward as he yanked on the trigger until the gun's cylinder was empty. In the process of doing this, he sliced open his hand in multiple places, the creature's razor-sharp teeth cutting through his flesh like butter. The pain was intense, but Tom didn't care.

The creature toppled over, falling dead at his feet.

A feeling of triumph surged through him, drawing forth another scream of righteous rage, but the feeling was short-lived. Still screeching, the other creature rose to its knees and came waddling toward him at high speed. That grinding sound recurred as its mouth opened, showing him the unnerving rotation of those inner rows of teeth. His gun was empty and if he couldn't come up with some alternate means of defending himself within about one more second, that terrible mass of grinding, rotating teeth would start chewing him to pieces. He would endure the same agony his children had experienced. Maybe it would be what he deserved after failing to protect them.

He spied a pitchfork propped up in a corner of the hayloft, but it was too far away. The creature launched itself into the air, springing upward off those pudgy legs like a circus performer bouncing off a trampoline. Tom fell onto his back, pulled a leg back, and kicked out at it at just the right moment, the hard heel of his boot smashing into the center of its round belly. Now the creature went sailing over the edge of the loft, landing with a heavy thud down below. Breathing heavily, Tom rolled over and crept up to the edge and glanced down. The creature was lying on its back, silent and unmoving, and for an instant Tom allowed himself the hope it'd broken its back in the fall.

This hope was shattered when the thing abruptly sat up on its plump rump and lifted its oval-shaped head to look up at him. The creature hissed, a long, forked tongue emerging and flitting about in the air a moment before retracting. This was followed by yet another repetition of the horrible grinding sound as the creature tried to stand.

Tom was on the verge of turning away to make a running grab for the pitchfork when he heard someone shout his name. Standing framed in the open barn door was Eleanor, clad in the kind of plain frock she often wore for working around the property. Clutched in her hands was a repeater rifle. She cast her gaze about, taking in the scene of unspeakable carnage. Doubtless she felt as he had in those first moments of seeing it all, scarcely able to comprehend any of it.

The creature turned toward her and made that hissing sound again. The grinding sound followed and though Tom could no longer see the creature's face, he knew it was showing Eleanor those rows of gnashing teeth.

Then it began racing toward her.

Tom screamed.

He spun about and made a dash for the pitchfork. A boom of rifle fire resonated inside the barn before his hands could close around the handle. The rounds fired from the rifle were just part of an overall cacophony of sound. Eleanor was screaming. The creature down below was loudly squealing in pain, at least one round from the Winchester apparently having perforated blue flesh. Tom was screaming.

Then he realized the noise from below had abruptly ceased.

For a moment, a terrible silence filled the barn, a period during which he felt certain his wife had joined his children in death. Then came the sound of her beloved voice, arriving like a life buoy thrown to a drowning man at sea.

"Tom? You alive up there?"

Sighing wearily, Tom let go of the pitchfork and approached the ladder. When his feet touched the ground below a few seconds later, he turned slowly around, facing Eleanor with glimmering eyes as tears spilled down his face.

He took a slow couple steps toward her, his hands spread wide. "I'm so sorry. Our babies were dead by the time I got here." He sniffled and sounded on the verge of descending into hysteria. "There was nothing I could do. You've got to believe me."

Eleanor still had the repeater rifle clutched stolidly in her hands. She eyed her husband warily, her face conveying surprisingly little emotion now. The strangest thing about her demeanor was how unsurprised she seemed about the situation in general. It was almost as if she'd expected something catastrophic to occur. But that was crazy.

Wasn't it?

Eleanor smiled. "Oh, I believe you, sweet husband of mine. Tireless provider and hero of the family. *Man* of the house."

Her voice dripped with sarcasm.

And now she giggled.

Tom frowned. "What has gotten into you? Don't you care that our children are dead?"

Eleanor raised the rifle and aimed it at him. "Oh, I care. I care about this wonderful gift bestowed upon me today. I'm finally free."

Tom gaped at her, stunned and unable to make sense of these new developments. His wife aiming a weapon at him with obvious deadly intent was, in its own way, just as shocking as anything else that had happened here today.

Tears streamed from his eyes as he shook his head. "I don't understand."

Eleanor smirked. "You never do."

Tom's confusion overwhelmed his grief, defeated any notion of self-defense before it could take shape in his head. Their children were *dead. Slaughtered.* How could there possibly be room in her heart and mind for anything other than that? And what was this madness about being free?

He would never know the answers to these things.

Eleanor's finger tightened on the Winchester's trigger until the rifle boomed again. Tom fell over and died, blood leaking from the hole in his head and mixing with the blood of his children on the ground.

SIX

SHERIFF NED KILMISTER sat alone at a table in the Last Chance Saloon. A glass of whiskey sat untouched several inches from his right hand, which was currently occupied with the idle task of shifting a coin from finger to finger without letting it fall to the table. The simple dexterity exercise was something he'd picked up as a younger man back east, while hanging out in drinking establishments after a day's work at an oyster packing-house on the waterfront in Baltimore.

Often other men from the packing-house joined him there in the evening. One of those men—a quiet and brooding older fellow whose name he no longer recalled—was pals with a friend of his. Thus they'd often find themselves seated at the same table. The older man would sit there and roll coins across his knuckles for hours at a time, rarely uttering more than a word or two at a time. One day Ned asked him why he did the coin roll thing so ceaselessly.

The man stared at him from the other side of the table and, in a serious tone, said, "You know what they say about the devil and idle hands. I do this because otherwise I might do bad things."

Ned wasn't so sure about that, yet the habit he'd picked up from watching coins roll across the man's knuckles remained. These days it mostly recurred when he was feeling unsettled, his thoughts scattered. Times like now. He did it to relax his spirit and bring things into focus.

Ned let the coin slip from his fingers and fall to the table. He picked up the glass of whiskey and took a big gulp. The saloon was close to empty now, most of the men who'd followed him inside earlier having departed to return to their daily routines.

Having told his wild and seemingly improbable tale, the exhausted bounty hunter was now tucked away in one of the rooms above the saloon. Quentin Brown and Cole Halford were also temporarily absent. They were off assisting Doc Richardson in transferring Angelina's corpse to Richardson's office across the street. Since it seemed possible the poor young lady's demise might in some way be related to the strange creatures described by Russ Harper, the doc wanted to perform a more thorough and professional examination of her corpse than could be conducted in the saloon's cellar.

As Ned downed the last of the whiskey in his glass, he heard a creaking of boards from outside the saloon's entrance. Seconds later, the batwing doors were thrust open and Quentin Brown came back into his saloon. Cole Halford was not with him.

Brown pulled out a chair and sat across the table from Ned. He stared straight ahead, with the kind of faraway look a man gets when lost in his own thoughts. Instead of prompting him to speak, Ned refilled his glass from the open bottle on the table, taking a contemplative sip of whiskey. After that, he tilted the glass slightly toward him, staring into the amber liquid, as if he could divine answers to the many mysteries facing him from within its depths.

The saloon keeper coughed. "Doc's a bit of an odd duck, ain't he?"

Ned chuckled. "Are you calling him a quack?"

Brown snorted and flipped a hand. "Nah, I don't mean like that. Man knows his business, far as I can tell. He's a damn sight better than that fraudulent sawbones we had here before him. Doc Hicks. You remember that sumbitch?"

LAST OF THE RAVAGERS

Ned nodded. "Aye, I do. A preening know-it-all without any actual skill to back up his highfalutin talk. Damn near every surgery he attempted had a fatal result. Lucky for him he absconded in the middle of the night." He held up a hand, displaying his thumb and forefinger, separated by a width of barely more than an eyelash. "I was *this close* to tying a noose around his damn fool neck after what happened to poor Nellie. Man didn't just get rid of her *bad blood*, as he called it. He rid the poor thing of every last drop she had."

Brown's gaze went to the open bottle. He eyed it with longing for a moment before getting up with a heavy sigh and making his weary way over to the bar. Returning with another glass and bottle a moment later, he settled into his chair again and filled the glass.

"That was a damn shame."

Ned grunted in agreement.

Brown tossed the contents of his glass down his throat and filled it again. "Woman wasn't even really sick. She was . . . what was the word Doc Richardson used when we told him about it?"

"Hypochondriac."

Brown nodded. "That's right. Someone who's always complaining about some ailment or other without any real symptoms."

Ned drank some more. "A sickness of the mind is all it really is. Imagining you're sick when ya ain't." He grunted. "Doc Richardson truly ain't like Hicks at all."

Brown nodded. "He's the closest we've ever had to a real city-type doctor. Educated and such. We're lucky to have him. But . . . "

He lapsed into silence and his eyes began to get that glazed look again.

Ned prompted him. "But?"

Brown filled his glass again and leaned back. "But . . . he just seems . . . *off*. You know? He's always like that, but he seemed to get particularly squirrely after hearing the bounty hunter's tale. Like something about it set off something in his head and got him all preoccupied. Some revelation. I asked him about it, but he wouldn't say anything. Now I can't shake the idea that he's got some big secret, which makes me nervous. You know what I mean?"

Ned laughed. "Oh, I know." His smile abruptly vanished. "Speaking of the story Russ told . . . you put any stock in anything he had to say?"

Brown pursed his lips a moment, considering it before shrugging. "He's always struck me as a straight shooter. I'll say that much. Not a big socializer, though. He'll sit at the bar with his nose in a book for hours sometimes." He sighed. "Russ loves his stories, proper stories written down in books by educated men, but one thing he ain't is a teller of tall tales. Man has a low tolerance for horseshit. I don't see him just making up anything like the story he told us, improbable as it seems on the surface"

Ned frowned, shaking his head. "I don't know him as well as you, but that's not far off from my appraisal of the man. I just don't see how the things he described could be real, though. Strange little midget demons feasting on coyotes out in the goddamn desert? Tearing the beasts apart with their bare hands? A days-old corpse returning to life? That's not just improbable, it's impossible."

Brown nodded. "I suppose so. But what was it Shakespeare said? 'There are more things in Heaven and earth, Horatio, than are dreamt of in your philosophy'?"

Ned snorted. "I reckon a literary allusion is appropriate, given this is Russ Harper we're discussing. But, hell, man, it's just as likely he hallucinated the whole thing. That happens to these lone riders in the desert sometimes, especially at night. You know that as well as I do. A man gets enough cactus wine in him, he's apt to start seeing all kinds of crazy things."

Brown looked slightly askance at him while refilling his

glass yet again. "I do know that. And I know how spirits of that type can mess with a man's head. Mess with it in mighty strange ways, yessiree." He sipped whiskey. "But my gut tells me that ain't the case here. And then there's the matter of Angelina. *Something* attacked her in the alley last night. A man or creature that tore her arm off like it was nothing. Quite the coincidence, ain't it?"

Ned frowned so hard he felt like the expression might etch itself into his features permanently. "The timing is interesting. I'll give you that. Just for the sake of argument, let's say the things Russ described were real and not some strange conjuration of a booze-addled mind. Well, then,who's to say there might not be more of them roaming around these parts? Maybe one even wandered into town last night."

Brown grimaced. "A sobering thought."

Ned knocked back a last gulp of whiskey, then groaned as he pushed back his chair and got to his feet. "Reckon I better get out and do some askin' around, see if anybody else saw anything unusual last night. You hear anything relevant from the regulars once they start to wander in, let Billy know. He should be around soon."

Billy Conway was one of two part-time deputies Ned employed.

Still in his chair, Brown nodded. "Will do."

The sheriff tipped his hat. "Take her easy."

He walked out of the Last Chance Saloon and into the bright morning sunshine.

SEVEN

THE NATURE OF Doc Richardson's work led to occasional squabbling with Eddie Horton, the barber who ran his business out of the bottom floor of the same building that housed Richardson's medical practice on the upper floor. Horton did not approve of the doctor conducting autopsies and research on cadavers directly above where he tended to the grooming habits of many of the men of Snakebite. His chief complaint was the often detectable stench of corpse rot wafting down from the upper floor. Some of his customers had a hard time focusing on their vanity with the smell of death clogging their nostrils, and his volume of business was beginning to fall off because of it.

Horton had recently proposed a solution. He would buy out the doctor's stake in the building, converting the second floor to other vanity-related usages. The doctor could use the buyout money to set up shop in one of the currently unoccupied buildings farther down Main Street.

Doc Richardson's response was succinct and blunt—*get fucked*.

In the last month alone, it was an answer he'd been forced to repeat numerous times. Horton's eagerness to force him from the building was veering toward desperation lately. Earlier this morning, as the men from the saloon were assisting him in the transference of

LAST OF THE RAVAGERS

Angelina's corpse, the barber had repeated the buyout offer yet again. The vehemence in his voice was greater than ever before, his face and the bald top of his head flushing a deep shade of red, a stark contrast to the tufts of snow-white hair ringing his barren scalp.

"You knew what you were getting into when we pooled our resources," Richardson told him this time, glancing at the furious barber as he followed Quentin Brown and Cole Halford into the building through the back entrance. "You were under no misapprehension about the nature of my work. If you want to breach the terms of our agreement, it's you who'll have to move down the street. Now if you'll kindly piss off, I've work to do."

Horton glowered. "Come on, man. What legitimate business could you possibly have with a corpse? You're a frontier sawbones, not a goldang university researcher. Take that cadaver to the undertaker."

Richardson flipped a dismissive wave at him and followed the other men up the stairs to his offices.

Now it was more than an hour later and the men from the saloon were gone. In the interest of doing some uninterrupted solitary work, the doctor hung a 'closed' sign on the door to the room where he typically met with his patients. After locking the door, he selected one of the older texts from his collection of books on medicinal theory, poured himself a glass of water from a jug, and sat down to do some reading.

This particular slim volume was entitled *Rejuvenation of the Dead*. The author was a man named Thomas Harcourt, a long dead scholar who was once one of the most esteemed practitioners of medicine of his time. The high regard in which he was held came to an end in the wake of his book's publication in 1643. Harcourt believed it was possible, via chemical stimulation of the brain, to restore to life freshly deceased human beings and animals. He believed he could restore the dead to full health as well, provided a cadaver was no more than a day old and in good, intact condition prior to its moment of demise.

His assertion ignited a firestorm of controversy in that more superstitious time. It was believed that only God could ever possess the power of resurrection. To suggest anything else was heresy. Harcourt was arrested and hanged after a sham trial, a travesty that infuriated Richardson every time he thought about it. The old scholar was merely a man ahead of his time, an innovative forward thinker in an era and place that didn't allow for such things.

But his book, fortunately, survived.

And Doc Richardson believed it still had much to teach the world. All that was required was a new innovator to take up the torch of knowledge and bring Harcourt's ideas into this new and more daring age. Since coming to Snakebite, he'd intermittently attempted to continue and complete the work started by the shamefully misunderstood Harcourt, who'd not, in Richardson's estimation, been working to undermine or deny God. To the contrary. The man had merely utilized the natural gifts provided him by the Almighty. His intellect and advanced knowledge of the healing arts. If by using these things he was able to uncover secrets of the divine, then surely that must be God's will. Right?

Richardson smiled, nodding.

Right.

He closed *Rejuvenation of the Dead* and returned the prized volume to its spot on the shelf behind his desk. Perhaps sparked by the raving bounty hunter's tale of a spontaneous resurrection in the desert, he was eager to again renew his research after an unplanned lapse of a few months. Whether the bounty hunter's wild story was true or not was immaterial. What mattered was the conviction he'd heard in the man's voice, as well as his vivid way of describing the bizarre events. It'd fired up the doctor's imagination.

LAST OF THE RAVAGERS

Feeling refreshed and inspired, Richardson decided the time for his first attempt at human revivification had arrived. For years he'd gathered the ingredients and binding agents needed to formulate rejuvenation drugs. All according to the instructions in Harcourt's book, with some refinements of his own.

Richardson went into the room where he conducted most of his experimental work. The shelves in this room contained an array of medical and research equipment, as well as numerous dark vials filled with various tinctures and potions. Angelina's corpse, still wrapped in the bloody blanket, was stretched out on a long exam table in the middle of the room. On another, smaller table nearby was a microscope and a small metal storage box. The storage box was old and dented in numerous places, the damage incurred in a train wreck he'd survived long before his arrival in Snakebite. It was that narrow brush with death, in fact, that first ignited his obsession with corpse reanimation.

Because the blanket had been wound around the deceased saloon girl multiple times, removing it involved a fair amount of physical exertion. He had to heave her up and flip her over more than once, and at one point he nearly dumped her over the side of the table. Once he'd successfully removed the blanket, he noticed a section of it was smeared with feces from her bowels relaxing at the moment of death. Some of the mess had gotten on his hands.

After dropping the blanket in a bin for later disposal, he cleaned his hands and set about getting Angelina properly situated on the exam table. This process included fastening her remaining limbs to the table with attached leather straps, a gesture to basic pragmatism. Richardson did not expect to achieve unqualified success with his first foray into attempted human revivification. The scientific method rarely worked that way. All the big breakthroughs involved a great deal of trial and error, along with a lot of total, abject failure. Odds were nothing would come of today's experiment.

Just in case, however, the straps were there to keep a revived corpse from flailing about or assaulting him. To further guarantee safety, he shoved a thick wad of cloth into her mouth and secured it with another strap cinched tight over the lower part of her face.

In the highly unlikely event he was able to achieve human reanimation his first time around, every possible precaution should be in place. There were so many things he didn't know about what reanimation might be like, couldn't know until it actually occurred. His biggest worry involved the departure of the soul from a deceased body, an event that surely occurred at the moment of death. If a corpse was revived, would the soul remain in the afterlife or would it be recalled to the flesh that'd formerly hosted it? If so—and if the revived individual was somehow cognizant of this repeated transference between realms—would the person awaken enraged at having been robbed of her heavenly reward? That was one possibility and it was worrisome enough on its own merits. Another one struck Richardson as potentially even more troubling—the revival of a dead human body as only a dumb beast, entirely absent any semblance of analytical mind or soul.

But this was what science was about.

Discovering things.

Taking chances.

The time to begin his great experiment was just about nigh. Before retrieving his reanimation formula, however, Richardson allowed his eyes to roam over the lush planes and valleys of Angelina's exquisitely feminine form. He experienced an unexpected fresh stirring of libido, a development he attributed to the changed circumstances of this second examination. He was locked in his own offices this time, in no danger of being intruded upon and judged a pervert by some simple-minded witness.

LAST OF THE RAVAGERS

I can do whatever I want.

He placed a palm on the cool flesh of her flat belly. His hand continued downward and his fingertips soon glided through the thatch of pubic hair below. He shuddered and leaned over the table, taking one of Angelina's nipples between his teeth. A wild impulse to clamp his teeth together and tear the tough nub of flesh away from her breast flashed through his mind, simultaneously exciting and repulsing him.

In the next instant, he stood bolt upright, a wave of self-disgust surging through him as he gagged and backed away from the table.

What's wrong with me?

He'd taken that same nipple between his lips numerous times when the woman was alive, both as a paying customer at the Last Chance Saloon and in secret liaisons in this very building. A romance of sorts had blossomed between them, albeit a temporary one. She eventually ended it, saying she needed to focus on making a living, which of course meant fucking the filthy trailhands and miners who passed through the doors of the saloon each night.

There'd been some bitterness on his part.

Some angry words exchanged.

In the end he'd had no choice but to let it go. So that, he surmised, was the ugly thing inside driving these perverse impulses. He had her all to himself now. She could no longer deny him. Despite his reflexive display of disgust, the possibilities remained intriguing.

No, he thought, brow furrowing as he shook his head. *You are a man of science. You have a higher calling. And work to do. So get on with it.*

This latest self-admonishment did the trick.

Snapping out of the spell of perverse erotic fever, he went to the corner table, where he opened the little storage box and removed a long metal syringe already filled with his reanimation formula. He returned to the examination table, raised the syringe above his head, and slammed it home in a swift downward arc, his thumb simultaneously pressing down on the plunger, driving the needle into the dead woman's heart.

Angelina's eyes instantly snapped open while the needle was still deep inside her. As her head turned toward Richardson, she screamed behind the gag and began to thrash against her bonds. The doctor gasped in shock and sudden pain as her unbound elbow stub jabbed hard into his stomach.

He staggered backward, eyes agape at the dark and terrifying wonder his work had produced.

EIGHT

HER BEAUTIFUL FAMILY was dead and she felt nothing for them. This lack of feeling was such a strange thing. Until recently, Tom and her children were her whole world. She couldn't have imagined a life without them. The prospect of losing them in so horrific a fashion, if described to her, would have been impossible to comprehend. Before about a week and a half ago, she could not have believed any of it.

They were all gone now, though. Not just gone, but torn into countless unrecognizable pieces by those strange creatures her mysterious new lover had summoned into this world from some other realm of existence. She'd seen all of it with her own eyes. It was as real as the punishing heat of the morning sun beating down on her face as she rode Tom's horse at high speed toward the mystery man's valley lair in the desert. Right now she should feel nothing but all-consuming grief and hopelessness, but what she actually felt was excitement.

He'd first come to Eleanor on a day when the kids were at school and Tom was in town tending to various errands. She was in the main room of the house, scrubbing out the family's wood-burning stove when she heard a creaking of hinges signaling the opening of the front door. Her back was turned and she felt the fine hairs on the back of her neck prickling as she heard the first clomp of a boot heel on the floor. She knew at once this was not Tom returning from his trip into town. The time factor was the main reason. Her husband had departed less than an hour ago and would not be returning for some time yet.

No, this was someone else.

A stranger.

Someone who didn't belong in her home.

Her heart was pounding as she ceased scrubbing the stove and got to her feet. A tiny whimper came to her trembling lips as fear gripped her. Someone—some *man*—was in her house, unannounced and uninvited. No decent, civilized person with proper manners would do such a thing. She could only conclude this was *not* a civilized person. The heavy tread of the stranger's boots sounded again as he came a few steps farther into the house. Eleanor's entire body was wracked with tremors as she imagined the stranger ripping her dress away and throwing her to the floor. The terror of being raped brought words of pleading to her lips. She didn't want the hands of any man other than her husband on her body.

She turned around, ready to drop to her knees and beg.

That's when the strangeness started.

There was something unusually compelling in the stranger's smoky blue eyes, which looked as placid as the surface of a lake on a windless summer day. She shivered at the sight of them and began to feel something much different from fear. The stranger wasn't young. His whiskers were gray and there were age lines on his face, but he was nonetheless the most handsome man she'd ever seen. Desire bloomed inside her. Almost immediately it was stronger than anything she'd ever felt for her husband. Until then even the mere idea of desiring any man or woman half as much as she desired Tom would have struck her as laughable, and yet what she was feeling could not be denied.

The man removed his hat and dropped it on the dining table as he continued to approach Eleanor in his unhurried way. He'd left the front door standing open behind him, and at first she had an irrational sense of guilt and fear at the possibility of someone coming into the house and seeing them together. On one level, it was a silly concern. They were both still clothed. Nothing had happened yet.

But something would.

Even in those early moments she knew it beyond doubt.

The man removed his long duster and continued coming closer, just the hint of a smile tweaking the corners of his mouth. He draped the long coat over a chair and licked his lips, boldly and unashamedly looking her up and down, taking the full measure of her feminine form. She whimpered again, but this time it was not from fear. She clutched at the fabric of her dress, aching to have it torn away. There was nothing she wouldn't let him do to her. Nothing she wouldn't do for him if commanded.

Even in the midst of the powerful desire gripping her, she remained cognizant of how wrong it was. And how bizarre. She was under his spell, could feel him working some arcane form of magic on her. *Real* magic he was able to wield without witch-like storybook chants. She felt it seeping into her, invading every pore of her body, manipulating her mind and soul.

Changing her. Making her into something new.

"I'm yours," she told him.

He smiled and nodded. "I know."

Just hearing his deep voice for the first time was enough to bring her close to the brink of orgasm. She took his rough, callused hand and led him into her bedroom, where she disrobed with no prompting from the stranger. She stretched out on the bed where she'd only ever made love to one other man, her husband, displaying her body more wantonly than the lustiest city whore. She felt his gaze on her like a living thing, slowly caressing every soft inch of willing, pliable flesh.

Only on one other occasion had she ever felt anything remotely like what she felt in those moments. Six months earlier she went into town for a meeting with Sally Frederickson, the young school teacher. The purported purpose of the meeting was to discuss the progress her children were making in their schooling, but she and Sally wound up talking about everything under the sun but education, laughing and joking about silly things. At some point Sally got out a bottle of something strong and one thing led to another.

They wound up unclothed, sweaty, and tangled up in each other in a back room of the schoolhouse. Eleanor didn't return home until late that night. Explaining away both her drunkenness and tardiness to her worried sick husband was not an easy chore. There was thus no repeat of this single sinful dalliance with Sally, and she'd not seen the teacher again since then, sometimes going to great lengths to avoid her. She tried hard to make herself believe the incident never happened, that it was some perverse fever dream, but the lustful memories often haunted her dreams, reigniting the forbidden desires.

And now this.

A new and far more powerful temptation.

The man removed his clothes and came to her, making her first gasp and then scream as his hardness plunged into her wet center. The sense of being under the thrall of magic intensified as the man looked into her eyes and rode her with a savage passion that ruined Tom for her as a lover forever. He made her feel engulfed in endless waves of unparalleled pleasure. This was something she'd never truly experienced before, a real bull of a man who made her husband seem like a timid boy. The world around them seemed to disappear. The bed was a cloud floating through a warm nighttime sky. She felt weightless. Ethereal and ephemeral. Then that sensation abruptly disappeared and she was back in the bed with the stranger as the strongest orgasm she'd ever experienced crashed over her like a tidal wave.

After it was over, she curled herself around the man and lightly traced a fingertip over his muscular physique. She'd thought of him as a kind of magician in the beginning, but now she saw he was more like a god. One of the old gods, from long before the time of Jesus. She worshipped him already and knew there was nothing she wouldn't do for him.

As if sensing her thoughts, he told her of the sacrifice to come. He knew she would be troubled by the prospect once he was no longer in her presence, but if she wanted to be with him, sacrifice was necessary. The stranger was right about that. She didn't believe it in the beginning. Not in those early postcoital moments. She was certain there was nothing she wouldn't give up for him. She would kill anyone for him. Murder the entire world or die trying.

But the stranger was right.

Not long after he'd taken his leave of her—vanishing like a wisp of vapor after departing through the front door—she was overcome with an almost crippling sense of guilt and doubt. Her love for her children reasserted itself somewhat, but she could tell that love was now a twisted, lessened thing. Vulnerable. In danger of breaking at any moment. In the days that followed, she tried to strengthen that love. Not just for her children, but for Tom, the man she'd betrayed without the slightest hint of hesitation. The effort continued all the way up to this morning, when she'd tried so hard to seduce Tom, a part of her hoping he'd rise to the occasion and make her feel something akin to what the stranger made her feel that day. All along another part of her knew he wasn't capable of it, a part that only wanted to be with the stranger again. Still, she kept at it even as she heard the first shrieks of terror coming from her doomed children, knowing already they were moments away from death.

Now it was all over and, yes, she felt nothing for them. Nothing for Tom, either.

What she felt was truly free for the first time in her life, no longer bound by ordinary expectations or the strictures of moral, "normal" society.

She rode Tom's horse far into the desert, pushing the beast to its limits in an effort to get to her new lover's lair as quickly as possible. He'd told her the animal would know the way, an idea that would've made her scoff from the lips of virtually anyone else, but it did seem to be true. The horse raced across the rough terrain with an unswerving sense of drive and purpose, only finally beginning to slow as it carried her deep into a narrow valley flanked by towering rocky hills. Plodding along now, the horse kept going until it arrived outside the wide entrance to a cave.

The stranger was not yet visible, but she knew he awaited her inside the cave. Even from this distance, she felt his presence. It made her shiver with desire and a deliciously pleasurable fear of all that was yet to come. Because this was just the beginning. The massacre of her family wasn't the end of anything. It was a prelude to something darkly wondrous and magical.

After dismounting, she lifted the hem of her long dress and carefully made her way up a rocky incline to the cave entrance. She saw the stranger sitting on his haunches next to a crackling fire. He was wearing the duster and the hat she remembered from his first visit to her house. His back was to her as she came into the cave. She sighed at the sight of him, desire surging once again. He poked at the fire with a stick, causing the kindling he'd used to shift and emit sparks. Instead of immediately disappearing, the sparks floated slowly in the air and glowed with unusual brightness for an unusually extended period of time. More evidence of the field of magic projected by the stranger.

They were not alone in the cave.

LAST OF THE RAVAGERS

A tall and sturdy wooden cross was driven into the ground several feet beyond the fire, in the shadowy recesses of the cave. The light from the fire, however, was more than sufficient to see who was upon the cross. It was Sally Frederickson. The school teacher was nude and tightly bound to the beams of the cross with lengths of heavy, thick rope, her bare flesh covered in a sheen of sweat. Her eyes widened when she saw Eleanor. She writhed against her bonds and cried out behind a cloth gag. Her words were indecipherable, but Eleanor easily sensed their meaning. She pleaded for mercy.

For rescue.

Upon seeing her, Eleanor felt a twinge of something faintly resembling empathy and regret, which was more than she'd felt at the loss of her family. Despite her desperate efforts to never think of it again, the sensation of the teacher's soft hands gliding over her flesh was rarely far from the front of her mind. The woman had awakened things within her she'd never known were there. Strange desires and a universe of untapped potential. A capacity for raw pleasure she'd never imagined. Her devotion to the charismatic stranger, however, far surpassed any lingering feelings she had for Sally.

After poking at the crackling fire one more time, the stranger rose to his full height and turned to face Eleanor. His eyes narrowed to inscrutable slits and the corners of his mouth tweaked slightly upward at the sight of her. He took a dagger from a sheath on his belt and offered it to her. She stared at his outhrust hand, chest heaving a little as she saw how long the sliver of sharpened steel was, somewhere right in between a normal dagger and a sword. It had an ornamental, jewel-encrusted handle and looked like a relic from ancient times.

Her hand trembled as she accepted the dagger and curled her fingers around its handle.

The stranger's sun-browned countenance took on a

crueler cast now as he said, "You've been brave today, woman. Your devotion is not in doubt. But I require a further sacrifice before taking you as my wife."

He turned and swept a hand toward Sally.

Eleanor frowned. "You want me to kill her?"

The man nodded. "Yes, but do it slow. Make her suffer. To be like me—to be *worthy* of my love—you must revel in cruelty and suffering."

Eleanor smiled. "Anything for you."

He nodded again, but said nothing in reply.

Eleanor approached the school teacher. The woman's whimpering grew louder, the writhing against her bonds more desperate. The silent plea in her eyes again stirred something faint inside Eleanor, but she shoved the flickering feeling away. Once she was within two feet of the woman, she placed the dagger's sharp tip against Sally's heaving belly, about an inch to the left of her navel. It was the gentlest of touches, yet even that was sufficient to draw forth the first trickle of blood. A line of crimson slid down to her pubis.

Sally cried out as another half-inch of the steel poking at her flesh pushed into her, an accidental escalation of torture that happened as Eleanor swayed on her feet, lost in a heady rush of pleasure. She looked at the place where steel pierced vulnerable flesh, nostrils flaring as sexual desire bloomed. Being born without a cock didn't mean she couldn't penetrate a lover. She moaned as she pushed the blade in another two inches. Sally screamed behind her gag and tried to twist away from the blade, but that wasn't possible.

Eleanor bit her lip and moaned many more times as she slowly retracted the dagger and pushed it forward again and again, never fully removing it from Sally's quivering flesh. The thin trickle of blood thickened and spread across her belly. Eleanor gasped and shivered in orgasmic delight and continued the violation of flesh with steel. The blade went in deeper, the penetrating jabs becoming hard thrusts. She was close to losing herself entirely in the storm of twisted passion engulfing her, but somehow she managed to avoid getting carried away. Sally was in terrible pain. That much was clear from the increasingly frantic and loud sounds issuing from behind the gag.

But she wasn't close to dying.

Not yet.

Eleanor sensed the presence of the stranger behind her. His erect cock poked at her behind even as she pushed the steel inside Sally again. Seconds later, he was inside her, making her whimper and writhe in helpless ecstasy. Instead of fucking her roughly as he had last time, his thrusts were slow and measured. In another moment, she realized he was matching the rhythm of her own thrusts with the dagger. As he slowly quickened his pace, she did the same with the dagger, sliding it in and out of the teacher more rapidly. While riding a wave of arousal so intense it almost defied comprehension, she lifted her chin and looked up into Sally's eyes, saw how they were starting to glaze over even as they continued to leak tears.

Eleanor thrust the dagger in harder than ever and gave it a vicious twist, causing Sally's eyes to snap open wide, making her scream again. She arched her back and her body went rigid, her muscles bulging as if she'd been jolted with electricity.

Eleanor laughed.

She withdrew the dagger fully from Sally's body for the first time and immediately rammed it back in again. The teacher screamed and screamed. In between the screams were more desperate pleas for mercy, but it was far too late for that. Eleanor fully withdrew the dagger and thrust it back in many more times, becoming frenzied as she felt blood slide down her arm and spatter against her own belly. She was so immersed in murderous rage she missed the moment when Sally finally died. At a certain point, the dagger's handle became so slick with blood she eventually did lose her grasp on it. By then, as the blade tumbled to the floor of the cave, Sally's abdomen was so severely shredded that a long loop of guts was spilling out of it. Eleanor thrust her hands through the gaping holes in the ruined flesh and tore at her insides.

She felt like a beast.

Or like a woman possessed by a demon.

Maybe both.

Whatever the case, it was *glorious*.

The stranger released his seed inside her as she ripped out a kidney and sank her teeth into it.

Later, when things were calm again, as they lay in each other's arms by the crackling fire, she ran her fingers over the hard muscles of his abdomen and spoke in a hushed tone. "You're not like a normal man at all. You're full of magic. Dark magic."

He laughed. "The best kind of magic."

She smiled. "Yes."

A period of contemplative silence ensued. A few of the man's strange, blue-skinned minions eventually came into the cave. They sat on their haunches in the dark recesses of the space, sloppily feasting on the remains of the teacher.

Eleanor looked into the stranger's eyes. "What happens now? Will you take me away from here?"

The man grunted. "We'll leave by daybreak tomorrow, but first I have business to attend to in your town. Dark business."

Eleanor sighed, smiling again. "Will we kill more people?"

"We'll kill everyone here, love. *Everyone*."

NINE

AFTER SPENDING MOST of the morning walking the streets of Snakebite and talking to too many people who could only give him funny looks when he asked if they'd seen anything strange the night before, Ned Kilmister gave up and began making his way back toward the center of town. By then it was almost noon and a hell of a lot hotter than when he'd started. The sun felt like a malevolent presence up there in the powder blue sky, relentlessly punishing the land and all who lived upon it. On days like this he often wished he'd chosen a life in one of the colder regions of the continent over life in the desert.

As he walked down the middle of Main St. at a much slower pace than he'd managed earlier in the morning, Ned removed his hat and wiped sweat from his brow with a sleeve already sopping wet with perspiration. He set the hat atop his head again without wedging it down tight, which made the scorching heat slightly more bearable. On a windier day, this wouldn't have been an option, but the air in Snakebite today felt as still as death, with barely any perceptible breeze swirling about. As he neared the building that housed his office and the town jail, he considered stopping in for a chat with Billy Conway, the deputy on duty today. The parched condition of his throat prompted him to veer off toward the Last Chance Saloon.

Before he could climb the steps to the saloon's porch,

however, a door on the opposite side of the street was thrown open and a little man with tufts of white hair ringing his bald scalp came running outside. Ned grimaced when he saw the bug-eyed, frantic look on Eddie Horton's face. The barber was an ornery son of a bitch, unpleasant to deal with even on the best of days, and his expression made it clear this was shaping up to be one of his not-so-good days.

Goddammit.

"Sheriff! Sheriff" The angry little man ran with one arm held up in the air, like a schoolboy signaling for a teacher's attention from the back of a classroom. "Sheriff! Come quick! You gots to come with me."

Ned forced a smile.

Like hell I do.

"Tell me about it over a drink, Eddie." He turned away from the barber and mounted the steps to the saloon's porch, never breaking stride as he continued toward the batwing doors. "I'm afraid I've worked up a hell of a thirst, and I mean to quench it before tending to any other business."

He heard the clatter of Eddie's feet on the boards as he raced up the steps behind him. "But it's an emergency!"

Ned banged through the flapping doors and headed for the bar. He restrained an impulse to abruptly turn around, grab hold of the barber, and toss his ass out on the street. Eddie was the classic boy who cried wolf, only he was a wee bit older than the boy in the fable. If the man had a genuine emergency on his hands, Ned would eat his hat. Odds were his "emergency" was just another complaint about Doc Richarson. The old man was like a dog with a bone where that tired old subject was concerned. He would not let it go.

Quentin Brown stood behind the bar with his arms folded and a toothpick wedged in a corner of his mouth. The placid, almost bored look on his face changed when he heard the grating sound of Horton's warbling voice. His eyes flicked toward Ned and the men exchanged weary, wary expressions. Ned was far from the only person in town sick unto death of listening to the barber's complaints.

The barkeep grabbed a bottle and poured whiskey into a glass without the sheriff asking for it. Ned tipped the brim of his hat in appreciation and grabbed the glass as he arrived at the bar, knocking the whiskey back in one quick toss.

Brown filled his glass again and set the bottle on the bar.

The barber stepped up beside Ned and rapped his knuckles against the bartop. "Sheriff! Ain't you listenin' to me? You got to come quick."

He sounded angrier than Ned had ever heard him. Agitated. More than that, actually. That wasn't just anger in his histrionic tone. The man sounded like he was on the verge of a nervous breakdown.

Ned and the barkeep made eye contact again.

Ned arched an eyebrow as he turned toward the barber. "Come quick? Eddie, you know better than to believe anything Quentin's whores tell you. I can last for *hours*."

Brown spluttered laughter, nearly choking on his own mouthful of liquor.

Ned chuckled and refilled his glass from the open bottle.

Eddie thumped a fist on the bar. "Goddamn both of you! This is not a joke. Something funny is happening up in that quack's offices!"

Ned decided to humor the old man. "Funny how?"

A look of grim frustration was on the barber's face as he shook his head. "Funny as in some loud form of deviltry, and I'm not even sure it's the quack making all the dadblamed noise."

Ned frowned.

He got an uneasy feeling in his gut and for the first time worried there might be some substance to the barber's complaint this time. "Describe this deviltry."

The barber made an exasperated noise. "Hollering. Crashing sounds. Screams that sound like they're comin' from far away, but I know they're from upstairs."

Ned bit back a curse.

Much as he hated to admit it, there might be something to this. It definitely was nothing like Eddie's usual complaints about the doctor.

Shit.

He looked at Quentin Brown. "Reckon I better go have a look. You mind running across the street right quick to tell Billy and send him after me?"

The barkeep nodded. "Will do."

Ned downed the liquor in his glass and sighed heavily. "All right, then. Let's go see what this commotion is all about."

TEN

UP IN HIS room above the Last Chance Saloon, Russ Harper writhed about in his sleep, reliving his harrowing experience in the desert, but this time through the distorted lens of dreams. Much of what he saw in his head was as it had really happened, but there were significant differences. There were more of the strange little creatures gathered along the edge of the rocky outcropping. He saw them more clearly now, their strangely shaped heads and the horrible inner rings of spinning teeth, the blue shade of their leathery-looking skin.

They were like nothing he'd ever seen in the desert or anywhere else, nor did they resemble any descriptions of creatures he'd read about in texts on mythology or tales of the macabre. All of which seemed to validate his initial impression of being faced with creatures not of this world. Whether they came from the stars or from Hell itself, he could not say, but he felt more certain than ever they were not of earthly origin.

There was another presence up there with them on the outcropping, one that had not been there in reality, unless this was another instance of his dream illuminating something the darkness had hidden from him. This was a thing that looked like a man, someone of his own world, but the chill that went through him as he gazed upon the stranger suggested otherwise. His dream self suspected it was instead another kind of otherworldly being wearing the guise of a man. A creature capable of looking any way it wished. Right now the thing looked like an older man of impressive physical stature. He had gray whiskers and wore a long duster over typical trail hand garb. A hat with a wide, flat brim rested atop his head, loosely-tied drawstrings hanging beneath his chin. Even from down on the ground, the man's eyes projected a level of malevolence and danger that shouldn't have been perceptible in the dark.

In the dream, the man who was not a man stepped over the edge of the outcropping and spread his arms wide, the long tail of his coat flapping in the wind like the wings of a prehistoric beast as he glided slowly downward. The soles of his boots touched the ground seconds later, a landing of unnatural smoothness. Bedelia whinnied loudly as the man lowered his arms and smiled in a predatory way. The man raised a hand and snapped his fingers, an action that caused Russ's horse to whinny again and bolt away into the desert. As the horse departed, the other creatures—ugly minions to this far more powerful thing—also stepped over the edge of the outcropping. None of them landed with anything resembling the grace exhibited by their master. They squealed in pain as they hit the ground and rolled awkwardly around before regaining their feet.

Russ knew he should draw his gun, but his fingers felt frozen stiff. He trembled as the man and his minions came closer. "Who are you? What do you want from me?"

The man chuckled and smoothed the gray whiskers of his chin. "I am known here as Doyle. I am from beyond the veil. A harvester of souls. King of the Ravagers. It's reaping time, bounty hunter. I'll start with you."

Doyle pointed a finger at Russ. The wind picked up and the air felt charged with electricity. His dark eyes changed, glowing now with a bright light that also lit up the rest of his head from within, revealing a blackened skull beneath the mask of flesh. Sparks jumped from the tips of his fingers. The man's grinning skeleton mouth opened wide as he began to laugh. Then a bolt of light jumped from the tip of his finger and arced fast toward Russ's face . . .

Russ gasped and abruptly sat upright in bed, panting heavily from the terror induced by the nightmare. Before he could begin making any sense of what he'd experienced in the world of dreams, he was distracted by a startled shriek from someone else. His head snapped toward the sound and he frowned when he saw a saloon girl rooting through his things on the floor. Some kind soul had evidently retrieved his pack from wherever Bedelia was stabled and brought it here, quietly depositing it in the room while he was asleep.

He knew the would-be thief was a saloon girl from her painted face and the frilly little undergarment she wore in place of a proper dress. She wore stockings and scuffed-up white shoes with high heels. The girl was slender and had the malnourished look of a laudanum addict, with bags under her eyes the powder on her face couldn't quite obscure.

She jumped to her feet and made a run for the closed door. Russ hopped off the bed and caught up to her before she could get there. He spun her about and clapped a hand across her face, propelling her toward the bed. Her ass hit the mattress and she flopped backward. Instead of immediately getting up again, she lifted her torso up slightly, bracing her elbows on the mattress as she stared up at him. "You better not hit me again. There are people here who wouldn't look too kindly on that."

Russ snorted. "I only hit you because I caught you in the act of robbing me. I bet the man who runs this place wouldn't look kindly on that."

The girl gave him a blank-faced look for a moment. Then she spread her legs and pulled up the hem of her negligee, revealing the bare private parts beneath. "Let's not fight about it. Stick your cock in me and then give me some money. We'll both be happy. I need the coin and you have the look of a man who hasn't had a woman in a while. Come on, what do you say?"

A smile replaced the frown on Russ's face. "I reckon you've got a deal."

Clad only in dungarees, he was already halfway to naked. Under other circumstances, he might have sent her on her way, but the way she'd exposed herself got something started inside him that needed finishing. Otherwise he wouldn't be able to think straight the rest of the day. The lady was right, of course. It'd been a while.

Shed of his clothes now, he climbed up on the bed with the whore and plunged into her.

After it was all done, they lay sprawled on the bed together, Russ lighting a fresh stogie from a match as the whore stared up at the ceiling. She seemed in no hurry to leave the room now, which was strange. In his experience, saloon girls tended not to stick around after the deed was done and they were paid. And why would they? What they'd done together wasn't an act of love or mutual lust. It was a transaction. Work. Nothing else.

He exhaled a stream of sweet-smelling smoke and looked at her. "You plan to leave any time soon?"

Her head turned slowly toward him. "Don't you want to know why I was robbin' you?"

Russ grunted. "Not particularly."

She grabbed his wilting cock and squeezed hard. "You bastard. I should tear this thing off you."

Russ laughed. "Better watch it with the sweet talk. You'll have me ready to go again faster than you expect."

She arched an eyebrow. "Oh, really?"

Russ exhaled another stream of smoke. "Yep."

Some silent minutes ticked by. The whore's hand remained wrapped tight around his cock, which wasn't wilting anymore.

LAST OF THE RAVAGERS

She sighed. "I was robbin' you because I want out of this town."

"Is that right?"

She let go of his cock and rolled toward him, draping a leg over his midsection. "That's right, all right. This is a dead-end nowhere town. That copper mine where so many of the fellas work is gonna tap out soon. I hear them talk about it all the time. Snakebite ain't ever gonna be anything but a stop between places that matter. A girl like me's got no future here no matter what. I was gonna have to leave sooner or later." A troubled look contorted her features, which had the odd effect of making her look prettier than she normally did. "Now, though, with what happened to Angelina, I'm thinkin' the sooner I get out of here, the better."

"Angelina? That some whore friend of yours?"

She nodded. "Uh-huh. The one who got attacked last night, in the alley out back. Died this morning. They're sayin' it was an animal attack, but I don't believe that."

This reminded Russ of his conversation with the sheriff. He'd been apprised of the attack on the saloon girl at that time. There'd been some conjecture among the men gathered in the bar regarding the possibility of the assailant being a creature like the ones he'd seen in the desert. He'd heard nothing resembling real conviction in their voices as they discussed the matter, however, which wasn't surprising. The tale he'd told the men was a fantastical one. He couldn't rightly blame them for believing he'd hallucinated all of it, perhaps in the midst of a peyote trance. After all, he rode into town delirious from exhaustion. Even absent some mind-altering substance in his system, it was possible a mind pushed to the brink and beyond might conjure images of frightening things that did not actually exist.

Russ desperately wanted to believe this was possible. But he did not.

He knew and trusted his own mind. He'd spent a lot of lonely, empty days and nights in the desert, sometimes going without proper sleep or even food and water for extended periods. At no point had he ever imagined seeing things that weren't actually there. What he'd seen out there last night was real, no question about it as far as he was concerned. That being the case, it was also possible one or more of those things was already in Snakebite.

"What you thinkin' about, mister?"

Russ looked at her. "I don't believe your friend was attacked by an animal either. Not any ordinary beast anyway. When were you thinking about getting out of town?"

She touched his face, tracing the edge of his jawline with the ball of her thumb. "There's a stagecoach comin' through tomorrow on the way to Tombstone."

He grunted. "How much is the fare?"

She told him.

Then she added, "Which I've got already, but my plans don't stop there. Passenger trains run through Tombstone. I want to catch one and get to San Francisco. I have some friends already out there. I was gonna stay here another year and save up some more, but I've got this rotten feeling deep in my bones that if I do that, I'll wind up dying here."

Russ nodded. "What's your name, girl?"

"It's Charlotte. Why?"

Russ carefully disengaged himself from the prostitute and got up off the bed. On the floor, his unfurled pack was in disarray, but she'd not had time to locate the drawstring bag filled with gold coins. Soon enough, he was able to determine the bag was in its usual location.

Still squatting, he glanced up at the whore and saw her watching what he was doing with more than mild interest. "Close your eyes, Charlotte."

She sighed. "I'm not gonna rob you later or nothin'. Honest."

"Just close 'em, please."

Charlotte made a sound of mild annoyance, but did as he asked.

Russ took out some coins and put the bag away again. He stood. "Open your eyes and hold out your hand."

Again, she did as instructed, but this time she was smiling. Her eyes widened and she gasped in surprise as he dumped the coins in her hand. "Oh, sweet Jesus. That's gold. How much is this in dollars?"

Russ took her gently by the wrist and guided her off the bed. "Enough to get you where you're going and then some."

She gave him a puzzled look as he opened the door and ushered her out into the hallway. "Why are you doin' this? Was I that good a lay?"

He chuckled. "You were indeed. But I also know a thing or two about those deep down rotten feelings. I've learned it's best to pay close attention when they occur. Be on that stagecoach tomorrow, Charlotte. You hear me?"

Before she could answer, he closed and locked the door.

ELEVEN

THE THING ON the table in Doc Richardson's post-mortem examination room looked like a human woman but was not one. It was a living dead thing unnaturally possessed of animation, but it was devoid of the special spark that distinguished human intelligence from the rudimentary minds of beasts. The thing was driven by primitive instinct and a murderous rage the disappointed doctor could only interpret as an indication of a departed soul, a damning realization of his greatest fear.

At the most basic level, what he'd achieved here was extraordinary, a triumph of scientific innovation and human ingenuity over one of the most fundamental laws of nature. Death of the flesh was reversible. He'd shown that conclusively. As far as he knew, no one else ever had. No one but God, anyway. But what good was revived flesh absent any semblance of the person who'd inhabited it?

None whatsoever.

The strapped-down living dead woman was making one hell of a racket. The gag in her mouth was next to useless, suppressing barely any of her screaming. Some agitated yelling was audible from downstairs for a few minutes before it abruptly ceased. Richardson had no doubt Eddie Horton had heard more than enough to know something wasn't right up here. This left the doctor with little choice but to extinguish the miracle he'd accomplished. The barber had probably run off in search of Ned Kilmister, who would at first scoff at the man's tale, but would eventually feel compelled to investigate anyway.

Angelina could not still be in her state of reanimation when Ned arrived. He did not want to have to explain how this startling development had come to pass. The prospect filled him with nerve-shredding anxiety. Though Ned was not his equal in the realm of intellectual thought and discourse, he was smart in his own way, a good and competent lawman blessed with the natural gift of sussing out the truth of things in almost any given situation. Whether that would remain true when the matter at hand was so abnormal and beyond the experience of any lawman on Earth was impossible to say. He did know the sheriff was unlikely to take an understanding view of his experiments. Richardson did not feel inclined to leave any of it to chance.

The saloon girl would have to die a second time.

And soon.

But how to go about it?

The good news was Ned had already seen with his own eyes that Angelina was unquestionably deceased before being carried across the street for further examination. If he arrived here and found her dead again, he'd be none the wiser regarding any temporary change in her mortality status in the interim. The noise described by Horton he could dismiss as more of the barber's usual slander. With this semi-comforting thought in mind, he was able to calm down enough to start taking practical steps to bring the situation under control. Getting that syringe out of the thrashing woman's chest was his first order of business. The damn thing would make for an awfully conspicuous sight if it remained there.

The living dead woman stopped screaming and glared at him as he edged closer to the table again. She snarled and growled like a beast, her formerly pretty eyes projecting nothing but hatred. That she'd do her damnedest to tear him to pieces if freed of her bonds was a given. He wiped moisture from his mouth and forced himself to creep a few steps closer, feeling unsteady on his trembling legs. Remembering how she'd jabbed him with surprising force with the arm stump, he made his approach from the opposite side of the table. His hand shook badly as he reached out and tried to get a grip on the syringe. Before his fingers could curl around the metal cylinder, however, something shocking happened.

Angelina stopped thrashing.

Her eyes cleared and became imbued with a previously absent intelligence as she uttered actual words behind the cloth gag in her mouth. Richardson reeled backward a step or two, as startled by this development as anything that had occurred since the initial moment of reanimation. Tears leaked from the corners of her eyes and she sniffled as she tried to speak again.

Some moments passed.

The doctor finally remembered to breathe again. He remained keenly aware of time ticking by. This change in Angelina was astonishing and possibly indicative of a major breakthrough. He supposed it was possible the initial feral period after reanimation was a necessary transitional stage in the restoration of life and not a permanent state. During the transition, the soul might resist being called back to the flesh but in the end had no choice but to return. He deemed this the most logical explanation for what was now happening. A grin spread across his face as his heart filled with joy and hope. Despite the initial strong evidence of failure, he'd succeeded after all.

His genius was confirmed.

His smile faded, however, as he realized it changed nothing about the current situation. Any revelation of this nature to simple men such as Ned Kilmister or anyone else

LAST OF THE RAVAGERS

in Snakebite would have to be preceded by a long and detailed explanation of his research and scientific method. He would have to guide them through all of it step by careful step. It was not a thing men like that could walk in on and be expected to understand. They would react with strong emotion and perhaps condemnation. He'd be accused of doing the devil's work. It was not out of the realm of possibility that he might find himself fitted for a hangman's noose before the day was done.

Angelina still had to die again.

Richardson approached the table and this time did not shrink away when the revived saloon girl again tried to speak to him. He could make out some of her words if not complete sentences. She sounded scared and confused. He couldn't blame her. He even felt a bit of genuine sorrow on her behalf, but he could not allow that to sway him from the job at hand. The thick needle of the syringe was lodged deep inside the muscles beneath her chest wall. Prying it loose took some doing, but he finally managed it, noting with dismay how blood dribbled from the hole in her flesh. That would need dealing with, but first things first.

He returned the syringe to the dented metal box and hurried out of the post-mortem room. From his bedroom he retrieved a pillow and from his office a scrap of white cloth. As he moved through these rooms, he faintly heard Angelina calling out to him, a pronounced note of distress in her muffled voice. She was likely confused about her restoration, as well as scared about why she was strapped to the exam table. He wondered whether she retained any memory of being dead and gone or anything about the realm beyond death. It was an intriguing question, but there was no time to query her about it.

Back in the post-mortem room now, he dropped the scrap of white cloth between her spread legs and took a deep breath as he tried hard to summon the strength to do what was necessary. His plan was simple. He would force her head back down on the table and press the pillow down over her face. Smothering her would leave no additional trace of bodily violation and therefore less to explain. It was still a nasty bit of business. Murder was murder, regardless of the method employed. He did not relish anything about it, but it had to be done. After she'd expired a second time, he would use the cloth to wipe away the blood leaking from the hole in her chest.

As he approached the head of the table with the pillow clutched in his hands, he reminded himself he would need to undo the straps binding her to the table as soon as the deed was done. Not doing so would be an unfortunate oversight, one an interloper would certainly not miss. He couldn't imagine how he might explain the purpose in strapping a dead person to the table without giving away everything.

Standing directly over her now, he began to raise the pillow.

She looked up at him with tears flowing from her eyes and said something. A single word he thought he recognized. At first what she was saying didn't fully register, but then she repeated the word, taking care to enunciate it clearly, in a way that allowed no room for misinterpretation, even behind the gag.

Alfie.

Richardson felt something yield inside him. The internal barrier he'd erected against his emotions began to falter. During his brief romance with Angelina, Alfie had been her pet name for him. This despite pointing out to her on multiple occasions that his name was Albert and not Alfred, in which case it would have made more sense, but she didn't care, using the pet name constantly when they were alone together. In truth, he found it endearing, even when he pretended to be annoyed by it. When she ended things between them, he was surprised to discover how much he missed her whispering it in his ear.

LAST OF THE RAVAGERS

Now she said it again, even more clearly than before. "Alfie."

Sighing, he took one hand from the pillow, undid the strap cinched over her face, and began to pluck at the wadded-up cloth lodged in her mouth. She gagged and coughed as it began to come free of her oral cavity.

Once it'd been fully removed, she smiled and said, "Thank you."

Richardson nodded, hand trembling as he tossed the gag aside. "You're welcome."

The doctor's anxiety level soared again as his normally agile mind struggled to adjust to the wildly changing circumstances. Engaging with the newly cognizant revived woman to any degree complicated things. He was no longer at all certain he could go through with what he'd had in mind mere moments ago. Snuffing a suffering woman on the edge of death, as he'd done in the saloon's cellar a few hours earlier, was a different thing entirely. That'd been an act of mercy. Now, however, her formerly suppurating wounds were no longer oozing pus or showing other signs of infection. The extreme fever that had gripped her was gone and her pallor had returned to normal.

Perhaps there was a simple way out of his dilemma. He could tell Ned his pronouncement of death was premature, maybe utilize some pseudo-scientific mumbo-jumbo to convince him the girl had instead been in a deeply comatose state, one so profound it'd fooled even him. Then add that he'd detected some telltale signs of enduring life after being left alone with the apparent corpse, at which point he'd started working frantically to revive her, ultimately succeeding. There'd be no need for the sheriff to know anything about his experimental work. The approach could work, *if* he sold it hard enough.

Richardson sighed heavily, resigned to the attempt.

Angelina's relieved smile slowly shifted, becoming an accusatory smirk. "I mean it, darling. Thank you *so much*.

I saw it all, you know. What you did before suffocating me. The way you molested my broken body and played with your tiny cock as I lay there dying in the cellar. I know you believed I was beyond knowing or feeling anything in those moments, but you were wrong." Her laughter then had an insidious edge to it. "I can't wait to tell the sheriff all about your act of hideous perversion." She laughed again, sneering. "He should be here in about five seconds."

Richardson gaped at her in astonished horror. Something wasn't right. This was not the Angelina he'd known, who was, after all, only a simple saloon girl. Never before had she spoken with anything approaching this level of articulation. Something else was speaking through her, using her revived flesh as a conduit. As a man of reason, he'd never believed in demons, but it was the only explanation that fit. Something evil was in possession of her body, making her say things the real Angelina would never say.

He started shaking, but this time it was from anger as much as fear. "That's a lie."

She laughed heartily, taunting him. "Is it? Wait . . . listen."

Before he could reply, he heard muffled voices from down below. Then a faint creaking sound as multiple sets of booted feet began to ascend the stairs.

The thing possessing Angelina laughed again. "The hangman's noose won't kill you right away, doctor. Did you know that? Your consciousness will linger several seconds at least, a short period that will seem like a thousand horrible eternities."

Richardson slapped the pillow down over the demon's sneering face, gripping it tight with both hands as the thing began to scream and thrash about again. It repeatedly wrenched its head from side to side with such force that maintaining his grip on the pillow became an almost impossible chore. Already leaning over her, he realized he'd have to climb up on the table and straddle her to have any hope of keeping the pillow in place long enough to get the job done.

He was about to attempt it when the thrashing thing's right arm stump jabbed him hard in the side of the head, causing him to stagger away from the table and cry out from the pain. The pillow fell from his hands and the demon inside Angelina started screaming again. The sound was more like the howling of a wild and wounded animal than anything human. Hearing it unnerved the doctor nearly to the point of making him piss his pants. The thing's thrashing became more agitated than ever, and as he watched the thick leather straps stretched and snapped.

Richardson screamed and reeled backward, feeling his back meet the wall as the thing on the table sat up and turned its head toward him. The ghastly, contorted expression on the thing's face revealed its evil nature as it opened its mouth wide and unleashed another of those unearthly howls. The doctor felt a small trickle of pee stain the front of his trousers. His hands clawed at the wall behind him in desperate search of a way out that wasn't there. He knew he'd never make it to the post-mortem room's closed door before the thing could pounce on him.

This was it. There was no way out.

He was staring his doom in the face. Death was seconds away.

From one of the outer rooms came a frantic pounding on the door. The thing on the table roared again and launched itself at Dr. Albert Richardson.

TWELVE

NED KILMISTER TOOK out his Colt Peacemaker and told everybody crowded around him on the second floor landing to get the hell back. He aimed the gun an inch to the left of the lock on Doc Richardson's door and fired twice, damaging the wood around the mechanism sufficiently to render it vulnerable. Then he kicked the door open and raced inside, the others following right on his heels.

He stopped and stood still for a moment inside the doc's office, trying to track the source of the terrible sounds.

At the back wall were two closed doors, one to either side of a large desk, behind which was a bookcase stuffed to bursting with volumes mostly academic or intellectual in nature.

Billy Conway pointed to the door on the left. "That way."

Ned remained uncertain but decided to trust the younger man's hearing over his own. By lucky coincidence, the deputy had been on his way over to the saloon when they met in the street, the men conferring for a moment before heading over to the building shared by the doctor and barber. Quentin Brown came out of the saloon and joined them on the way, drawn both by genuine curiosity and a desire to lend assistance if necessary. Ned was grateful for their company. He wasn't ordinarily a fearful man, but what he was hearing now was disturbing enough to rattle any sane person. Having Eddie Horton trailing along in their wake was less than ideal, however, and he could only hope the dimwitted barber would stay out of their way.

The door on the left was not as sturdy-looking as the outer door. The simpler lock yielded to a single kick. Ned and the other men rushed into a larger room outfitted for performing all manner of basic medical examinations. There was also a surgical table surrounded by an array of equipment that made Ned feel sorry for any poor bastard ever in need of that level of help. Among these items were numerous tools designed for cutting into human flesh, including a hacksaw flecked with rust and what might have been old blood stains.

On the opposite side of this room was another door. The terrible screaming could be heard much more clearly now and was obviously emanating from the other side of that door. After only the slightest of hesitations, Ned led the other men through the exam chamber and kicked the door open.

Like any other lawman working in the wild and untamed areas between large cities, Ned had seen some disturbing things in his time. Senseless murders and the occasional mutilated corpse. These things didn't happen with great frequency, not out here in this largely empty part of the desert, but they *did* happen from time to time. As a result, he'd believed himself hardened enough to never be shocked by anything. He was taken aback, however, by the inexplicable sight that greeted him in the post-mortem room.

The dead saloon girl, Angelina, was somehow alive again and had the doc pinned against the wall, clearly engaged in an attempt to kill him. She was the source of that awful, unearthly howling. She turned her head and growled like a wild beast as Ned and the other men piled into the room. The rejuvenated woman's features were strangely contorted, twisted in ways that mirrored no normal human expression.

Billy Conway made a noise of disgust. "This is devil's work right here. Lady's been turned into a got-damned abomination."

Ned ignored this and aimed the Peacemaker at Angelina. "I'd rather not have to shoot you, miss, but I will if you don't let go of the doc and back the hell off right this minute."

In a sick-sounding voice fraught with dismay, Eddie Horton said, "Dear lord. She's got a demon inside her."

The barber went into a swoon and fell back against the frame of the open door.

The revived saloon girl still had a firm grasp on Richardson and thus far didn't seem inclined to release him any time soon.

Ned cocked the Peacemaker's hammer. "Lady, I'm gonna give you five more seconds to take your hands off the doc. I've warned you fair and square. What happens next is on you."

Richardson's eyes looked glassy as his head swiveled toward the sheriff. "Don't wait. Shoot her now."

The woman's contorted lips formed a strange mockery of a smile. What happened next occurred too swiftly to stop. She pushed a finger into one of the doctor's eye sockets, slipping it in beneath the eyelid and hooking it around the ocular orb. Richardson screamed and stamped his feet against the floor as she ripped the eyeball out and held it up for all to see.

Ned flinched at the boom of a pistol.

Then he realized his deputy, Billy, had his own gun out and was already firing. The first slug from his weapon punched a hole through one of Angelina's cheeks. Any normal woman would've dropped instantly to the floor, but the thing inhabiting her body remained upright and started cackling like a lunatic. Then it reared back an arm and whipped it forward, flinging the blood-dripping eyeball across the room with startling force. The orb smacked a still delirious Eddie Horton right in the middle of his forehead, adhering there a moment before beginning to slide down the bridge of his nose. Having an eyeball stuck to his face brought him all the way out of his swoon as he unleashed a shriek shriller than that of any schoolgirl. He batted at the thing until it flew away from his face and hit the back of Quentin Brown's shiny black saloon keeper's vest, where it also adhered a moment before finally dropping to the floor.

Billy's gun roared again and then Ned started firing his Peacemaker. Nearly every bullet found its mark, puncturing flesh and jerking the possessed body this way and that. Ned had no experience with the supernatural and until just now would not have believed such things actually existed. Demon possession was the stuff of superstition. Only those lost in the depths of intractable religious mania could possibly believe in it. Even in the midst of this moment of profound violence, he understood this was an opinion in need of revising. Clearly demons did exist.

How else to explain any of this madness?

The lawmen continued firing their guns until they clicked empty. Though they hadn't managed to drop the possessed body with their combined firepower, they'd driven her up against the back wall. The numerous holes in the naked female flesh oozed a combination of yellow pus and a black, oily substance that vaguely looked like blood.

Cackling again, the thing pushed itself away from the wall and charged at them. More precisely, charged straight at Ned.

Ned groaned. "Goddammit."

The creature hit him hard enough to blast the air from his lungs as it drove him to the floor. She—or *it*, whatever—

bared bloody teeth and hissed at him like a serpent. Instinct told him she meant to tear out a chunk of his neck. Before she could do that, he got his hands between them, palms turned upward to brace against her chest. Quite by accident, he'd grabbed hold of both her breasts. There was no accompanying moment of reflexive sexual excitement, only revulsion and terror as the thing's teeth snapped and clacked again and again, straining to reach his vulnerable flesh.

Ned's focus was necessarily on the life-and-death struggle in which he was currently engaged, but he had some sense of the chaos taking place around him. He heard yelling and a pounding of boots on the floor as the others—most of them, anyway—raced to his aid. Billy and Quentin grabbed hold of the demon's host body and tried pulling it away from him. When that didn't work, Billy resorted to repeatedly slamming a fist into the side of her head. That approach also did not work.

Next came a pause of a few seconds.

Then, once again, came the booming report of a pistol. Billy had stopped to reload. This time he put the muzzle of his gun against the side of Angelina's head and fired twice. Both bullets went right through her skull, blowing out chunks of it as they exited the other side. Bone fragments and gooey bits of brain matter decorated the nearest wall. This greater level of damage finally weakened the demon. Quentin and Billy grabbed hold of it and again tried pulling it away.

The creature still thrashed and growled at them—albeit more weakly than before—but they were finally able to get it away from Ned. Still working together, the deputy and saloon keeper pushed the demon onto its back, pinning it to the floor and holding it there. Both men looked confused as to what to do next. Ned figured this was understandable. As far as he could tell, the goddamn thing was unkillable.

Ned sat up, wincing at the many aches throughout his

body. After a few seconds, he realized there was no sign of the doctor. Then he heard a sound of pounding feet again as the doctor came racing back into the room.

Gripped in his hands was the rusty hacksaw from the exam room. One side of his face was a mask of crimson, thanks to the flow of blood from the empty eye socket. Ned couldn't help flinching at the ghastly transformation of his visage. How the man was functioning at all given the amount of pain he must be in was a mystery. Perhaps it was the pain itself spurring him to action, along with a desire to avenge the act of mutilation. As he knelt between the men holding the demon down, he placed the blade of the hacksaw against Angelina's throat and began to saw away at the flesh, more of that oily black blood-like substance emerging from this fresh wound.

Then the howling stopped and the woman on the floor whimpered. "Please don't hurt me."

Richardson continued sawing away at her.

The woman's face was no longer a contorted and bruised-looking mockery of a normal human face. It'd returned entirely to normal, or as close to normal as possible with a bullet hole in her cheek. Tears leaked from her eyes as she continued to whimper and plead for mercy. Even the blood flowing from the deepening gash in her neck had regained a normal reddish hue. Perhaps sensing the imminent demise of its human host, the demon had departed, which meant the doc was now in the process of murdering an innocent woman.

One who'd already died once today.

Ned could make no sense of that, nor of how she could possibly have reverted to normal with a large portion of her brain matter stuck to the wall, but figuring any of that out would have to wait for later. He had to stop Richardson and couldn't afford to hesitate any longer. It might already be too late.

Before he could try, the woman abruptly ceased

whimpering and started in with that soul-shriveling howling again. This time the sound was shriller and even more unnerving than before. The noise sounded like something directly connected to the blackest depths of hell, the screaming, enraged voice of Lucifer himself perhaps. Hearing it pushed Ned to the brink of abandoning any sense of duty He longed to run from the room, find his horse, and ride away from Snakebite just as fast as he could.

The other men weren't faring much better. Eddie Horton was passed out on the floor. Billy and Brown had each relinquished their grip on the demon in favor of clapping their hands over their tortured ears. The look on Richardson's face was an agonized one, but he was still trying his best to complete the task of severing the woman's head, an effort that ended a moment later when she ripped the hacksaw from his hands and, still on her back, started swinging it about in rapid, vicious arcs. The blade chopped into Richardson, Conway, and Brown in multiple places as they tried to shield themselves with upraised arms.

Ned got to his feet. Spying the dented metal box on the smaller of the room's two tables, he snatched it up and raced forward again, smashing a side of it against the side of Angelina's head already reduced to a pulpy mess by the exit wounds from Billy Conway's bullets. The heavy blow quieted the weakening demon and Ned pushed the advantage, slamming the box down into the same place again. *Still* not dead, but getting weaker all the time.

He straddled the demon and raised the box high over his head.

Then he slammed it down again.

And again.

Over and over until there was nothing left of Angelina's head but a squishy, bloody, pulpy mess on the floor.

Panting heavily, Ned got shakily to his feet and tossed

the metal box aside. It hit the floor with a clatter, its lid coming open as several syringes rolled out of it.

Billy shook his head and whistled. "Holy goddamn moly. I think the bitch is finally dead."

Doc Richardson dropped to his knees and started sobbing.

THIRTEEN

ELEANOR AWOKE ALONE by the crackling flames of the fire, which now felt too hot within the confines of the cave and in the aftermath of aggressive sexual coupling. Her body was covered in sweat and sticky, drying blood. As she dragged herself toward the sunlight beyond the cave entrance, she desired nothing more desperately than a good, cleansing bath. She felt drained and at the brink of total exhaustion. Tom's horse was still waiting for her somewhere beyond the entrance to the cave. She could hear the animal softly whinnying, as if sensing her lethargic attempt to reach it.

This effort had nothing to do with regret over anything she'd done. There'd been no sudden swelling of remorse for knowingly standing by while her family was slaughtered, nor did she regret torturing and butchering Sally. All these things had occurred at the behest of her new master, for whom she still felt a deep and unswerving devotion. She would do anything he asked of her, no matter how perverse and disgusting.

Unlike her master, however, she was only human, and there was a limit to what her body could take. She was simply overwhelmed and depleted, in both body and mind. A period of rest and recuperation was needed. Though he was human only in appearance, surely the stranger must understand that.

She was reaching forward to claw at the cave floor

again and drag herself a little closer to the entrance when she felt one of his big hands close around her right ankle. A soft, defeated whimper escaped her lips as he dragged her back deeper into the cave. He didn't stop pulling her along the uneven, pitted ground until they were again within a few feet of the fire.

"You are not to leave without my permission."

Eleanor sighed. "Okay. I'm sorry. I'm just tired. I need to sleep. I need a bath."

He grunted, letting go of her ankle. "You require replenishment."

She grimaced as she turned her head to look at him. "Yes. Please. If I can't leave, please let me sleep."

"There is no time for that. Wait here."

"Okay. Whatever you say."

The stranger moved away from her, passing from her field of vision as he returned to the back of the cave. His blue-skinned minions were still back there and they started making excited chittering and grinding sounds at his approach. Though she knew the strange creatures wouldn't hurt her without his permission, they nonetheless made her nervous. Their alienness triggered an involuntary sense of revulsion, something she would've felt even without knowledge of their murderous capabilities. They had no fear of normal men, of that much she was sure, but they both deeply feared and revered their master.

From the back of the cave came some loud cracking and popping sounds. At the same time, the chittering of the stranger's minions grew louder and more high-pitched. They sounded like birds fighting over crumbs on the ground. In a few more seconds there came a final, louder pop. Then she heard the man's footsteps again as returned to her.

He nudged her ass with his foot. "Sit up."

Eleanor groaned tiredly, but did as she was told.

She frowned.

The popping and cracking sounds she'd heard were a product of the stranger removing Sally Frederickson's head from her body with his bare hands. The stretched flesh of her throat had a gruesomely twisted look to it. The head dangled from the fingers of his right hand, which were entwined in the dead woman's long dark hair.

The stranger sat across from Eleanor in a cross-legged position, their knees nearly touching. "You require a meal. One that will restore you to full vitality within moments of ingestion."

Eleanor stared at the severed head clutched in his hands, frowning in confusion. "What, am I supposed to eat her face or something? How's that supposed to revitalize me?"

The thought of it triggered a sick twinge in her guts. The reaction was an odd and unexpected one, considering she'd already taken multiple bites out of one of the dead woman's kidneys after ripping it from her dying body moments earlier. That, however, had been in the heat of the moment, in the midst of a dark and thrilling dive into perverse revelry, with the stranger fucking her and telling her what to do. In those moments, she was completely in his thrall, incapable of feeling sickened by anything he required of her, but she was no longer in that state of depraved frenzy.

The stranger smirked. "Eating her face would not bring about the rejuvenation you require. Watch."

He clutched Sally's head tightly in his hands while pushing his thumbs into her eye sockets. Eleanor heard liquid popping noises as the eyeballs yielded to the intense pressure, bursting apart. Blood and other fluids oozed out around his thumbs. Once his thumbs were fully inside the sockets up to their top knuckles, he began pulling his hands in opposite directions. At first nothing happened as the stranger's face became a mask of sneering concentration, but in a few more seconds Eleanor heard popping sounds again.

LAST OF THE RAVAGERS

The man was cracking Sally's head open like a gourd. Eleanor felt another of those little twinges in her gut, only this time the feeling was overridden by a deepening curiosity about what he had in mind. The cracking sounds got louder as he continued ripping Sally's skull apart. As the process continued, the flesh covering the front of the skull began to stretch and tear apart like thin tissue paper.

Moments later, the two halves of Sally's skull came fully apart and the stranger roared in hungry triumph, sounding more like a beast than a man. He scooped out a big handful of gooey brain matter from Sally's cracked-open skull and shoveled some of it into his mouth, making snorting, hungry sounds as he chewed and swallowed.

Next he reached out to Eleanor, a big, heaping glop of brains held in his outstretched hand. "Eat."

It was a simple command. Just one word. Easy to understand. And this was a man one should never even think of disobeying, not if one wished to go on living much longer.

Eleanor, feeling genuinely queasy now, hesitated anyway. "Um . . . "

The stranger laughed, licking tiny bits of brain matter from his lips. "I understand. Even after all you have done today, after all the taboos you have transcended, this feels like one step too far, but trust me when I tell you you'll never feel even a shadow of that loathing again after your first taste of this most uncommon of delicacies."

Eleanor frowned, still not fully convinced. "Is that right?"

The stranger chuckled. "Oh, yes. Devouring the brain of someone you have killed conveys power and insight. You will feel stronger than you ever have before. And you will know your victim's thoughts, everything they ever knew. When amplified by my power, there is no greater pathway to knowledge, no greater conduit of energy." He stretched his hand a little closer and a few tiny morsels of brain slopped over his fingers and dripped to the cave floor. "Go on now. Eat."

Despite her queasiness, Eleanor was officially intrigued. "I'll know everything she thought? Really?"

The stranger nodded, his dark eyes twinkling with mischief in the dying light of the fire. "Yes. Really. As I already do."

Eleanor let out a shuddery breath and tentatively reached out, dipping her slender fingers in the pile of gelatinous glop held in the stranger's much larger hand. She experienced another moment of reflexive disgust, but she shoved aside the feeling and pushed a handful of brain matter into her mouth. The moment the large helping of it touched her tongue, she knew the stranger was once again right about everything. Never in her life had she tasted anything finer. She groaned in almost sexual ecstasy as her taste buds lit up. As the first bits of it slid down her gullet, she felt electrified, bursting with eager energy and a renewed and strengthened desire to give herself fully to her new master, with no hesitation or shame.

She flopped over and rolled about on the ground. Images, thoughts, and feelings that did not belong to her invaded her consciousness with the force of a tornado, a torrent of raw and unfiltered information that for a period of several moments overwhelmed and frightened her. This was the totality of everything Sally had ever been filling her up to the point where she feared it might overtake and obliterate her own identity. In addition, she felt the dead woman's psychic essence flitting about in the midst of it all, filled with confusion and teetering on the edge of living again. This essence, Eleanor instinctively realized, was what people meant when they talked about the soul. Unanchored from its own body, however, the soul was an ephemeral thing. It required that strong connection with its birth body to remain in the earthly realm. Before long, Eleanor sensed the woman's essence start to dissipate and drift away.

LAST OF THE RAVAGERS

Then it was gone.

Eleanor's eyes snapped open and she sighed heavily in relief. She sat up, feeling more alert than she could remember feeling in a long time, possibly ever, and suffused with so much strength and energy she felt capable of fighting mountain lions with her bare hands . . . and winning. Power coursed in her veins, crackled in her nerve-endings. She looked at her hands and flexed her fingers, feeling and reveling in a new and massively elevated capacity for brutal violence. Curling one hand into a fist, she felt that new strength gather and focus itself, eager for a target. In that moment, she felt fully capable of ramming that fist right through a man and ripping out his heart.

In the absence of a fresh victim to kill, she relaxed her fist and looked inwardly, delving into that section of her mind that now contained Sally's thoughts and memories. This time she was able to examine it all in a more leisurely fashion. The information was already there. She accessed it simply by focusing.

As it turned out, the school teacher's carnal interest in Eleanor was not a fleeting or impulsive thing fueled by the consumption of alcohol. Sally was a woman who liked women exclusively. She became smitten with Eleanor the first time they met and immediately began scheming potential methods of seduction. This despite being fully aware of Eleanor's status as a devoted family woman and respected member of the community. Sally simply did not care about any of that, believing she sensed something in Eleanor that was just waiting to be awakened.

She succeeded in seducing Eleanor, which filled her with elation. This wondrous feeling was, unfortunately, followed by the shattering disappointment of rejection as the object of her intense desire took extreme measures to avoid ever being in her presence again. The repudiation destroyed Sally. The worst part of it was how she had to work so hard at hiding her pain from the citizens of

Snakebite, an almost impossible thing that led to excessive drinking and suicidal thoughts. The teacher went to her death truly believing she was in love with Eleanor.

It was a strange thing, being in the grip of memories that were not her own. One could lose oneself in them if one wasn't careful. Eleanor focused on the face of the stranger, who was watching her with a look of intense concentration and curiosity. In a few seconds, the illusion of being someone else faded and she was herself again, albeit not exactly the same as she'd been before.

A shiver went through her and she laughed softly. "That was . . . incredible. I felt . . . lost for a few minutes. Not myself." She laughed again. "I can't believe some of the things in Sally's head. She really loved me. Also, she killed an ex-husband back east before fleeing to this desolate place. Never would've imagined anything so lurid in her background."

The stranger nodded knowingly, smiling again as he licked slimy brain goo from his fingers. "Humans are full of surprises. The interesting ones, anyway. Devouring the brains of the dull-witted ones is less fulfilling."

Eleanor's brow furrowed as she thought about it. "That makes sense, I suppose, but I can't help wondering . . . what are you? If not human, I mean. What makes you so powerful?"

The stranger shrugged. "The answer to your question is simple and complicated at the same time. Here in your world, I am called Doyle. In other places, I am called other things. Sometimes similar things. Sometimes not."

Eleanor leaned to one side slightly and spent a few seconds staring at Doyle's minions, who were quiet now and regarding her with an equal amount of curiosity.

She met Doyle's gaze again. "Okay, so I know your name now. You still haven't told me *what* you are. While I'm at it, what are they?"

She indicated the minions with a lift of her chin.

LAST OF THE RAVAGERS

He clasped hands with her. "I am like you. A living creature. Flesh. Blood. Imbued with what your kind thinks of as a soul. But I am more than that. Something better. Something stronger. I'm from a different world, one that scarcely resembles this one, but to which it is nonetheless intimately connected. There I am like a god. In your world, I *am* a god. I am a harvester of souls, an annihilator of the flesh. I am the Lord of the Dead. Last of the Ravagers. I can raise dead things, reanimate them, and use them in any way I see fit. My minions, for instance."

Eleanor's confusion continued to deepen. "What about them?"

Doyle chuckled. "I am able to reconstitute the bodies of those I kill in any form that pleases or amuses me. The minions, the way they look . . . it is a creation of mine. They are former humans and other mortal beings from other worlds. All of them. Remade and bestowed with a new purpose."

Upon hearing this revelation, Eleanor felt distaste and fascination in equal measures. She had no reason to doubt anything Doyle was telling her, not after all the verifiably real dark wonders he'd exposed her to so far.

"And what is that purpose?"

Doyle kissed the back of one of her hands. "Isn't it obvious by now, my queen? They serve as an advance guard in my army of the dead."

Eleanor was on the verge of continuing to pursue the same line of questioning when what he'd said fully registered.

"Hold on . . . did you just call me your queen?"

He pulled her into his arms and she felt his once again rigid cock prod at her belly. "I did. Every king needs a loyal queen to serve at his side. Soon we will ride into glory together. But first . . . "

Eleanor smiled. "Yes. First."

She climbed atop him and soon screams reverberated in the cave again.

FOURTEEN

L **ESS THAN AN** hour after her encounter with
the bounty hunter, Charlotte Blanchard decided she
wanted to go outside and get some fresh air, so she
went out to the saloon's porch. It was around half past
noon and there weren't many people out and about. A few
buildings down on the other side of the street, two men
came out of the hardware store carrying either end of a
heavy wooden crate. They loaded the crate into the back of
a wagon and shook hands.

She recognized the leaner of the two men. He was
Jacob Montgomery, owner of the hardware store and a
married man. She didn't know much about Montgomery's
wife, Kathy, but she felt sorry for the woman, doubting she
derived much satisfaction from her husband's unusually
tiny cock. Jacob had paid for Charlotte's company on a few
occasions and always had difficulty getting the thing inside
her. The difficulty wasn't a matter of arousal. He got hard
with no problem. His little stub of a penis, however, was
rarely able to penetrate her deeply enough to matter. It had
to be embarrassing for the man, but that didn't stop him
from trying.

Sensing scrutiny from somewhere, he craned his head
around until he saw her standing outside the saloon. She
smiled and raised a hand in a silent greeting, but he quickly
glanced away, murmured some parting words to his
customer, and hurried back into the hardware store. The

customer unhitched his mules from the post outside the store, climbed up onto the riding bench, and rode away.

Once the wagon was out of sight, Charlotte descended the porch steps to the dusty street. She was acting out of a combination of boredom and an intuitive sense that with her time in this nowhere town growing short there might be something to be gained by pressuring Jacob. Ordinarily she'd never think of putting the screws to any of Snakebite's relatively upstanding citizens. There'd be hell to pay if word of it ever got back to Miss Agatha, madam of the girls who worked at the saloon. She'd be cut loose from the Last Chance and possibly even thrown in jail on trumped-up charges, ones that wouldn't quite reveal the true nature of her offense.

As she headed in the direction of that hardware store, she became aware of some hollering emerging from the building across the street from the saloon. She paid this little mind. That doctor and barber were always going at each other and their squabbling often got loud and heated. This was just more of the usual, as far as she was concerned. Certainly nothing to be alarmed about.

She continued on down the street and, in another few moments, entered the hardware store. Inside were neat rows of shelving with various types of tools and items for the home arranged in an orderly fashion. In the back was a large pile of lumber and a table for custom cutting of the lumber, which was often purchased in large quantities by homesteaders who built their own barns and houses outside of town.

Jacob was behind the counter at the front of the store. He was examining entries in a ledger, a frown of concentration on his face when she came through the door. He grimaced when he saw her. "What are you doing here?"

Charlotte pooched out her bottom lip in a look of mock offense. "Jakey, darling, I'm hurt. Is that any way to talk to a woman you've been intimate with so many times? I had you figured for more of a gentleman than that."

Jacob made a sound of annoyance, glancing around as if afraid someone might have heard this, but there was no one else in the store. "You need to keep your mouth shut, you stupid whore. If you don't, someone might shut it for you." A corner of his mouth twitched. "Forever."

Blunt words designed to instill fear.

In truth, they troubled her, but Charlotte was determined not to let him see that. "Oh, big words. Big, scary words. Kind of funny coming from a man so small where it really counts."

Jacob was seething now

She could see him grinding his teeth and trying not to blow his stack.

"How dare you come into my place of business and talk to me this way. This is a respectable establishment patronized by god-fearing people. And you waltz in here in your harlot's clothing, running your filthy mouth." He sneered. "This isn't Saturday night at the saloon, bitch. Get out of here before I decide to have a little talk with the head whore over at that den of iniquity."

Charlotte laughed. "Oh, please. You're playing to an audience of one here, Jakey, and I damn well know you don't have any morals. You've spent lots of time at that so-called 'den of iniquity', ya goddamn hypocrite."

Jacob glared at her a moment longer.

Then he sighed and shook his head. "What do you want from me, Charlotte?"

She smiled. "Money. What else?"

Her heart started beating a little faster. Until uttering these words, she'd still been on the safe side of a dangerous line, one she could step back and walk away from with no damage done. Well, it was too late for that now. The craziest part of it was how she'd arrived at this point purely on impulse. What she was attempting wasn't even necessary to facilitate her escape from Snakebite. With the gold coins the bounty hunter had given her, she already had enough to get where she was going and start a new life. On the other hand, an additional bit of money would make her new beginning even more comfortable.

Jacob muttered a curse, spraying the counter with spittle. "I can give you some money, Charlotte, but only a little." He lifted the ledger, displaying it for a second as if it meant anything to her, which it did not. "This is a meticulously run enterprise. Everything is accounted for. If I give you more than just a little, it will cause problems."

Charlotte rolled her eyes. "I truly do not care. Just give me what you can. If I'm happy with it, I'll never need to have a talk with your wife."

Still glowering at her, Jacob stepped out from behind the counter and moved past her, starting down one of the aisles. He turned back and glanced at her with a raised eyebrow. "You coming? I'd like to get this over with, please."

She smiled. "Lead the way."

She followed him down the aisle and then into a back room beyond the lumber pile. This was a cluttered room filled with additional stock of many of the items for sale out front. Jacob went to a table pushed against the back wall, upon which sat, among other things, a safe. Charlotte crowded in close and tried to peer over his shoulder as he opened it and reached inside.

"What have you got for me, Jakey, dear?"

He turned around and showed her the most evil, tight-lipped grin she'd ever seen.

Her mouth dropped open.

She was terrified, but there was no time to flee.

He shoved the derringer into her mouth and pulled the trigger.

FIFTEEN

AIDED BY QUENTIN BROWN, Ned Kilmister guided a woozy Doc Richardson through the back entrance of the smithy. They could feel the heat from the forge before they entered. Sweat rose on Ned's brow within seconds. The shop was owned by Gareth Blackmore, one of just two blacksmiths operating a full-service smithy in Snakebite. Of the two, Gareth had by far the better reputation.

He also owed Ned a favor.

Heaving a breath as the trio of men came to a stop, Ned looked the blacksmith in the eye and simply said, "Roscoe."

Roscoe Jones was the man who'd raped Gareth's wife two years earlier. A longtime thorn in the side of the entire community, Roscoe was known for making lewd and lecherous comments to the womenfolk of Snakebite. It was one thing to talk that way to saloon girls. That was frowned upon, but a man could get away with it, especially on rowdy weekend evenings. Addressing the more respectable ladies—the wives and the mothers—well, that was more than frowned upon. A man could get the shit kicked out of him for that. Roscoe did it anyway. Repeatedly. Even after taking his beatings. The behavior got him locked up overnight for indecency numerous times. Still, no one ever thought Roscoe's crudity would one day lead to transgressions of a more extreme nature.

Until that spring day in 1875, when Roscoe went to the

LAST OF THE RAVAGERS

home the Blackmores owned on the outskirts of town. Gareth was busy with a major project and the Blackmores' only child was at school. Knowing no one would be around to get in the way, Roscoe let himself into the house and accosted Lydia, taking her with violence and afterward warning her to keep her mouth shut about the incident, saying he'd come back to slit her throat if she blabbed about it.

Lydia, however, did not keep her mouth shut.

She told Gareth.

Gareth told Ned.

And shortly afterward, Roscoe Jones ceased to exist. No one missed him. His mysterious disappearance was never discussed, at least not in public. It was as if he'd never walked the face of the earth at all.

Gareth nodded, his gaze flicking briefly to Richardson. "What happened to him?"

Ned sighed, shifting his weight as the woozy doctor leaned a little more heavily into him. "Trust me when I say you'd never believe a word of it. The bottom line is something messed the hell up happened and the doc here is missing an eyeball."

He told Gareth what they had in mind.

Gareth listened with a stoic reaction. Then he nodded. He'd do it. Of course he would. He'd probably do anything for Ned Kilmister. "That's gonna hurt. A lot."

Richardson let out an audible sob.

Ned grimaced. "We know."

This thing they had in mind was almost unspeakably horrific. No question. It was also unquestionably necessary, because the doc's violated eye socket wouldn't stop bleeding. Right now a wadded-up scrap of cloth soaked in laudanum was packed inside it. This had seemed to help at first, but now the cloth was soaked through and a steady stream of blood was seeping out of the socket again. Before this, they'd tried sulfur, also to no avail.

These were normally reliable ways of getting the blood from an open wound to clot, but nothing was working. Prior to his departure, Billy ventured the theory that perhaps the problem was in some way related to its infliction by a supernatural entity. Some unseen and abnormal extra form of infection, one that could not easily be treated in the normal ways.

Hence this visit to Blackmore's Smithy.

Ned felt more tired than he had in a long time and it was barely past one in the afternoon. After spending some time tending to their many cuts and abrasions, Ned Kilmister assisted the other men in wrapping up what was left of Angelina's corpse and carrying it into the alley out back of the building shared by Horton and Richardson. This was after the reluctant barber, at the sheriff's behest, first went downstairs and put up a 'CLOSED' sign on the front door.

Once it became apparent that death at the hands of an inexplicable supernatural phenomenon was no longer an imminent threat, Ned started rethinking his original idea of burning Angelina's remains in the alley. He had enough to worry about already without facing a barrage of questions from the superstitious contingent of the town's population. The alley afforded a higher level of privacy than the open street, but folks were still apt to wander through it at any given time.

Some level of discretion was obviously in order. With that in mind, he directed Billy to take the blanket-wrapped corpse miles out of town, to some unpopulated patch of land with no one around, and set the remains ablaze. The deputy agreed to this assignment without complaint, which was typical for him. A short while later, he rode out of town with the body lashed to his horse.

That left the unpleasant task of dealing with Doc Richardson, who by then had already helped himself to a generous portion of laudanum from his professional supply. He'd also consumed most of a bottle of whiskey. Given the amount of pain caused by the demon's horrific act of mutilation, Ned judged all this well within reason. After a while, the doc's head was wobbling so much it looked as if it might soon separate from his neck and float away.

He was likely as numb as a man could get and still be alive. In Ned's estimation, he was about as ready to face the grim reality of this desperate measure as he'd ever be. Even in this drugged state, the agony would be severe, possibly beyond the man's ability to endure. Ned put the man's odds of surviving the shock to his system at somewhere around 50/50.

At best.

The shop's entrance and exit were wide enough to allow admission to stagecoaches and covered wagons in need of repairs, though none were present at the moment. Gareth spent a few minutes getting the doors pulled shut and latched. He knew without being told it'd be best not to perform this procedure in full view of anyone who might walk by.

Once this was taken care of, the blacksmith ushered his guests over to the forge. Though the embers within had cooled somewhat since he'd paused in his work some twenty minutes earlier, the forge was still putting out significant heat. Some work with the bellows got the temperature up even higher. All the men sweated profusely as they stood within six feet of the forge. Ned glanced at Richardson and saw his remaining good eye turning glassy, a sure sign of an impending lapse into unconsciousness. Given what was about to happen, any such lapse would be short-lived. He felt sorry for the poor son of a bitch, even though he harbored suspicions regarding the doc's possible role in the inexplicable shit that had happened in his offices. He had a lot of questions, but they'd have to wait for a better time.

If one ever arrived, that is.

After donning thick protective gloves, Gareth took a thin iron rod and began to heat it in the forge. The rod was black in color and remained so for the first few minutes. Before long, however, its tip began to glow a bright red. He kept the end of the rod immersed in the coals a while longer, allowing it to get even hotter.

As this process continued, Richardson's knees buckled and he began to sag toward the ground. After exchanging a glance, Ned and Quentin loosened their grips on the man's arms, allowing him to kneel.

Gareth glanced at them. "Ready when you are."

Ned nodded. "Just a second."

Grimacing, he dug a finger into the doctor's violated eye socket and tugged out the blood-soaked cloth. There was no trace of the fabric's original white color. Richardson shuddered and groaned as the cloth came free, wincing when the sticky blood forced Ned to tug harder. Once this task was complete, he made the doctor clamp his teeth down on a thick leather bit.

Gareth moved closer. "Get down on the ground with the man and grip him tight. Hold him as steady as you can. If he flails around too much, this thing is apt to go right up into his brain. And, well . . . "

The rest of it didn't need saying.

If they couldn't keep him under control, the doc would be a dead man.

Ned and Quentin knelt to either side of Richardson, each taking a strong, two-handed grip on an arm. Gareth let out a breath and moved the blazing tip of the iron rod close to the oozing socket. Now that the bloody cloth was no longer in place, the blood was streaming out more freely. The flow of it, in fact, seemed thicker than before. The agony of cauterization would be a hellish experience, but by now it was clear he'd die anyway if they didn't attempt it.

LAST OF THE RAVAGERS

Gareth directed one last hesitant glance at Ned, the tip of the rod now no more than an inch away from the puckered flesh of the eyelids. "No second thoughts? You definitely want to do this?"

Ned growled like an animal.

He wanted this exercise in barbarism over and done. "Do it."

Gareth nodded, but said no more.

The time for hesitation was over.

The blacksmith pushed the glowing tip of the rod into Richardson's eye socket. There was a sizzling sound and a thin column of smoke emerged from the socket. The smell of burning flesh triggered nausea in all those present, but the men pushed through this instinctive revulsion and put everything they had into keeping the doc relatively still, holding on for dear life as he struggled like a wild beast. The doc screamed and screamed behind the bit in his mouth, his teeth sinking so deeply inside the thick leather that it would later need to be pried free.

Gareth held the rod in place, rotating it with slow and careful precision inside the socket. The doc's screaming continued even as the blacksmith pulled the rod free and returned it to the forge. Ned and Quentin maintained their strong grips on the doctor until long after the horrendous procedure was finished, feeling him shake and whimper endlessly in their arms.

They didn't let go of him until he finally passed out.

SIXTEEN

A **HALF HOUR** of riding carried Billy Conway out to a shallow gully, where he tied his horse to a solitary tree with barren and withered-looking limbs bleached almost white by the unforgiving Arizona sun. Overlooking the gully, the lone tree stood above it like a dead sentinel, a guardian of forgotten things.

Of dead things.

Billy figured it was an appropriate place for disposing of the headless body. After removing the blanket-wrapped corpse from the back of his horse, he dumped it on the ground and rolled it into the sun-parched gully.

Best get on with it, he thought.

Careful of his footing, he descended into the gully with his tinderbox. Squatting on his haunches next to the unmoving corpse, he examined the blanket in which it was wrapped and judged it likely to ignite with relative ease. The dry parts of the fabric would act as effective kindling. He raised a hand, ready to hit the flint with the fire striker when something happened at the edge of his peripheral vision that caused him to turn his head to the right.

He frowned and stared at the dead saloon girl's bare feet, which were sticking out from the end of the blanket. Something barely perceptible had happened there. Something he'd almost missed. A tiny flicker of movement. His gaze remained on the exposed feet several moments longer as he waited for a repetition of whatever it was. As he did this, he became aware of his heart beating a little more quickly than before.

The girl was deader than a damn doornail. That much was an incontrovertible fact. Bodies didn't go on living without a head. Not for more than a few seconds. Billy was no man of medicine or science, but he didn't need to be one to know that. Maybe he hadn't really seen what he thought he'd seen. It was hotter than hell out here and it'd been a rough day. Could be his mind was playing tricks on him.

Sure.

It was possible.

But Billy didn't really believe he'd imagined or hallucinated that fleeting movement. He was certain it'd happened. A little twitch, nothing more than that. A twitch wasn't necessarily cause for alarm. He'd been around enough dead bodies to know they sometimes did unexpected things. Sometimes they twitched. Other times they farted or even belched. All these things were natural symptoms of muscle relaxation or internal gas releasing. One thing they definitely were not was evidence of a lingering demonic presence. What use, even to a demon, was a body with no brain to steer and otherwise manipulate the flesh?

Billy shook his head.

It was one thing to know these things as basic facts of existence, but in the context of the insane things he'd witnessed today, it was hard not to feel at least a little spooked. Knowing he'd feel a lot better once he was on his horse and riding away from here, he again raised the striker to hit the flint and get the fire going.

Then the corpse rolled over.

Billy gasped and leapt to his feet, staggering backward. "What the hell?"

After he'd dumped it into the gully, the corpse had landed on its back. Now, however, it was a couple feet farther away from him than it'd been, in what could no longer fairly be called a "facedown" position for more than one reason.

Billy was no coward, but he wasn't a stupid man either. His instinct now was to climb the hell up out of the gully, mount his steed, and ride away from this forsaken, empty place. He'd chosen the location specifically for its remoteness. There'd be no one around to see him set a corpse ablaze. Unfortunately, this also meant there was no one around to help him should he run into trouble.

Despite the growing urge to run away, he hesitated a bit longer, waiting in the vain hope of a rational explanation for what was happening to present itself. Maybe the wind did it, kicking up out of nowhere and causing the body to roll over. Except he already knew for a fact nothing of the sort had happened. The air in the vicinity of Snakebite was as still as it'd been all day. He would've felt a sudden gust of wind strong enough to move a goddamn dead body.

Nope. Something else was happening here.

Unfortunately.

Then the body flipped over a second time and rose up on its knees as the headless torso twisted in his direction.

Billy shook his head. "Nah. I've seen enough."

He turned around and started racing up the side of the gully as fast as he could while still trying to stay careful of his footing. His mind could make no sense of what his eyes had seen and was making no attempt to do so. All that mattered in those crazed, wild-eyed moments was survival. Getting away. He was almost back on level ground when he heard bare feet pounding across the rocky ground in pursuit of him.

A quick backward glance brought a helpless whine to his lips. The headless body had somehow managed to extricate itself from the blanket, thus treating him to the horrifying and surreal sight of a naked and animated female corpse pursuing him with what he could only assume was lethal intent. Even missing a head and forearm and perforated with multiple bullet holes, it retained some of the beauty it'd possessed in life, which only heightened the hallucinatory feel of what he was seeing. Also, the damn thing was moving with a quickness and agility far surpassing anything normal for a body so outwardly debilitated.

His head start, however, allowed him to get to his horse and untie it from the dead tree before the headless creature could reach him. Seconds later, he had a foot in a stirrup and was swinging himself up into the saddle. Before he could finish the maneuver, a hand grabbed at the back of his pants, fingers hooking inside the waistline and finding purchase. He tried twisting loose to no avail as he was yanked backward off the whinnying horse. His back hit the ground hard an instant later, sending sharp stabs of pain along his spine as his horse rose up on its rear legs and whinnied again, sounding distressed now. This was followed by the sound of its hooves beating on the ground as it took off running.

Billy looked up and saw the headless thing looming above him. Without its head or anything resembling a weapon, he couldn't fathom how it intended to harm or kill him. All at once, the sheer absurdity of what he was facing landed on him with the force of a falling anvil, eliciting an abrupt burst of laughter as he raised up on his elbows.

"What are you gonna do? Beat me up with one goddamn hand?"

The headless thing moved in close before he could react, displaying that unnatural speed again. It now stood directly overhead, partly blotting out the blazing sun. Before he could scrabble backward, it placed a foot on his throat, pinning him to the ground. He gurgled and grabbed at the thing's ankle, trying to dislodge it by twisting with all his strength. The effort failed to budge the foot by even the smallest fraction of an inch, and now it was pressing down harder, making him gag and choke as his airway closed. A desperate terror engulfed him as he realized he'd been tragically wrong to underestimate the threat this thing posed. His muscles strained as he redoubled the effort to dislodge the foot, but again met only with failure.

Time was growing short. He only had a few more seconds to make something happen before the lack of oxygen first robbed him of his remaining strength and then killed him. Remembering the gun holstered at his hip, he yanked the weapon free and turned the barrel upward, aiming at the middle of the headless thing's torso, in the general area of the heart. What good shooting the thing might do, he had no idea. It was already missing a head. A bullet through a heart that almost certainly wasn't beating anyway was unlikely to change anything, but he was running out of options.

He squeezed the trigger several times, continuing until the hammer landed on an empty chamber. Every bullet he fired found flesh. One went right through a titty, but the rest hit her dead center in the chest. A substance oozed from the holes, but it wasn't blood, not even that strange oily kind he remembered from the struggle in the doc's exam room. Some of it sprinkled over his face and fell into his mouth after sliding down the length of the body. What he felt on his tongue tasted like grains of sand.

The headless thing ripped the empty gun from his hand and tossed it into the gully. Despair consumed Billy as he realized he was defeated. Death was coming and it was mere moments away. He thought of his mama and daddy back home in Georgia and wished he could see them one last time, tell them he loved them and would see them in heaven. Tears welled from his eyes and spilled down the sides of his face at the sudden thought of seeing his little sister again, who'd died when she was only twelve. That was the only thing resembling a silver lining in this cloud of shit.

LAST OF THE RAVAGERS

Just as he was finally feeling ready to accept this rotten twist of fate, he again heard a pounding of hooves racing across the desert. This time the sound grew louder instead of fading away, reaching a thunderous level in a short span of time. He tried rolling his eyes around to see what was happening, but the firmness of the foot against his throat made seeing anything approaching from any other direction impossible. In another few seconds, he heard the whinnying of his horse again as it rose up on its back legs and kicked out at the headless thing with its front hooves. The reanimated corpse went flying into the air and then back into the gully, where it landed with a heavy thump. A gagging, gasping Billy just managed to roll out of the way in time to avoid being trampled by his own horse as its hooves struck the ground again.

His crushed windpipe made wheezing sounds as he got to his hands and knees and greedily sucked in as much air as he could manage. It took doing this several more times, breathing deeply in and out, before the stars dancing at the edges of his vision finally disappeared. His throat would be sore for weeks, maybe longer, but that was okay, because he was still alive.

He was shaking hard as he at last got to his feet and staggered over to his horse, which neighed softly at his approach. He patted the beast gingerly with a trembling hand and said, "Thanks for coming back for me, girl. You're like an angel from heaven." He laughed weakly. "It was lookin' like I was gonna be one myself for a minute there."

Feeling in dire need of a soothing taste of water, he removed a canteen from his saddle gear, opened it, and drank deeply. Before long, he was feeling restored and steady enough to risk creeping close to the side of the gully. As he did this, that admonishing inner voice rose up inside him again, telling him how stupid it was to linger here even one second longer when he could be riding back to safety right now.

Billy ignored the voice and crept closer still.
He looked down.
"Aw, shit."
The headless thing was gone.

SEVENTEEN

EARLY ON DURING that Saturday afternoon, Mary Kelleher was beginning the final stage of the weekly laundry cycle. The hard work of scrubbing with the washboard, rinsing, and scrubbing again was already done. All that remained was to hang everything on the clotheslines out back. Piling everything in a large metal tub, she went out through the back door and set the tub on the ground. She'd just pulled one of her husband's shirts from the tub when she was distracted by a faint sound of voices from somewhere nearby.

Her husband had gone into town to pick up some things at the general store and get some lumber from the hardware store for a new barn he wanted to build, in preparation of acquiring more livestock in the near future. She'd waved goodbye to him from the front porch maybe an hour ago as she watched him ride off in the wagon they used for hauling supplies, snapping the reins to get the mules moving at a good pace. He couldn't have returned yet. Even if he'd turned back before reaching town for some unknown reason, she at least would've heard the sounds of the wagon's approach—the creaking of wheel spokes, the not quite horse-like whinnying of the mules, and the hollering of her husband as he urged the animals onward. Mary felt certain he was still gone.

The faint voices were still talking, almost too softly to hear. She supposed one must belong to little Kevin, her nine-year-old son. An only child, it wasn't unusual to hear him talking to himself as he enacted imaginary battle scenarios while he was outside. Among other things, he liked to pretend he was the brave commander of a cavalry unit charged with hunting down bloodthirsty savages. She'd often hear him hollering out commands to his imaginary troops or making gun noises. He was always so boisterous about it. If his voice was indeed one of those she was hearing, something wasn't quite right.

Listening intently a moment longer, Mary determined the voices were coming from around the side of the house. Dropping her husband's shirt back in the tub, she moved with as much quiet stealth as she could manage in the direction of the voices and peeked around a corner. She wasn't truly scared just yet, not prior to glancing around that corner, but some common sense wariness did not feel unwarranted. People didn't come out to visit the Kelleher homestead often. On the rare occasions when it did happen, you could usually hear them coming well before they arrived, the most common indicator being a steadily rising sound of hoofbeats. In this case, she'd heard nothing of the sort.

A stone wellhead protruded above the ground some forty feet to the side of the house. Kevin and another person were standing next to the wellhead. Kevin had one of his little hands on the rope they used to pull up the bucket that went down to the bottom of the well. The other person was an adult woman. She was leaning in close to the boy, whispering something to him.

Mary initially believed the woman was clad in some tight, dark-colored garment. Distance and the angle of the sun enabled this illusion. She frowned and put a hand to her brow, squinting in an effort to see the forms by the well more clearly.

She gasped.

The woman was not wearing a dark-colored garment.

LAST OF THE RAVAGERS

In fact, she wasn't wearing anything at all. Much of the woman's flesh was smeared in some substance that might have been blood or mud or both, but none of it was obscured by even an inch of clothing. In addition, her large breasts were hanging only inches away from her son's face.

Stepping boldly out into the open now, Mary called out to Kevin as she raced toward the well, urging him to move away from the stranger. Instead of responding instantly to her shouted commands as he normally would, he stayed where he was, his back turned to his mother as the woman continued whispering words that were impossible to make out from a distance. Mary raised the volume of her voice, nearly screaming as she rapidly cut the gap between them.

Mary arrived at the well and grabbed her son by the shoulders, dragging him away from the bedraggled stranger, who now stood up straight and smiled. Once she felt she had Kevin a safe distance away, she stopped to berate the interloper. "Keep your grubby paws the hell off my boy! This is private property, which means you're trespassing. You need to skedaddle right now."

Kevin twisted in her grip, tugging at the front of her dress as he looked up at his mother with wide, innocent eyes. "Mama, it's okay."

Mary sneered.

Like hell it is.

Mary turned him around, steering him back in the direction of the house. "You go on inside, boy, and stay in until I say otherwise. You hear me?"

The boy frowned. "But, mama—"

"Right now!"

He cried out as she turned him fully toward the house and gave him a hard smack on his rear end, eliciting a yelp. After that, he started walking toward the house in a slump-shouldered, sullen way that wasn't like his normal self at all. She'd have to give him a good scolding later, but for now it was enough that he was yielding to parental authority at last. He glanced back one time, a look of confused hurt on his face that made her heart ache a little.

Mary turned back to the stranger as soon as Kevin was safely inside the house. The rage triggered by the woman's unexpected presence on her property was a fire threatening to burn out of control. It was in part a reaction to the inappropriateness of the woman's interaction with her son. The fear that had gripped her added more fuel to that rage. She did not care for the way she'd been made to feel afraid on her own property. Most people out here respected the boundaries of their neighbors. They didn't sneak up on people or behave strangely toward children. That kind of behavior was apt to get a person shot, a thought that made her wish fervently for a rifle in her hands.

Her hands clenched into fists as she took a threatening step toward the stranger. "Look, lady, I don't know who you are, but—"

"Yes, you do."

These were the first clearly enunciated words the woman had spoken in her presence. Mary's instinct was to scoff at the woman's absurd insinuation of acquaintanceship. No one she knew would ever voluntarily show up at another family's home looking like this. The family-oriented women she knew were all civilized and well-mannered. The woman standing before her was more like some island primitive or native person, a wild and feral thing seeking to deceive her or steal from her.

Then she realized there *was* something she recognized in the timbre of this person's voice. For the first time, the suspicion that her assumptions about this woman might be entirely wrong reared its head.

Mary frowned and moved another cautious step closer.

Then she gasped in shock.

"Eleanor McKinley? Is that really you?"

The filth-smeared woman whimpered pitifully and

limply held out her arms, begging for the comfort of an embrace. "Oh, Mary. Please help me. Something t-t-terrible has happened."

Eleanor's eyes were shiny with tears.

Seeing the woman in this obvious high state of distress dissolved much of the anger that had gripped Mary. She spread her arms wide, feeling her own eyes mist with tears as Eleanor staggered forward and fell into her embrace. The nude woman wrapped herself around Mary, gripping her tight as she wept into her shoulder. Mary patted the back of her head, making shushing and cooing sounds as she sought to comfort her neighbor, who'd endured some yet unnamed but obviously awful trauma.

If she'd seen how Eleanor was struggling not to laugh, she would've known she'd been right to fear her all along.

EIGHTEEN

DOC RICHARDSON REMAINED unconscious until shortly after Ned Kilmister and Quentin Brown carried him into the building he shared with Eddie Horton. He began to stir just as they were starting to climb the stairs to the second floor, crying out miserably as the pain made its presence known again. The doc struggled in their grip, temporarily confused in his state of semi-consciousness. One especially strong kick of his right leg staggered Ned for a moment as they were climbing the stairs. The trio of men came distressingly close to taking a painful tumble to the floor below. Ned sighed in relief after managing to steady himself. The last thing he needed on a day like this was a broken limb or two on top of everything else.

As soon as they got Richardson ensconced in his bed, the men plied him with additional generous portions of whiskey and laudanum. They kept at it until the doctor once again lapsed into unconsciousness. Ned then applied some ointment to the doc's cauterized eye before carefully wrapping a bandage around his head.

At that point, they decided to head across the street.

A woman dressed in form-fitting buckskin clothing was seated on a stool at the bar as Ned and Quentin entered the Last Chance Saloon. She stood up as soon as they were inside. Her skin was a bone-white shade of pale unusual in this climate. Ned hadn't seen anything like it

110

since he was back east. She had piercing blue eyes and long black hair. Atop her head was a wide-brimmed, maroon-colored hat. She was without question one of the most breathtakingly beautiful women Ned had ever set eyes on.

She also had a gun in her hand.

It was pointed at Cole Halford, who was sprawled on the floor of the saloon. He looked up at the other men as they came inside, a smear of blood on his chin from a busted lip, his wide eyes pleading with them for help.

Ned's right hand went to the handle of his gun.

The woman cocked the hammer of her gun and pointed it at him now. "Stop right there. I'd really hate to have to kill you, sheriff."

Ned exhaled slowly as he eased his hand away from the handle of the Peacemaker. "Easy, now. Nobody wants bloodshed. We've had a hell of a day already. Who are you and what do you want?"

Instead of answering Ned, she shifted her aim slightly, until the long barrel of her pistol was pointed at Quentin Brown's belly. "I'm sensing some anger on your part, barkeep. I apologize for the rough handling of your man here, but you best believe me when I say he had it coming. Now listen up. I've got business in this pissant town and I'm not leaving until it's settled."

The hammer of her pistol was still cocked, her forefinger resting lightly on the trigger. Ned was trying his best to maintain a calm exterior, but his heart was racing. Despite her undeniable beauty, the woman exuded a degree of menace he'd only ever encountered a few times. Those other times he'd been in the presence of hardened outlaws, the baddest of bad men. Bandits and killers willing to take a life over things as trivial as a game of cards or innocent remarks mistaken for insults. This was the first woman he'd ever met who gave him that same type of bone-deep bad feeling. A blustery, confrontational method of dealing with this type of person wasn't apt to accomplish anything positive.

Ned strove for an even tone while keeping his right hand out to his side, well away from his gun. "We don't want trouble, ma'am. We're reasonable men. We're willing to listen to anything you have to say. Isn't that right, Quentin?"

Brown's unflinching gaze remained on the woman as he nodded. "I reckon so."

Ned smiled. "See? Reasonable. Now, then. What's the nature of this business you say you have in our town?"

The woman took her finger off the trigger of her gun after easing the hammer back down. "Reasonable is good. It's also a good thing you're willing to listen, Ned Kilmister. I've come to you with a warning. A storm warning, I guess you could say. Trouble of the worst kind is coming to your town, sheriff. Most of your friends and neighbors will be dead by morning, but you can save some of them if you listen well and heed what I have to say."

Ned and the saloon keeper exchanged a doubtful glance.

Then Ned's head swiveled back in the direction of the gun-toting woman. "Most of the town will be dead."

He said it in a deadpan, disbelieving way.

The woman smirked. "That's what I just said, yes. Almost exactly. I realize it's a shocking thing to hear, but it's the absolute truth."

Ned shook his head. "It's a wild thing to say to a person you've just met, you've gotta admit. Are we just supposed to accept this at face value? And while I'm at it, you seemed to recognize the two of us on sight. I can't speak for my friend here." He directed a pointed glance at Quentin. "But I'm reasonably certain I've never been in the same damn room as you."

Quentin Brown nodded. "Me neither. Not in this lifetime, leastways."

The woman grunted. "I know everything there is to know about most of the people in this town, as well as all the secrets they hold. You'll learn how and why soon enough. In the meantime, gentlemen, we need to have a civilized discussion about some things. If I put my gun away, can I trust you to behave?"

Ned sighed and nodded. "I give you my word as a man of honor."

She gave him a long, hard look before nodding, too. "I hope you're not pulling my chain, sheriff. Because one thing I can guaran-damn-tee you, I am a faster draw than either of you men. You try anything stupid and you'll wind up on the floor like that boy. Only dead."

Ned frowned. "You already have my word, ma'am. If somehow you truly do know everything about me, you already know that's good enough."

The woman twirled her gun one time and dropped it smoothly into the holster on her hip. "My name is Raven Decker. I'm a bounty hunter of a sort and I'm here in pursuit of a man named Doyle. Only he's not really a man."

Ned and Quentin again exchanged confused glances.

Ned's frown deepened. "Not a man? What the hell is he, then?"

Raven's steely blue eyes fixated on him so intensely the scrutiny sent shivers down his back. "Something vastly different from anything in your experience. Doyle is not of this world. He likes to visit primitive realms such as this one and present himself as a god or a devil while wreaking as much bloody havoc as possible over a short time before jumping to another world to stay ahead of me. He is sheer chaos, but there is a purpose behind it all."

Ned looked her up and down. Despite some slightly unusual aspects to her manner and appearance, there was nothing about her that struck him as truly inexplicable or otherworldly.

Down on the floor, Cole was beginning to sit up.

Raven took a few quick strides toward him and kicked him in the side of his head, the heel of her boot sounding like a hammer as it connected. Crying out, Cole flopped back to the floor and didn't move.

Ned angrily stamped his own boot on the floor. "Goddammit, woman! Leave the boy alone! What could he possibly have done to make you so dadblamed pissed off?"

Raven looked at him. "It's more about who he's in league with than anything he did. I'll explain as best I can momentarily, but first I could use a drink. Maybe more than one. Care to join me?"

Ned and the saloon keeper again exchanged weary, confused looks.

They nodded.

And with that, they adjourned to the bar.

But not before Raven Decker viciously stomped Cole's head into the floor one more time. This time there was a cracking of bone as his jaw broke.

NINETEEN

THE **NUMBERS IN** the ledger no longer meant anything to Jacob Montgomery. They had morphed into indecipherable shapes and were no longer recognizable symbols with known values attached to them. His mind, temporarily or otherwise, seemed to have lost its ability to properly process and interpret information. On occasion, as he stood behind the counter at the front of his store, he would flip back a page or two and stare at more columns of newly meaningless figures, trying his damnedest not to let his fingers shake visibly as he turned the pages. He did this to appear preoccupied and therefore lessen the chances of direct interaction with any potential customers who might wander into the store. This was out of an abiding fear that any of them might, at any moment, immediately see or sense the horrible, indelible stain on his soul should eye contact occur.

Now and then as he stood there pretending to discern things from the ledger entries he would experience a moment of terrible, crystalline clarity, his traitorous brain deciding it was once again time to remind him that he was now a murderer. Right now, as he strove desperately to project an air of quiet normality, the body of a young woman was hidden away in the locked storeroom, covered by a canvas tarp. It was a fact and it wasn't going away.

The decision to kill Charlotte Blanchard was an unthinking impulse that happened in a moment of blind panic, her attempt to extort money from him filling him with an unreasoning fury. His mind ceased functioning in a logical way as he considered the unbearable prospect of his wife learning of his shameful nights spent in the company of whores. Nights when she'd believed he was working late at the store, either taking inventory or putting together a big order for an important customer. Never mind that there was no one in Snakebite in need of that level of assistance. Kathy accepted a lot of the things he said at face value, but she wasn't stupid. She also wasn't apt to simply brush off a betrayal of this magnitude.

Bottom line, there'd be hell to pay.

And Jacob Montgomery wanted no part of that.

So now Charlotte was dead and he was stuck with the thorny dilemma of figuring out how to deal with that. At some point, the body would have to be removed from the premises and disposed of in a permanent way. Just allowing it to rot in the storeroom was not a viable option. Even in his state of deep distress, he knew that. An unmistakable odor of death would be present before long, for one thing. There was also the complicating matter of everything he didn't know to consider.

Had anyone seen her entering the store? Did she tell anyone of her destination before walking out of the saloon? If the answer to either of these questions was yes, then he had very little time to figure out a solution, because as soon as her friends realized she was missing, even a cursory investigation would lead to his door in short order Jacob fervently wished he had someone—anyone at all—with whom he could confide, some close friend willing to do anything to help even in matters of questionable morality.

Unfortunately, he had no one like that in his life.

He briefly entertained the notion of paying a visit to the Last Chance Saloon tonight. Men of dubious moral character were known to frequent most frontier drinking establishments, especially in the evenings. Among them might be someone open to the idea of transporting a body out of town under the cover of night. For the right price, of course.

Jacob quickly dismissed the idea, however, realizing how dangerous it'd be to attempt something like that in the dead whore's place of work. She had friends there, including men who'd fucked her and likely enjoyed it far more than he ever had. There were other saloons in town, though. Smaller places with an even seedier clientele. He could try his luck at one of them, he supposed, but the idea didn't hold much appeal. If anything, it'd be even more dangerous. The men who spent time in places like that were apt to knock him over the head and take his money.

Hell, they might even kill him.

Nope.

As much as he hated it, he'd have to take care of the matter himself. He felt a small bit of the tension drain out of his body as he accepted the notion. The decision was made. Next time the store was clear of shoppers, he'd lock up and put up the 'closed' sign.

Then he'd go into the back and hack Charlotte's body into manageable bits with an axe.

Charlotte's eyes opened beneath the tarp in the storeroom, consciousness returning in a subdued, undramatic way, as if she'd only drifted out of a light nap. The main thing she experienced in those first moments of renewed life was an overriding confusion. She didn't know where she was and at first remembered nothing of what had happened to her. There was an odd and troubling sense of something wrong at the back of her throat. She felt it whenever she tried to swallow. It wasn't long before she became aware of a similar sensation at the back of her neck. She had an impression of the flesh there not being fully intact, which scared her, but what was even odder was how she felt no pain in association with this mysterious damage to her body.

As she lay there in darkness, she became more cognizant of other basic aspects of her situation. She was flat on her back on a hard wooden floor, with what she assumed was a heavy bed sheet or blanket covering her entire body. The rough fabric on her face felt oppressive and she began to experience a mild bout of claustrophobia. Intent on pulling the sheet away from her face in order to breathe more freely, she grabbed hold of it and tugged but encountered significant resistance.

A slowly simmering sense of alarm yielded to outright panic as she tugged harder and harder at the sheet. There was some give now, but she was still encountering that resistance. At first she wondered if some other person might be asleep on the other side of the sheet, weighing it down. Then, as she continued pulling at it, she heard something sliding across the floor. It belatedly hit her that someone had used heavy objects of some sort to weigh the blanket down, an insight that was not at all reassuring.

She pulled at the blanket in a more frenzied way until at last a corner of it came free from whatever was pinning it in place. She yanked the blanket away from her face and sat up gasping in the middle of a room she did not immediately recognize. Despite its initial unfamiliarity, there was something about the space that made her feel anxious and desperate to be somewhere—anywhere—else.

The thing she'd assumed was a blanket was instead a heavy canvas tarp. Someone had piled bricks at the corners to weigh it down. She took a look around and saw piles of wood, crates and barrels filled with unknown things, a work table with a cluttered surface, and various types of tools piled up on shelves. Tools of a sort meant for building things. From there, it didn't take long to figure out where she probably was—the storeroom in Montgomery Hardware.

LAST OF THE RAVAGERS

This was no great feat of deduction. The hardware store was the only local business likely to stock the kind of items she was seeing in such quantity. The greater mystery, however, remained.

What the hell am I doing here?

An impulse caused her to reach around to the back of her neck and delicately probe the damage she sensed there. Using the tip of a finger, she traced the ragged outline of a hole. Chunks of some form of wet matter lodged in her hair brushed against the back of her hand. She brought her hand away from her neck and frowned at the coagulated blood smeared across her finger. It was wet and lumpy. Tears welled in her eyes as she deduced something else.

Somebody shot me!

Someone had shoved a gun into her mouth and pulled the trigger. Given the nature of her wounds, nothing else made sense. What didn't make sense was how she could possibly still be alive. Not just still alive, but functioning normally in every way, at least as far as she could tell. It was incredible and disturbing at the same time, like some dark miracle. She was breathing in and out and her thoughts seemed in regular order, with no hints of mental disturbance or impairment.

She swept more of the tarp away from her body and got to her feet. Whatever had happened to her, she knew one thing with absolute clarity—she needed to get out of the goddamn hardware store right now.

The storeroom had two doors. One would lead back out to the main part of the store. She suspected the other would open onto the alley out back. The latter would be her best option, if she wished to escape without being violently assaulted again. There was a small window high up on one of the walls. She dragged a crate into position just beneath it and climbed up to look outside. One quick glimpse of the wide, junk-strewn alley was all she needed. The door to the left of the window was her way out. She'd suspected as much, but it was nice to have some confirmation rather than walking out blind.

She climbed down from the crate.

Before she could exit to the alley, she heard a heavy tread of booted feet from right outside the door. Panic again seized her as she cast a quick glance around in desperate search of anything she could use as a weapon. Atop one of the barrels was a hammer Jacob Montgomery appeared to have used for cracking open nuts. She saw a lot of shell debris atop the barrel and on the floor along its base. Snatching up the hammer, she raced over to the door and positioned herself so she'd be behind it as it opened.

The knob rattled and the hinges creaked as the door swung inward. Next came that thumping tread of Jacob's boots as he walked into the room. As soon as she saw his broad back and the gray hair curling around the bottoms of his ears, the previously obscured memories came flooding back into her mind. An image of the grim look on his face right before he killed her brought with it a rising tide of righteous anger. She remembered now how that stupid little gun felt in her mouth when he pulled the trigger.

She emerged quietly from behind the door and closed in on him as he stood in the middle of the room gaping confusedly at the spot occupied by a hidden body only minutes earlier. He sensed something at the last second and turned around in time to glimpse the hammer hanging in the air above his head.

Charlotte brought the hammer down, cracking the blunt end against his forehead. He staggered backward an awkward step or two before falling onto his ass. In the next instant, the woman he'd murdered kicked him in the face, smashing his nose and knocking him backward as blood erupted from his nostrils. Charlotte fell atop him, straddling him as she raised the hammer and brought it down again, making even more of a wreck of his already pulped nose. She squealed in delight as she watched blood jump into the air. More heavy blows from the hammer followed.

She laughed as she smashed Montgomery's teeth to bits. Giggled at the way he gurgled and coughed as he tried to talk, no doubt attempting to beg for mercy. The tears spilling from his eyes filled her not with empathy but contempt. She used the hammer to crush his eye sockets and pulp the tissue within.

After Jacob was dead, a voice spoke in her head. A voice belonging to someone named Doyle. At first this alien presence in her mind was unnerving, but soon she began to feel soothed by the things the voice said. She started understanding things that had been beyond her comprehension until then.

Cosmic truths.

Secrets from the heart of creation.

Doyle knew everything there was to know, it seemed, and Charlotte gave herself over to him without hesitation.

TWENTY

THUS FAR MARY hadn't managed to draw out much information from Eleanor about the events that led to her showing up at the Kelleher homestead in such a dreadful state. The woman's body was covered in so much grime and blood she looked as if she'd followed up surviving outside naked during a dust storm with a stroll through a slaughterhouse.

Nothing of the sort had happened, of course. There'd been no recent dust storms of any significance in the area and a lady like Eleanor wasn't apt to pay a casual visit to an abattoir, let alone roll around in the blood and muck of such a place. It seemed obvious something far more terrible had happened. She suspected one or more persons had died in violent fashion in close proximity to Eleanor. Several times while sponging the filth off her body, Mary gently pressed her distant neighbor for details. Each time the woman would attempt to answer only to start sobbing inconsolably once again.

After a while, Mary decided to stop interrogating her neighbor and focus on completing the task of cleaning her, a job she seemed in no condition to do for herself. Eleanor was fortunate the Kelleher household was outfitted with a dedicated washroom, an anomaly in frontier homes. Inside the room were two cast iron tubs and a barrel filled with water from the well. The larger of the two tubs had just enough space for Eleanor to sit in it without having to pull her knees all the way up to her chest. The water in the tub turned a dark shade of brown not long after Mary started scrubbing dirt from skin. Twice she had Eleanor get out of the tub long enough for Mary to dump the dirty water outside and haul the tub back inside.

Eleanor sniffled and smiled with gratitude as she climbed into the tub for a third time. "You're an absolute angel, Mary Kelleher. Bless you for being so kind. I'm sorry to have brought this bother into your life."

Mary began the process of filling the tub again, using a large bucket to transfer water from the barrel, a supply that would have to be replenished much sooner than usual after this was done. "It's no bother. I'm happy to help." She bit her bottom lip, hesitating a moment as she debated whether it was yet time to repeat her previous inquiries. "Do you feel able to tell me anything about what happened yet?"

She carried the bucket over to the tub and began pouring in the water.

Eleanor leaned back and draped her arms along the edges of the tub. "Soon. It's so terrible. So . . . tr-tragic . . . " Her bottom lip quivered and she began to weep again, but more quietly than before. "I wish I could spend the rest of my life believing it never happened, but I know I can't. I'll talk when we're done here, when I can sit with you in clean clothes like a civilized person and tell my story properly."

Mary nodded as she carried more water over to the tub. "I understand. Talk when you're ready."

Eleanor's lip stopped quivering and she smiled again. "You're so kind."

"No need to keep saying that," Mary said as she emptied the bucket again and knelt next to the tub. She picked up the squeezed-out sponge and dipped it back in the water. "It wouldn't be very Christian of me not to help a neighbor in need. Pretty sure there's even a Commandment about it."

She moved the sponge firmly along the length of Eleanor's left leg, pressing harder as she scrubbed at the inner thigh. The coating of gunk was thicker there for some reason. As she did this, Eleanor's head fell back and she visibly shivered. "Oh. Oh. That feels so nice."

Mary nodded. "I bet it feels good to get all that gunk off of you."

Eleanor moaned softly. "Oh, it does. Feels so good."

She abruptly seized Mary's wrist and pulled her hand lower, guiding the sponge to her sex. "Wash me here."

The other woman's grip was firmer than she would've guessed, given her supposedly weakened state. She looked at Eleanor's upturned face, studying the almost sensuously relaxed set of her features. The closed eyes. The parted lips. The ongoing low moan. A sense of something not right invaded Mary's consciousness for the first time since initially catching sight of Eleanor by the well, as the disheveled, unrecognizable-looking woman whispered into her son's ear. She'd survived some kind of trauma, yes, which excused a lot, but now Mary wondered if she'd been right to be wary of her after all. Because no amount of trauma, regardless of how severe, could explain away what seemed to be happening here.

She tried to pull her hand away, but Eleanor held fast to it as she spread her legs as wide apart as she could manage in the tub. "What's the matter, dear? You've been doing such a marvelous job of comforting me. Now isn't the time to stop."

Another moan escaped her lips.

She forced Mary to press the sponge harder against her sex.

"Stop it! This isn't right."

Eleanor laughed.

Mary tried yanking her hand away a second time, putting all her strength into it now. The renewed attempt failed utterly at loosening the other woman's grip by even the smallest degree. Her wrist felt as if it was caught in a steel trap rather than one made of flesh.

"Let go of me!" She was becoming frantic, yanking at her wrist again and again to no effect. "Let go or I'll scream!"

Eleanor opened her eyes, turned her head, and met Mary's gaze. The cast of her features conveyed only malevolence now, revealing an inner capacity for evil that must have been there all along, hidden from everyone. Even her family, who Mary now believed were all dead. All three children and her husband, killed by the one they'd believed loved them the most. "Oh, you'll scream. There's no doubt of that."

Growing desperate, Mary made a fist of her other hand and raised it in preparation of striking at the woman's face.

Then she heard a creak from somewhere behind her. She turned her head in that direction and saw Kevin slipping into the room. A large kitchen knife was clutched loosely in his right hand. Her son was smiling in an odd way as he inched farther into the room. The expression was unlike anything she'd ever seen on his sweet, innocent face before. It was a smile devoid of love or anything even remotely resembling affection.

Instead, it was filled with hate.

After a long moment frozen with fear, Mary sucked in a reedy breath and yelled at the boy, attempting to assert motherly authority. "Kevin Kelleher, you get out of here right this instant! And put that knife down!"

Kevin shook his head and continued his slow advance. "No."

Mary whimpered through her tears. "Kevin, you're being naughty. Listen to your mother."

Kevin giggled. "You're the naughty one, Mommy. Miss Eleanor told me so out by the well."

Mary's heart raced faster and faster. She felt close to hyperventilating. An image of Eleanor bent over and

BRYAN SMITH

whispering into her son's ear came to her then, a taunting reminder of what she now recognized as a damning failure on her part. She'd been tragically wrong to place neighborly kindness over what her instincts were telling her at the time. Now she realized something diabolical had occurred during that first interaction between her son and Eleanor McKinley. The woman had exerted some demonic, devilish influence over him merely by speaking into his ear. How that was possible she didn't know, but she believed it.

Eleanor sat up straight in the tub, maintaining her unnaturally strong grip on Mary's wrist. "Remember what I told you, boy. The time has come. Stick the knife in your mommy's neck."

Kevin grinned.

And did as he was told.

Mary gasped and then gurgled as the big blade punched into the soft and vulnerable flesh in the hollow of her throat. Letting out a shout of excitement, Eleanor pulled her close and yanked the knife away with her free hand. She grabbed hold of Mary's neck and forced her down into the space between her spread legs. Blood gushed from the hole in her flesh, pattering into the water and staining it red.

Eleanor held her there until the blood flow ceased.

Then she looked at the boy and smiled. "You did good, son. Just like you were told. Now go outside and do the other thing."

The boy nodded and went outside.

Minutes later, he climbed atop the wellhead and jumped into the well. As his bones shattered and a faint sound of screams emanated from the bottom, Eleanor used the knife to dig out Mary's eyes. One by one, she popped them into her mouth, savoring the tough, squishy flavor.

TWENTY-ONE

IN ORDER TO assure privacy while Raven Decker told her story, Quentin Brown closed and locked his saloon's outer front door. This was something that was only ever done for a few hours deep in the dead of night. There were often long stretches of days or even weeks where the saloon didn't close at all. Ned couldn't remember ever being inside the place when it was shut up tight like this during daylight hours. Seeing the inner batwing doors pressed up against the back of the outer door was a strange thing, which Ned figured was only appropriate given the overall bizarre tone of the day.

The woman's gun rested on the surface of the table where she sat now with Ned. In a basic way, it resembled many of the more popular pistols circulating throughout the western territories, but with a few obvious differences. The length of the barrel was standard, but its width was not. The loaded chambers of the cylinder were also visibly much larger than the norm. He didn't know what caliber the cartridges in those cylinders were, but they looked capable of stopping a charging rhino in its tracks. The gun and the bullets looked like custom jobs, with fancy scrollwork along the barrel and on the cylinder. Fitted in the center of each of the gun's black grips was a small silver skull. There were flecks of blood on the barrel from where she'd smashed it across Cole's face.

"Admiring my weapon, sheriff?"

"Indeed. It's very . . . unique." Ned scratched a match across the rough and pitted surface of the table, applying the tiny flame that arose to the stogie already wedged into a corner of his mouth. "Mind if I ask where you got it?"

She shrugged. "Not from this world, but from one of the many that closely resemble it. And by that I don't mean from some other continent elsewhere on this planet. I literally mean another world entirely."

Ned exhaled a cloud of smoke, turning his head slightly so as not to blow it directly into her face. He frowned as he took the stogie from his mouth, holding it between his fingers as he shifted uncomfortably in the chair. A lot of what she'd told them so far was hard to swallow, even on a day as rife with the strange and inexplicable as this one. He'd spent the early stages of his time in this woman's company in a credulous state of awe, so entranced by her that he was almost too willing to believe anything that came out of her mouth, but now a bit of his natural tendency toward skepticism had returned.

He took another puff off the stogie and exhaled again. "Huh. And how is it you travel so easily from one world to another? Hot air balloon?"

Raven laughed. "Moving from one realm to the other isn't really a matter of traversing physical distances, Ned. Or not always. There are countless other worlds, infinite layers of reality. Some of these alternate realities are so much like your own world you'd need a while to start picking up on the differences. Others are wildly divergent, some in ways that would shatter your sanity in an instant."

"And you've been to such places?"

She nodded. "I hear the doubt in your voice. That's okay. It won't be long before your skepticism melts away like morning dew. But, yes, I've been to some of the stranger realms, though I avoid the ones with the harshest conditions whenever possible. For a few rare individuals, myself among them, travel between the realms is as simple as stepping through a door."

At that exact moment, Quentin Brown came out of a door at the back of the saloon, stepping into the area behind the bar.

Ned and Raven glanced that way, then shared an amused look.

Raven smirked. "Not quite *that* simple, but not far off either."

Quentin grabbed a bottle of mescal and three glasses before joining them at the table, where he sighed heavily after pulling out a chair and sitting down. "Talked to Miss Agatha," he said, looking at Ned. "She'll make sure the girls stay up there and out of the way until we're done here. And they've got Cole chained up in the special room they have for the fellas who like the, uh . . . well, the out of the ordinary stuff. Being whipped by the ladies and that sort of thing." He frowned. "Something strange, though. Charlotte's missing."

Ned grunted. "Probably just went out for a stroll. Stretch her legs a little before things get busy later." He chuckled. "She'll be banging on that door soon, wanting to know why she's been locked out."

Quentin was still frowning, but he nodded. "Yeah, maybe."

Ned's gaze returned to the woman on the other side of the table. Even if it turned out the dark-haired beauty was a giant bullshitter, there was already overwhelming evidence of an unnatural menace present in Snakebite. The sooner they started putting together a plan on how to handle it, the better. He'd listen to what Raven had to say for a bit. There was a chance she'd definitely reveal herself as a con artist or raving lunatic soon enough, in which case he'd either lock her up in one of the cells across the street or advise her to head on out of town, whichever option seemed safer in the moment. Conversely, if he deemed what she had to say credible to any degree, he would act accordingly. Get the mayor involved. Maybe even call a hasty town meeting.

Brown and the lady bounty hunter had already helped themselves to some mescal.

After setting his stogie in an ashtray, Ned tipped some of the clear liquid in the remaining glass and pulled it close. "So let's hear more about Doyle. You said if we didn't heed your warning about him, a whole lot of folks in Snakebite would be dead come tomorrow."

Raven stared back at him evenly. "That's right."

"And you're serious about that?"

"Yep."

Ned leaned back in his chair and sighed heavily in an exaggerated way, directing a smirking glance at Quentin before continuing. "Well, hell, in that case I reckon we ought to evacuate the town immediately. Send some men around on horseback, get the word out now before the magic devil-man from another world kills us all."

Quentin chuckled and shook his head.

Raven sneered. "It's not as simple as that, sheriff. This is a threat your people can't outrun. No way you'd get far enough away in time."

Ned took another quick draw off his stogie and returned it to the ashtray. "You don't sound like you're joking."

"I'm not."

Ned squeezed his eyes shut a moment before allowing them to flutter open again. Early afternoon and he was feeling as drained as he'd normally start feeling around midnight. If it turned out there was more than just a small grain of truth to what this woman was telling him, he might have to head back over to Doc Richardson's office and help himself to some of the stimulants in the man's medicinal supply. A small bit of cocaine would suffice.

He looked Raven in the eye again. "Are we just doomed then?"

LAST OF THE RAVAGERS

She shrugged. "Some of your people will die tonight at the hands of Doyle and his minions. That's unavoidable. Others might live. How many will depend on the actions we take between now and tonight. Before anything is done, you'll need a fuller understanding of what you're facing."

Ned nodded. "That's a point I'll happily concede. I must admit I'm having a hard time buying the idea of Doyle as some kind of god or devil."

Raven sighed. "I didn't say he was either of those things. In fact, I told you the opposite. Pay closer attention, please." Ned bristled at her brusque phrasing, but she pressed on before he could interject. "I said he's *like* a god or a devil, not that he *is* one. He enjoys visiting the lesser developed worlds and *presenting* himself as one. The inhabitants of primitive realms tend to believe him because he possesses abilities beyond their understanding. They think he's a god because in their experience mortal men and women aren't able to do the things he does."

The scowl on Ned's face softened by a miniscule degree. "Okay, so what is he then?"

Raven downed the rest of her mescal and returned the glass to the table without refilling it. "Doyle is the last surviving member of an outlawed necromancy cult called the Ravagers."

Ned tilted his hat back and regarded her with a raised eyebrow. "Necromancy? What is that?"

"A dangerous form of dark magic. Skilled practitioners of the art are able to communicate with and manipulate the spirits of the recent dead."

Raven's gaze was unwavering as she pointedly eyed each of the men in turn. There was nothing overtly shifty in those steely blue eyes. She was either telling the truth, Ned believed, or was one of the best liars he'd ever met.

"There are necromancers even in your realm," she continued, her gaze settling on Ned again. "Have been for centuries, including a few especially determined individuals who occasionally manage a few moments of real interaction with departed spirits. Compared to Doyle, however, they're akin to children playing with toys. It's different where he's from. Where we're *both* from. In that world, magic in all forms is more potent than it is here. Anyone there familiar with the rites of necromancy can talk to the dead virtually at will, but with the Ravagers it goes much further than that. They are also able to resurrect the recent dead and use them as ghoulish puppets."

Ned and Quentin glanced at each other.

Raven nodded, smiling almost imperceptibly. "You've both seen some things today you can't explain. I don't need to read minds to know that. It's right there in your eyes. Let me ask you this. Have you had any recent experience with corpses behaving in ways corpses normally don't? As in getting up and moving around?"

Ned grimaced. "You could say that."

He spent a few moments sketching out the highlights of their struggle to subdue Angelina's resurrected corpse.

Raven's expression darkened as she gnawed on her bottom lip a moment. "What that tells me is Doyle has grown even more powerful than I feared. He's clearly been harvesting souls at a faster rate than ever since jumping to this world."

Ned didn't like the troubled look on her face. "Well . . . what does that mean for us?"

Raven shrugged. "It's like I already told you, sheriff. What it means is trouble. Trouble with a capital T. Doyle's only able to achieve that level of corpse manipulation by absolutely *gorging* on life energy. This means he has most likely been slaughtering large numbers of your kind over just the last few days. Ravagers grow stronger by feasting on the souls of living things they personally kill, as well as things killed by the minions in their thrall. If that's what Doyle has been doing, it means he's gearing up for a fight."

Ned shook his head, frowning again. "Why would

LAST OF THE RAVAGERS

Doyle come looking for a fight in Snakebite? What could the son of a bitch possibly have against us?"

A pained expression crossed Raven's face. "It's not anything against you or anyone else here personally. He knows a secret thing about this town, something he uncovered only recently, I believe. This is knowledge I possess as well. And he's tired of being hunted. He wants rid of me, because I'm the only person in all of existence who can possibly kill him. The people here just have the misfortune of being in his path at the wrong time. In *our* path, I suppose."

A silent moment ensued as the men digested that.

Then Ned said, "What is this secret knowledge?"

A hint of a smile returned to Raven's lips. "Your town is special in a way you know nothing about. Doyle wants access to what makes Snakebite special and knows he'll have to go through me to get it."

Ned gave her a doubtful look. "Something special. Here in Snakebite. In the middle of goddamn nowhere. Really?"

Raven nodded. "Yes."

Ned waited a beat.

"Well, what is this special thing?"

Her smile brightened. "The Infinity Engine."

Ned gaped at her a moment before saying, "You intend on explaining what that is?"

She shook her head. "When the time is right. When you're ready to truly understand. In the meantime, I'll need some help to make sure it all goes off the right way. Reinforcement here at the Last Chance Saloon in the form of a squad of men handpicked by you. Ones able to fire a weapon with a reasonable degree of accuracy. Does that sound like something you'd be willing to orchestrate?"

Ned downed the contents of his glass.

He thumped it on the table. "This is still my town we're talking about. Of course I'm willing. Listen, folks are gonna need some kind of warning, even if we don't tell them everything."

Raven's smile disappeared. "Not a good idea. You'll needlessly start a commotion and the warning won't do anyone any good anyway when Doyle sends in his vanguard of blue meanies."

"Blue . . . what?"

Raven turned in her seat and stretched her long legs out, the spurs on her boots jangling. "Also known as 'Mogs,' as in the transmogrified. Blue meanies is just what I call them. Like a nickname. Fits because they're mean and, well, blue, as in blue-skinned. Warning or not, they'll sweep in here and kill a bunch of your people and there's pretty much no way to stop them. Our only hope is to hunker down in here and fight them off along with whatever else Doyle throws at us until I can initiate the final stage of my plan."

"Which somehow involves this Infinity Engine thing you won't tell us about?"

She nodded. "Yep."

Ned squeezed his eyes shut again.

When he opened them, he got woozily to his feet. "Despite what my common sense keeps trying to tell me, I guess I believe most of the crazy shit you just unloaded on us. Which leaves me with no choice but to go along with anything you want us to do. I hope like hell I'm not making the biggest mistake of my life by putting my faith in you."

Raven reached for the bottle of mescal and filled her glass. "You're not."

Ned was done discussing the matter for the time being because he was running out of steam and becoming in more dire need of medicinal cocaine with each passing moment. "I'm headed across the street for just a minute. Will be back as soon as my mind is sharp again."

He'd started moving away from the table as he spoke and wasn't fully turned around until he arrived at the saloon's street entrance. This was unfortunate, because in his deepening state of inebriation he'd forgotten something important. Instead of passing easily through the swinging batwings as he normally did, he ran smack into the closed outer door, staggered backward a few steps, and fell to the floor, landing hard on his ass before flopping onto his back.

After muttering a curse, he held a hand up in the air and said, "Some help, please."

Raven and Quentin came to his aid.

Eventually.

After they stopped laughing at him.

TWENTY-TWO

FOLLOWING THE DISAPPEARANCE of his one-armed, headless adversary, Billy Conway descended into the gully again to retrieve his pistol. Sure, lingering here even a short while after his close call was a big risk, but he wanted that gun. He could replace it easily enough, of course, but this gun was special. It was engraved with the name of his favorite ever dog along the barrel. *Big Boomer*, it read, in a fancy script.

Down in the gully, he experienced a few moments of additional distress, failing to spot the gun right away, but then, turning slowly about, he spied a glint of sunlight on metal on the far side of the gully. He moved in that direction and in another moment spotted the gun on the ground, partially hidden behind a rock. He snatched up the pistol and climbed up out of the gully as fast as he could manage.

There was still no sign of the crazy walking corpse with no damn head. After loading his pistol, he holstered the weapon, mounted his horse, and rode away. As Billy and the beast raced back toward town, all he could think about was how he'd failed to accomplish the job he'd been given. Sure, there were extenuating circumstances. Unforeseen developments that complicated things. When a man was charged with the task of disposing of a dead body, he didn't go into it expecting that body to get up and fight back. That went double for a dead body with no goddamn head. Given his experiences earlier in the morning, however, perhaps he shouldn't have been so nonchalant about it. He'd let his guard down a little. Okay, a *lot*.

And as a result, he'd not only failed utterly at what had been asked of him, he'd soon be faced with the dispiriting responsibility of telling Ned Kilmister that he had no idea what had become of the reanimated bitch. She could be anywhere, maybe even back in town, transported there by whatever kind of black magic had lifted her out of the gully. It pained him to imagine the disappointed look on the sheriff's face. Ned was the closest thing to a father figure he had these days and he hated letting the man down.

He was still stewing over it when he heard a cawing sound from somewhere above him. The cawing of carrion birds was a commonplace thing in the desert. He paid it little mind at all until a shadow fell over him. As he looked up, a pattering of birdshit struck him in the face, a little of it getting in his mouth. The disgust he would normally feel in that moment, however, was overridden by a much larger concern. At first he couldn't believe what he was seeing, it was so surreal, like something out of the kind of weird dreams he sometimes had when he got a little too drunk on bad rotgut. Twisted nightmares visions that occasionally made him swear off drink for up to three or four days.

The two vultures flying high above him were the largest such creatures he'd ever seen. They were so unnaturally huge he was reminded of drawings he'd seen of long-extinct flying dinosaurs. Pterodactyls, they were called. These were not resurrected beasts from an ancient, bygone age, however, though that wouldn't have surprised him at this point. They were vultures, all right, with feathers as black as the inside of Satan's butthole.

Their unusual size, however, did not trouble him nearly as much as what was clutched in the massive claws of one of the flying beasts—the slender wrist of the headless woman's sole remaining intact arm. The legs of the thing that was once Angelina the saloon girl kicked wildly in midair.

As Billy peered up at this bizarre sight in disbelieving awe, the vulture holding the headless woman aloft began to descend slightly, angling to match the course of his galloping horse. Its companion in flight remained at a higher altitude. In another few moments, it descended even lower. The vulture and the flailing corpse were a scant twenty feet above the deputy by the time it finally hit him what the actual intent was here.

"Oh, shit."

Even more disconcerting was the way the kicking of the headless body's legs grew steadily more frantic as the vulture dipped lower and lower. He had the distinctly disquieting impression she meant to kick his own head clean off his shoulders. On a normal day, he'd never believe she possessed enough leg strength to accomplish such a thing, but on a day like today he couldn't take one damn thing for granted. He'd learned that, if nothing else.

When the vulture dropped to an altitude of no more than ten feet directly overhead, he dug a heel hard into the flank of his horse. The horse whinnied but moved no faster, apparently incapable of it. Billy tugged on the animal's reins, directing it to turn sharply to the left instead of continuing in a straight line back toward town. He was just trying to buy time. By then he knew he had no chance of evading his strange pursuers. The time for running was almost over. The time to stop and fight was nearly at hand.

He was reaching to draw his rifle from its saddle scabbard when he felt wind from the flapping wings of the vulture touch the back of his neck. It'd descended even lower faster than he'd anticipated. The rifle came clear of the scabbard in almost the same instant a weight dropped into place behind him. His heart lurched in his chest as he realized the headless woman was now astride the horse with him. Her fingers reached around and clawed at one side of his face, drawing blood as her nails scratched grooves in his shit-smeared cheek. Billy screamed and dropped the rifle as the horse abruptly reared up on its back legs, whinnying loudly.

Billy tumbled out of the saddle and hit the ground hard, tasting dirt as he rolled over a few times. He wound up flat on his back, staring at the sky as he watched the big vulture flap its wings and achieve altitude again before flying off toward the horizon with its companion.

He coughed and spat out dirt. "That's right, fly on back to hell, you goddamn ugly birdies."

Sitting up, he saw the headless woman on the ground less than ten feet from where he'd come to a rest. The ravaged, mutilated corpse sat up seconds after he did, its torso twisting in his direction. He again had the impression the thing was looking at him despite having no obvious physical means of doing so. It was strange and unnerving, but now he understood it must truly be observing him by some unnatural method. Not Angelina, of course. She was gone, departed to heaven, hell, or wherever. Instead he was being watched by the supernatural force manipulating her body.

Billy and the headless corpse got to their feet at roughly the same time, but Billy managed it with significantly greater ease than his bizarre adversary. The headless thing moved with great awkwardness, nearly toppling back to the ground more than once. Billy tilted his head as he moved a cautious step closer, sighing in relief as he studied the twisted angle of the thing's right leg, which appeared to have broken upon impact with the ground. A bloody shard of bone peeked through broken flesh.

The thing took a hobbling step toward him and dropped to its knees.

Billy laughed. "Luck ran out, huh? About damn time, if you ask me, which you didn't, because you don't have a dadblamed mouth." He strode forward rapidly and kicked the thing in the belly, causing it to flop backward. "That's for scaring my horse."

The horse whinnied softly, standing nearby and watching in its steady, unjudging way as the final phase of this struggle played out.

As the headless thing again tried to get to its feet, Billy scanned the ground for his rifle. Spotting it a ways off to his left, he started in that direction. He was about halfway there when his mangled adversary finally managed to get upright. The thing immediately started hobbling toward him, lurching awkwardly forward with each step as that damaged right leg continually threatened to crumple beneath it.

And yet somehow it kept coming.

Billy snatched the rifle off the ground.

When he turned around again, the headless thing was only a few feet away. He levered a round into the rifle's chamber, aimed at the thing's messed up leg, and pulled the trigger. The bullet ripped into the knee, dispersing bits of bone and ligament. Wobbling sideways while pinwheeling its arms for balance, the reanimated nightmare lady somehow was able to stay upright a few moments longer. This shouldn't have been possible. That knee was no longer functional, not in any normal way. He cranked the rifle's lever and fired again, aiming for the same spot. The second bullet ripped away more of the ruined knee. Once again, the thing flailed about with its arms, its whole body lurching around in a spastic, desperate way.

Billy shifted his aim and fired multiple times at the thing's other knee.

This time it fell down and didn't get up.

Billy spat at the thing's unmoving form. "Almost got me, didn't you? But it's me who got you in the end. You tangled with the wrong hombre, you demonic piece of lowdown monkey shit."

LAST OF THE RAVAGERS

The thing shakily raised its one good hand and showed him its middle finger.

Billy raised the rifle and shot the finger off.

"Fuck you, too."

He whistled over his horse, returned the rifle to its scabbard, and climbed back into the saddle. Seconds later, man and animal were racing back toward Snakebite once again.

TWENTY-THREE

DOC RICHARDSON WAS semi-conscious when the sheriff came in and started rummaging through his supply of medicines. Even in his drugged state, he knew this was actually happening and not something from a dream. It was also clear the man was inebriated from the way he was stumbling about the place. Whatever he was looking for, it seemed he was having a hard time locating it. The bumbling about got annoying enough to temporarily rouse Richardson out of his stupor.

He shifted about on his bed, raising up on an elbow as he called out to the man. "What're you trying to find, you drunken fool?"

The sheriff poked his head around the corner of the open bedroom door. "Go back to sleep, doc. Just looking for your cocaine."

Richardson told him where to find it and flopped back down on the mattress. The lid of his one remaining good eye fluttered as he drifted back down toward unconsciousness, though he remained faintly aware of Ned's boots thumping around the place. At long last, apparently having found his supply of the drug many in Snakebite considered a miracle cure for just about everything, he called out a goodbye and departed, slamming a door shut behind him.

"About damn time," Richardson muttered, his good

eye fully shut now. "Give a sick man some goddamn peace."

He was genuinely annoyed. The man had chosen to barge into his offices and noisily upend the place when he could easily have gone down the street to the drug store to get what he wanted. The drug store sold cocaine candies in a wide assortment of flavors. Surely that would've been preferable to what he kept here for medicinal purposes. Then again, the man was clearly drunk and drunk people had a funny habit of not thinking in straight lines. He supposed it may have been a matter of expediency, just giving him a slight benefit of the doubt. The drug store *was* farther away and maybe he was too drunk to walk the extra distance. Whatever the case, it was a ridiculous state of affairs. A large portion of the man's working existence involved controlling and penalizing rowdy drunks. Maybe their bad behavior was rubbing off on him. Or he was just under a lot of damn stress and all-day drinking was the only way he knew of dealing with it.

Either way, Richardson was glad he was gone.

He floated in and out of consciousness after that, never staying in the dream realm more than a few minutes at a time. Pain was the culprit, robbing him of a long period of deep, healing sleep. The laudanum, whiskey, and whatever else they'd poured down his throat was keeping it at a distance for now, but he could feel it poking in at him around the edges of that wall of numbness. As time went on, the pokes started feeling a little sharper and slightly more protracted. The stages of near-wakefulness became longer and he didn't want to be awake yet.

To stave off that dreaded state, he heaved himself up and swung his legs over the side of the bed. Someone had left a bottle of laudanum and a spoon on the little side table next to his bed. How thoughtful. The spoon almost made him laugh. He was in no condition for carefully measured quantities. Grabbing the bottle, he removed the cap and took a few big swallows before returning it to the table and lying down again.

He sighed in relief a few minutes later as the fresh influx of the drug made him drowsy and pushed the pain further away. Reality turned soft around the edges and began to yield once again to the permeable pseudo-realities of dreams. His sleeping mind returned to those horrible moments spent on his knees in the blacksmith's shop, awaiting the insertion of the glowing-hot rod into his eye socket. As the heat invaded his wounded flesh, a searing wave of molten pain made him scream behind the leather bit lodged in his mouth. The unbearably hot nub of metal remained in his eye socket for what felt like an eternity, far longer than it had in reality.

In the dream, he looked up with his good eye and saw the leering, diabolically delighted face of the blacksmith. Only it wasn't Gareth Blackmore's face he was seeing. His visage had transformed, becoming the face of an older man, one with deep lines and sharper angles, with gray whiskers along his jutting jaw. With skin turned a bright shade of red from overexposure to the sun, he looked more like a devil than a man. The devil laughed at him as the rod pushed in deeper, angling upward toward his brain. His muffled screams were continuous now as the hands holding him down gripped him tighter, preventing him from twisting free.

Even when the devil-man finally took the glowing end of the rod out of his eye socket, there was no relief from his suffering, because he immediately swung it over to Richardson's remaining good eye. He squirmed mightily in the grip of the men holding him, desperate to get away as the rod began to advance again. Laughter resounded all around him, some of which sounded inhuman and abrasive. He twisted his head enough to see he was no longer being held by his friends. In their place was a team of fat blue dwarfish things, with heads like flattened pumpkins and mouths lined with too many teeth. The advance of that glowing metal tip was slower this time, but before long he could feel the intense heat singeing his eyelashes. In another moment, the glowing nub of metal blotted out everything else.

Doc Richardson abruptly awakened with a scream at the tip of his tongue, but the sound didn't quite reach his lips, because now something else inexplicable was happening. Looming over him was a saloon girl. Not Angelina, but one of the others. She was dressed in the salacious way they all were when working at the saloon, with stockings visible beneath the short hem of an undergarment that marginally functioned as a dress, with a feather boa wrapped around her neck. There were flecks of what looked suspiciously like blood on the undergarment. That was troubling, but there were no other obvious indications of anything amiss. Other than the mere fact of her presence here, that is, which was unexpected, to say the least. He'd been told Eddie Horton would turn away any potential patients who showed up today.

He frowned. "What are you doing here, Charlotte?"

"I heard you weren't feeling well, Doc." She smiled as she said this, holding her hands behind her back as she swayed slightly and rolled her bare shoulders in a vaguely seductive way. "I was thinking maybe I could help you feel better if you do me a teensy little favor."

Something was off about her voice. She also appeared to be having some difficulty swallowing. He figured she had some swollen nodes. Some opium would soothe that nicely, if his diagnosis was correct. With his perceptions still fogged by sleep and drugs, it was possible he was wrong, but it didn't matter. Either way, he'd give the lady opium and send her on her way.

He sighed. "I'll get you some medicine, Charlotte, but after that you need to go and leave me in peace. I need my rest."

"It's not medicine I need, Doc." She frowned after saying this, as if reconsidering. Her voice still sounded off, emerging slightly distorted now in a way he couldn't quite attribute to swollen nodes. In addition, there were occasional strange clicking noises. "Or not *just* medicine, least ways. I have a bit of an ouchie place on the back of my neck and was hoping you could help me with it." She removed the boa from her neck, lifted up the hair at the back of her head, and turned around as she lowered her rear end to the edge of the mattress. "There. Do you see?"

Richardson raised up on an elbow for a closer look.

Then he gaped for several seconds in silent disbelief at what looked like the messy exit wound of a bullet. At first he thought he must be mistaken, that his perceptions were still off-kilter from whiskey and laudanum. He squeezed his eye shut in an attempt to dispel the bleariness from his vision, but when he opened it again, the ragged, bloody hole at the back of her neck was still there. He kept staring at the wound, wishing the gruesome sight away.

But that didn't happen.

"What do you think, Doc? Can you fix it?"

As she spoke, Richardson saw—through the hole in the back of her neck— ragged muscles in her throat attempting to move. At least now he understood why her voice didn't sound right. He was amazed she could speak at all. The caliber of weapon used hadn't been a large one, but it'd done enough damage to kill her. Not only shouldn't she be talking, she shouldn't be up and moving around at all.

A sick feeling stirred in his gut as he realized this must in some way be connected to the other bizarre events of the day. He wished fervently he could roll back time and never inject Angelina's corpse with his experimental reanimation formula. Or roll it even further back and never read Harcourt's *Rejuvenation of the Dead* in the first place. None of this day's madness would be occurring had the old book never planted such dangerous ideas in his head. On an objective level, yes, what he'd accomplished was an impressive triumph of science and intellect. Clearly he was blessed with a greater level of genius than he'd ever dared imagine. Unfortunately, his achievement came at too steep a price. He'd been maimed, and an experiment performed with the intent of reviving one woman instead awakened evil forces. Even worse, it now appeared the evil was not confined to that one possessed body. It had spread outward like a disease, infecting other members of the community.

Charlotte turned her head and looked at him, a sly smile playing at the edges of her mouth. "You look lost in thought, doctor. Are you thinking about how you'll fix me? You better be."

Richardson frowned. "That sounds like a threat."

Charlotte nodded. "Mmm-hmm. It definitely is. Doyle says you have to fix me." She made a grating noise that probably started out as a girlish giggle. "Or else."

"Who is Doyle?"

Charlotte shifted around on the edge of the mattress until she was facing him more directly. "Doyle is your new god. He is the Lord of Death and he owns this town now."

Richardson kept quiet as he absorbed this information and mulled it over. His instinct was to dismiss what she was saying as delusional lunacy, but when looked at in context with the other unusual events of the day, he realized doing so wouldn't be wise. Perhaps there was some nugget of truth in the outlandish-sounding claim. An entity of some kind had possessed Angelina. That much was undeniable. He'd seen the proof for himself. Maybe an actual demon, maybe not. Demons had names, at least according to many ancient religious texts. He supposed it was possible Doyle was a simpler, anglicized version of something that sounded very different in its original language.

Beyond that consideration, the truth was he had no genuine knowledge regarding the actual nature of things that existed beyond the mortal realm. He also had no informed concept of how powerful such an entity might be in reality. That being the case, he had to concede it was possible a spirit or demon calling itself the 'Lord of the Dead' might truly exist, regardless of how preposterous the idea might seem on the surface.

And maybe it did think of itself as a god.

As disturbing as these possibilities were, another was troubling above all the rest—that he, a mere mortal, had drawn the malevolent being to Snakebite by having the temerity to attempt god-like things.

Dear God, please forgive me. I knew not what I was doing.

"Doyle says you are a lustful man, cursed with appetites you have trouble controlling."

Richardson, lost in thought until that moment, again focused on the obviously dead but reanimated saloon girl. "How could he know that?"

"Doyle knows all."

Richardson sighed. "Of course he does."

Despite the flippancy of his reply, he once again felt unsettled by the words emerging from Charlotte's mouth. In this case, he knew for a fact she was speaking incontestable truth. He shuddered as he recalled his libidinous behavior in the presence of Angelina's corpse earlier in the day. He felt ashamed now. Not just for what he'd actually done, but for how far he knew he might have gone if he'd been just slightly less in control.

Charlotte laughed in that grating way again that set his teeth on edge. "Doyle says if you still want to fuck a dead girl, you can have your way with me, but you have to agree to fix me first."

Richardson grimaced. "I don't want to do that."

"Which part of it?"

Richardson groaned in aggravation. "Either one, for god's sake. One is an abomination. The other is impossible."

LAST OF THE RAVAGERS

Charlotte rolled her eyes. "Abomination. Please. Don't be ridiculous, doctor. We both know you'll be singing a different tune once your cock's inside me. As for fixing me, you're not being asked to repair that which cannot be repaired. What we're looking for here is a cosmetic fix, one that'll fool people for a while when I go back to the saloon. Because that's important. That's my big task. To get back inside the Last Chance before nightfall." She smiled and leaned closer after that, puckering her lips and exposing the tops of her breasts as the slinky garment's fabric shifted slightly downward. "So what do you say, Doc? Do you think you can do that?"

The doctor's brow furrowed as he paused to give the matter a few moments of actual consideration. Now that he knew he wasn't being asked to perform intricate surgery of a type that couldn't possibly be pulled off successfully, he supposed there might be at least one practical way of fulfilling her bizarre request, but there was a problem. Assuming the girl's story about Doyle was true, by doing as she asked, he would essentially be doing the bidding of a malign entity with undoubtedly nefarious motivations.

"Why does Doyle want you back inside the saloon?"

Charlotte sighed, shaking her head. "Come on, Doc. Stop torturing yourself with the inner debate. You know why. A big showdown is happening at the Last Chance Saloon tonight and he wants an operative on the inside." She smiled again. "And that would be me. Now, I can see the wheels spinning in your head. You've thought of a way to fix me, haven't you?" She smacked him on the arm in a way that was slightly harder than playful. "So let's hear it. What's your big idea?"

He winced. "That hurt."

Before he could react, she leaned over him and pressed the ball of a thumb against the wrinkly flesh just below his remaining good eye. "I can hurt you a lot worse than that, Doc. You're going to fix me. I know you're worried about your friends, but you have to realize you can't help them. They're doomed no matter what. The good news is you can still help yourself by helping me. Do as you're told and I won't have to sink my thumb into your eye socket and slowly dig out this other eye." She laughed softly. "You're not nearly strong enough to stop me. I think you know that."

Her thumbed pressed down harder.

He whimpered. "All right!"

The pressure eased some. "You're ready to help, then?"

He swallowed hard and huffed out a big breath. "Yes, damn you, yes."

A shudder went through Richardson as he peered into her eyes and saw an intensity of focus that had never been there before. His heart started thumping harder as he realized this wasn't just Charlotte he was dealing with here. She was still in there, clearly, but the malign entity was observing through her eyes and occasionally coming forward to guide her actions and speech.

God help me, I'm in the presence of evil.

Her hand came away from his face as she again shifted around on the edge of the bed. A moment later, she thrust a hand inside his trousers, making him gasp as cold fingers curled around his cock. Because he was still under the influence of laudanum and whiskey, he was surprised by the physical reaction that occurred. He alternately groaned and whimpered as she squeezed his thickening shaft.

"Tell me about how you plan to fix me, Doc."

He needed a few moments to get his breathing under control and gather his thoughts.

Then he told her what he had in mind.

TWENTY-FOUR

AFTER DEVOURING MARY'S EYES, Eleanor pulled the woman's lifeless body into the tub with her. Because the tub was small this required a fair amount of maneuvering, which caused a good bit of bloody bath water to slosh out of the tub. In the end, however, she was able to get the corpse in with her. The fit was a tight but pleasurable one. She spent several moments caressing and kissing the woman's lifeless flesh, as well as inserting her tongue inside the hole in her throat, moaning and probing deeply as she tasted blood and shredded tissue.

Her tongue was still inside the hole when the moment of reanimation occurred. The woman's body jerked and a gurgle came from her throat as Eleanor pulled her mouth away from the wound. She tried rising up, but Eleanor gripped her shoulders and held her in place. "Be still," she commanded, utilizing the stern tone she'd used with her children when they were misbehaving. "You belong to me now. Do you understand?"

The corpse was absolutely still for a moment.

Then it nodded.

Eleanor smiled. "Good, because I'm not even close to done with you yet. I told your stupid son to throw himself down the well and he did. They have such soft little minds at that age. If you listen close, you can still hear him screaming."

She allowed a short moment of silence to elapse.

Then she laughed. "Did you hear that?"

Another wet gurgle came from the throat of the eyeless corpse.

Then it nodded again.

"Isn't it the loveliest sound you've ever heard?"

Another nod.

Eleanor laughed again. "What a dumb sack of beautiful meat you are."

She gripped one of the woman's hands and guided it between her legs. "There," she said, gasping softly. "Do that until I tell you to stop." She raised up slightly as the revived corpse mindlessly did her bidding, then leaned forward and slid her tongue into one of those deliciously juicy empty eye sockets. "Mmm. What a treat you are, my lovely."

The living dead woman gurgled in response.

From somewhere outside the washroom came a heavy clomping of boots on the wooden floor. The sound came closer. The interloper whistled a slow, mournful tune. Eleanor moaned softly in pleasure and continued to swirl her tongue about inside an eye socket as the door to the washroom opened slowly with a loud creaking of hinges. She withdrew her tongue from the eye socket and pressed her mouth firmly around the vacated space, suctioning out as much of the remaining blood as she could. Her excitement increased as she sensed Doyle observing her from the doorway.

She hoped he was proud of her.

He scratched a match against the door and lit up a stogie. "Enjoying yourself?"

Eleanor shivered and gripped the sides of the tub as she abruptly surged to the brink of orgasm. As much as she was enjoying defiling her rejuvenated victim, it was hearing his voice again that helplessly pushed her to that point. It was a powerful reminder of the brazen way he'd walked into her life and effortlessly taken control of her. Every nerve-ending in her body felt inflamed with raw pleasure. She was his slave every bit as much as the dead woman belonged to her. There was nothing she wouldn't do for him, no act of debauched depravity in which she would not willingly wallow and come back begging for more, more, more.

She looked at him and smiled. "Yes. Very much so."

He puffed on his stogie and nodded. "Good. Not that I'm surprised. Through the ages, I've found that once a person gets a taste for this kind of thing, they tend to embrace it with vigor." He chuckled. "Though I don't know if I've ever seen anyone take to it so wholeheartedly in so short a time."

Eleanor licked blood from her fingers and smiled. "Thank you."

Doyle turned his head and cocked it at an angle, as if listening for something. Aside from the faint, barely audible screams of the boy in the well, Eleanor heard nothing, but that didn't mean anything. Doyle saw and heard things no else could.

"The woman's husband approaches. I believe I'll go out and greet him."

He turned away from her and walked out of the washroom without another word. In another few moments, Eleanor began to faintly perceive the sounds of a wagon drawn by horses or mules approaching the house. Doyle's transformative magic had changed her in a number of ways, including a heightening of all her senses. She was already something beyond human, something better and more powerful than that, but her own magic was still only in its infancy. Doyle, her master and teacher, remained a god by comparison. He was capable of almost anything, including hearing things from miles away. An impressive thing, yes, but child's play compared to his ability to communicate with the dead across far greater distances.

BRYAN SMITH

Her deepest desire at this point was to remain by his side forever, learning from him and, perhaps one day deep into the distant future, becoming nearly as powerful.

The sounds from outside grew louder and more distinct. A wagon was definitely approaching, one drawn by mules rather than horses. The loud creaking of its wheels indicated it was heavily loaded down with supplies. A man's voice became audible. He was speaking to the animals. From his tone, it was clear he still had no inkling of the nightmare awaiting him.

From the well, the broken boy's screams grew a little louder. Upon hearing them, Eleanor shivered and moaned. She moaned again when Mary flexed her fingers inside her vagina.

The wagon came to a stop somewhere outside the house.

Doyle opened the front door and stepped out onto the porch.

Within seconds, an exchange of words began.

Mary's husband sounded wary of Doyle and surprised by the unexpected presence of a stranger. He did not, however, sound frightened. Not at first. That changed when he finally heard the screams coming from the well. Sounds of a small commotion ensued. Eleanor could envision it in her head—the husband jumping down from the wagon's riding bench and racing toward the well, followed by his anguished reaction as he looked down and saw the broken and battered form lying at the bottom.

Then Doyle caught up to him and a struggle occurred.

The man's loud words of anger quickly gave way to even louder screams of agony.

Eleanor twisted herself about in the small tub and within a few sloppy moments was able to disengage herself from her undead lover. She climbed out of the tub and walked outside dripping wet and naked, the bottoms of her feet becoming caked with dirt as she trod across the dry

154

soil. She went around the side of the house toward the well, where she found Doyle looming over the crumpled form of Mary's husband. The man was still alive, but it was clear that wouldn't remain the case for much longer. Loops of intestine were hanging out of a large, ragged hole in his abdomen.

His lips quivered and his eyes were glassy as he looked up at Eleanor. "Wh-why?"

She and Doyle exchanged a glance.

Eleanor looked at the man and shrugged. "These things aren't meant for you to understand. You're only a man, after all."

Positioned directly over his head now, she raised up a foot and smashed her heel down against his nose, breaking it and sending a shard of bone into his brain. She watched him for a few moments until he stopped twitching and went still.

Then she smiled and looked at Doyle. "Well, this has been an enjoyable way to spend an afternoon. What's next?"

The man who'd described himself as 'The Last Ravager' laughed softly and shook his head. As he began to describe the next phase of his plans, a few of those strange blue-skinned creatures climbed up out of the well with blood smeared all over their faces.

TWENTY-FIVE

MUCH TO BILLY CONWAY'S relief, no additional airborne assaults occurred as his horse carried him the rest of the way back to Snakebite. He was, however, on edge for the remainder of the return journey. More than once he nearly jumped out of his saddle upon hearing the cawing of some bird soaring overhead. Each time it happened, he looked to the sky, half-expecting to see the freakishly overgrown vultures on his trail again. Sure, he'd shot the no-headed bitch's legs damn near off her body, but that didn't mean she couldn't be dropped behind him on the horse again. If that happened, she wouldn't need her legs to try attacking him one last time. She could reach around and claw at his face again, maybe try to tear out his throat with her unnatural strength. This thought made him wish he'd shot her whole hand off while he had the chance instead of just that one damn finger.

Each time he glanced heavenward, however, the sky was empty save for a few slowly drifting white clouds. He pulled on the reins of his horse as they arrived at the outskirts of town, indicating for the animal to slow to a trot as they reached Main Street. A few minutes later, he hitched the horse to a post outside the sheriff's office.

Above the door was a sign with just the word SHERIFF painted on it in large block letters. The sign was pockmarked with bullet holes that'd been there since

156

LAST OF THE RAVAGERS

before his time in Snakebite. Billy went inside and found the big outer room empty, with no sign of either Ned or Trey Walker, the other part-time deputy, having been in lately. Leaving the place unattended without at least locking up wasn't like Ned. Trey had the day off, but that didn't mean anything when a real crisis was brewing. Someone should've been sent to fetch the kid by now. It was possible he was in the back, cleaning out the cells.

"Trey? You in here, boy?"

Billy waited a beat, giving him a chance to answer. He raised his voice and repeated the query when no response came.

Still no answer.

Billy went through a door at the back of the room and down a short hallway to the holding cells There were just two side-by-side cells, each outfitted with two rickety cots that weren't much more comfortable than sleeping on a bed of nails. Billy knew this from experience, having slept off more than one night of heavy boozing here.

One cell was empty.

The other was not.

At first Billy couldn't tell exactly what was happening in the cell to his left as he came out of the hallway. Something wasn't right about it, that much he could discern right away, but his eyes and brain could make no sense of it. After gawping at the bizarre tableau for several seconds, a first impression belatedly took shape in his head. Riley McKay, notorious drunkard and Civil War vet, was sprawled out on the cot against the back wall of the cell. His mouth was wide open and his head was thrown back. One leg was hanging off the side of the cot. Pieces of fabric were scattered all over the floor. Riley was not alone in the cell. Someone—or some*thing*—appeared to be kneeling at the side of the cot between the drunkard's scrawny legs.

Billy's face twisted in an expression of disgust.

He still wasn't completely sure what was happening, but it looked . . . well, it sort of looked like a blue-skinned midget was sucking McKay's cock.

"Hey!" the deputy called out, taking a tentative step closer to the cell. "This ain't a got-damn brothel for freaks. Break it up before I come in there and crack skulls!"

Some moments passed. Neither of the cell's occupants gave any indication of being on the verge of heeding his command. Getting angry now, Billy approached the cell and gripped two iron bars to rattle the door.

"Hey!" Being ignored got under Billy's skin like nothing else. That went double for when the person or persons ignoring him were scum-sucking reprobates like Riley and his strange companion here. His face reddened with rage as he shook the cell door again. "Look at me, goddamn you!"

Only then did Billy begin to realize there was more amiss here than he'd originally believed. The blue-skinned thing wasn't some sideshow freak that happened to have an odd pigmentation disorder. People were sometimes born messed-up in various ways, with weird-shaped heads, extra fingers, or a flipper where an arm should be. Too much inbreeding caused it most of the time. If they weren't mercy-killed at birth, they were mostly kept out of sight of regular people. It was sad and unfortunate, but they were still human beings. This thing, however, whatever it was, wasn't human, Billy felt pretty sure of that.

The slurping sounds the creature had been making ceased as its oval-shaped head came away from Riley's crotch. Billy felt his balls shrivel as the head turned toward him and he finally got a look at the thing's wide mouth. Wedged between some of its seemingly hundreds of big, sharp teeth were shredded bits of pink and bloody flesh. Billy needed approximately one more second to recognize the bits of tissue for what they were—the masticated remnants of Riley McKay's cock. Now that the creature's head was no longer fully obscuring it, he caught a glimpse of the drunkard's crotch, gulping when he saw the ragged, bloody mess there.

Billy's stomach churned as he took an instinctive step back and reached for the grip of his pistol. The creature turned fully toward him now and took a few waddling steps toward the cell door. He saw now it'd been standing the whole time rather than kneeling. The thing was short and squat, like a Buddha statue. A horrible grinding sound came from its mouth as it opened wider. The shrill noise hurt his head. It felt like a nail being slowly driven into the base of his skull.

When the thing waddled closer to the cell door. Billy took out his pistol and slipped the barrel between iron bars. "Don't come no closer. This is the only warning you're gonna get."

He cocked the hammer of the pistol, a simple but often effective method of intimidation. In the very next instant, however, the creature rushed toward the cell door with deceptive, surprising speed, snatching the gun from Billy's hand.

Billy gasped and backed away, angry with himself for having lost Big Boomer for the second time in one day. This time there was no clear way of retrieving the gun without putting himself in grave danger. Though the creature wasn't physically imposing—putting aside the matter of its terrifying mouth, that is—there was no doubt it was extremely dangerous. Facing off against it without a weapon would be a losing proposition. He was grateful at least for the locked door of iron bars that stood between them. The creature was too fat to slip out through them.

Billy frowned.

Wait just a dang minute . . .

The question he should've been asking himself from the beginning belatedly dawned in his beleaguered mind—*how did the little blue bastard get in there in the first place?*

No question the door was locked. Billy knew that from shaking it multiple times already. His gaze went to the window several feet above the cot and he grimaced when he saw that some of the bars there were severely bent out of shape. At least one appeared to be missing entirely. Somehow the creature had scaled the wall at the back of the building to take a peek inside. When it saw Riley sprawled out on the cot—still sleeping off the previous night's overindulgence, no doubt—it decided to let itself in and have a bite to eat. Clearly the thing was far more agile and stronger than it looked.

Strong enough to bend the bars of a cell door, in fact.

The blue-skinned creature fiddled awkwardly with the gun for a bit, dropping it twice and immediately scooping it up again. Billy couldn't help noticing it only had three stubby fingers on one hand and four on the other, all of which resembled swollen thumbs rather than regular fingers. They were hands made for gripping and tearing things apart and not for effectively wielding man-made weapons.

Making a noise of frustration, the creature dropped the gun, gripped two of the iron bars and began to pull them apart. The loud groaning sound of solid iron yielding to extreme pressure was enough to convince Billy it was time to go.

He turned tail and ran out of the building.

His mind was racing as he backed out into the dusty street. It wasn't at all clear what his next move should be. The creature in the cell was a deadly threat to everyone in town. Based on what he'd seen of its capabilities, there was a strong likelihood the same creature—or one like it—was responsible for the mauling of the saloon girl last night. People should be warned. A team of men should be raised to shoot the goddamn thing into oblivion. He needed to find Ned and tell him about what he'd seen.

A desperate, scared part of him wanted to jump up on

LAST OF THE RAVAGERS

his horse and ride out of this seemingly cursed town forever. Aside from maybe a few of his friends—the sheriff included—there wasn't anything here he couldn't easily leave behind with even a single regret. He could make his way to Tombstone, a bigger city with no shortage of opportunities.

Billy sucked in a big breath and slowly released it.

You're not going anywhere, son. You ain't no yellow-belly.

Feeling slightly calmer, he went to his horse and took the repeater rifle from its scabbard. After reloading it, he stepped back up onto the porch and peered in through the window on the door, turning his head this way and that for any sign of the fat blue cocksucker. Or cock*eater*, rather.

The outer room appeared empty.

Billy opened the door and went back inside. Holding the long barrel of the weapon out in front of him, he conducted a careful search, checking under the desks in the outer room. The blue creature wasn't hiding under either of them. Billy stood up straight and approached the door leading to the cells, pausing before entering the hallway.

Either the creature was already out of the cell and still lurking back there for some reason, or it had fled the building through the window over the cot. Those were the only possibilities that made any sense. Unless, of course, it'd done something else extra damn weird, like vanishing into thin fucking air. At this point, he felt ready to believe almost anything. Whatever the case, it needed checking out.

And yet he hesitated.

Go on, ya big baby. You've come this far. Be a man and get your ass back there.

Just as he was finally about to step into the hallway, the blue-skinned creature appeared suddenly at the opposite end of the passage. Billy damn near jumped out of his skin when he saw it, by then having nearly convinced himself it'd fled the place. Its unnaturally wide mouth curved upward at the corners, taunting him with a deviously demonic grin. It picked a piece of bloody flesh from between two of the shark-like fangs and flung it the length of the hallway. An instinctive twitch of his head at the last second was the only thing that kept Billy from being smacked in the face with a bloody morsel of chewed-up cock meat. In the next instant, the thing came charging down the hallway.

Billy snorted. "Yeah, you bastard. Come get some!"

He aimed the rifle and fired.

The waddling but somehow fast-moving creature bobbed and weaved its way down the passage. Bullets flew past its stout body without so much as nicking it. By the time it made it to the halfway point without getting hit, Billy began to fear he was within seconds of dying. His only consolation was he hadn't run off like a coward.

He kept shifting his aim, frantically attempting to match the creature's rapid movements. Finally, when it was about three quarters of the way down the hallway, a bullet found its target, blasting a hole through the creature's swollen throat. It squealed in pain and that terrible grinding sound Billy had heard before started up again. He tracked the creature's movement as it staggered sideways and bounced off a wall. Firing again, he hit it in the side of the head this time, obliterating one of those pointy ears. Now it spun away from him and tried to retreat, weaving around like a drunk.

As he gave chase, Billy was able to take his time and aim with better precision. His next shot hit the creature square in the back of the head. It flew forward, hit the floor on its portly belly, and slid forward a few more feet. Now it squealed weakly and clawed at the floor. Billy approached with caution in case it was playing possum. When he was convinced it wasn't about to miraculously spring up off the floor and tear out his throat, he inched even closer, until he was standing directly over the thing.

He fired one more time into the back of the creature's head, making extra sure it was kaput for good. Then he kicked it.

Nothing happened.

Billy sneered. "One of these days you and your freaky kin are gonna learn not to mess with me. If you all have to learn the hard way, so be it."

After retrieving Big Boomer from the cell in back, he hurried back down the hallway and walked out of the building.

TWENTY-SIX

THE ONLY BOOK remaining from Russ Harper's small personal library was a volume of short stories by Edgar Allan Poe. All the others were still out there in the desert, abandoned in his haste to get away from the strange blue-skinned creatures, which he steadfastly continued to believe were not of this world. He still had no explanation for what they were or from whence they came, but the lack of answers could not sway him from his opinion. They were from *somewhere else*, some realm of mystery beyond simple human comprehension.

As was often the case, Russ read tales of the macabre to shut out the world around him. Unfortunately, the collection of stories by the renowned scribe from Baltimore was not casting its usual transportative spell. His ability to focus on the stories drifted in and out, never quite reaching that magical point of full immersion.

Contributing to his lack of focus was the way his thoughts kept going back to the saloon girl who'd tried to rob him earlier. He knew better than to fall in love with whores, of course. They were mercenaries of the heart. A girl like Charlotte wasn't made for getting married and raising a family. Still, there was something about her that made her less easy to forget than other saloon girls he'd fucked. The sense of longing for something better than what she had resonated with him. He spent so much time telling himself he was content with his life of wandering the western territories and killing men, some who maybe deserved it and at least a few who didn't. Mostly he was able to make himself believe it. A little less lately, though.

Maybe it was time to try something else.

Like follow her to San Francisco and see what happened next.

A couple times he put down his book and went out of his room to look for Charlotte. There was a sitting room on the floor above the saloon where some of the working girls lounged around in their underwear. Despite the early hour, most were drinking already. A few were smoking opium. Each time he asked if they'd seen her around, they responded with shrugs. Their bored, apathetic expressions told him no one really cared. He got the impression Charlotte wasn't that popular with the other ladies here. Could be all sorts of reasons for that. Maybe they resented her for wanting to leave Snakebite. Russ didn't know or care why.

The second time he came around asking, one of the ladies wanted to know why he was so concerned with the whereabouts of one particular whore when there were so many others available right then and there. This woman had a mass of black hair piled atop her head and a sultry expression. "Stop sniffing around for that dumb bitch. Any lady here could make you feel just as good. Better, probably." She started to stand up. "Come on, I'll prove it to you."

Russ backed away, raising his hands with his palms facing out. "Sorry, ain't in the mood.. I really just want to talk to her."

The black-haired woman shrugged and sat down. "Your loss."

Another of the women—a blonde in a tiny green slip—turned her head and looked at him, her drugged features twisting slightly in confusion. "Why do you wanna talk to

Charlotte anyway? Ain't anything interesting ever come out of that cunt's mouth. Unless you think spitting out a man's baby batter is interesting."

This prompted a round of giggles from the other women.

Russ took his leave of them without bothering to retort, walking on down the hall in the direction of the staircase that would take him down to the saloon. To get to the staircase, it was necessary to first pass through a door guarded by a man of impressive girth and height. The man had his arms folded over his giant gut and was standing with his back against the door. He wore a tight-fitting white shirt with the sleeves pushed up to the elbows, showing off massive forearms. His bearded face betrayed no emotion whatsoever at Russ's approach.

"I need to go down to the saloon."

The big man's face remained impassive as he shook his head. "No."

Russ frowned. "What?"

The big man grunted. "No. It's a simple word. Not hard to figure out."

There was no malice in the man's words or in the way he was looking at him.

Just resoluteness.

Russ sighed. "Any good reason why?"

The big man nodded. "Private meeting. I was told not to let anyone down until it's over. So that's what I'm doing."

"So I'm not being held prisoner here?"

For the first time, the man's expression registered something other than impassiveness, his brow furrowing in confusion. "Of course not. If you have to leave the building, you can go out the back way."

Russ asked how he could do that and the big man told him.

He walked back down the hallway, ignoring snickers from a few of the ladies as he passed by the sitting room.

LAST OF THE RAVAGERS

After stopping off in his room to retrieve his hat, he resumed his trek down the hallway, which branched off to the right at the back of the building. At the end of this shorter passage was another staircase. He started moving toward it but stopped and backed up as he passed by a room with an open door. He hadn't gotten a good look at what was inside, but his brain perceived something as off and compelled him to take a closer look.

Dark curtains hung over the room's lone window, blotting out the afternoon sunlight. The only source of illumination was a gas-lit lantern sitting atop a dresser. A naked man was sprawled out on the bed, with his hands tied to the slatted headboard and his ankles lashed to the corner posts at the foot of the bed. His jaw looked unnaturally crooked, as if it'd been broken just recently. He was alternately moaning and muttering what sounded like gibberish, but Russ did pick out one word that made him gasp.

Doyle.

It was the name from his dream. Hearing it uttered by someone else here in the waking world sent a cold shiver down his spine.

The bound man was not alone in the room. Two women were in there with him. Both wore black masks partially obscuring their faces. One was larger and clearly older. Something in the younger one's manner made Russ believe she was an assistant to the older, pudgier woman. Both were outfitted in what he at first perceived as black lingerie, but on closer look the garments appeared made of leather. The larger woman was standing on the bed, brandishing a whip as she loomed over the bound man. Judging from the many livid marks on his body, he'd already been lashed nearly to the point of oblivion.

Russ took a step closer to the door. He wasn't quite sure what was going on here, except that it was like nothing he'd ever seen before. Despite the implied violence of the situation, there was something almost titillating about it. As he got closer, he realized the young man on the bed looked familiar. In another moment, he recognized him as the barkeep's employee.

Cole. That's his name. What the hell has happened to him?

Before Russ could devote much more thought to that, the younger woman appeared to sense his scrutiny and turned away from the bed. For a moment, she only stared at him from behind the mask obscuring the top part of her face. She came unhurriedly to the door and eased it shut, maintaining eye contact with him until the door blocked her from view. He then heard a click that signaled the turning of a lock.

Russ spent another moment puzzling over what he'd seen before deciding it was none of his business.

Just move along, he thought. *Keep your mouth shut and act like you never saw it.*

He turned away from the closed door and put the mysteries it shielded out of his mind. In another few seconds he descended the staircase to the back door. He gripped the doorknob and found it locked.

Unlocking it, he stepped outside and did a double-take when he encountered Charlotte on the back stoop.

He laughed after gasping in surprise. "Well, shit. Ain't this a coincidence? I was just about to go looking for you."

Charlotte smiled. "How lucky for me. And just when I was about to give up on getting back inside. It's like fate or something. Let's go up to your room, Russ. I have something special to show you."

Russ chuckled. "I could say the same."

She smiled at his mildly crude joke, but said nothing.

Shrugging, he stepped aside and ushered her inside with a wave of his hand. A few minutes later, they were back inside his room, with the door shut and locked at her request. Then she showed him the knife she said she'd gotten at the hardware store. It was an ordinary knife.

He frowned. "Ah . . . I hate to say it, but I don't see what's so special about that thing."

She smiled again. "Here. Let me show you what's special about it."

Her hand moved like a lightning flash.

Before Russ knew what was happening, the blade was buried in his flesh up to the hilt.

TWENTY-SEVEN

THE **MULTIPLE GUNSHOT** reports brought Ned out to the porch of the Last Chance Saloon. He was quickly joined there by Raven Decker and Quentin Brown. All three stood there with weapons drawn, scanning the mostly empty street for signs of recent violent conflict, but there was nothing. No bodies in the street. No horse ridden by a perpetrator galloping away in the distance amidst a cloud of dust. Not a damn thing.

After looking up and down the street multiple times, Ned's gaze finally settled on the horse hitched to the post outside his own office. His heart-rate quickened as recognition dawned at last. That was Billy Conway's black filly. He hadn't seen the deputy for hours, not since sending him out to the desert to burn the saloon girl's headless corpse. The horse wasn't there just a short while ago. He remembered that from his trip back across the street from Doc Richardson's office.

Before he could share this insight with anyone, an agitated-looking Billy Conway came out of the sheriff's office with a Winchester rifle clutched in his hands. He had the wild-eyed expression of a man who'd been through a lot in a short span of time. It didn't take a huge leap of deduction to figure the rifle was the likely source of the gunshots they'd heard moments earlier.

Catching sight of them, Billy started across the street

with a purposeful gait. "Y'all ain't gonna believe half the crazy-ass shit I've been through since last we set eyes on each other, but I swear on my sweet grandmama's grave every got-damn word of it is true." He stopped abruptly in the middle of the street, turning his rifle toward the sky upon hearing the cawing of a bird. "Oh, hey, it's you again! Well come and get me, you ugly son of a bitch!"

He sighted along the barrel of the rifle and squeezed the trigger.

Nothing happened.

Billy's features drew downward in dismay. "Ah, shit."

The cawing sound came again as a large shadow passed over the street. Confused about why his deputy was so jumpy about a bird circling overhead, Ned stepped to the edge of the porch and turned his own gaze skyward. He'd just started squinting against the glare of the sun when something big came swooping downward.

Ned gasped in shock as the largest vulture he'd ever seen took a screeching dive at the deputy's head with its claws outstretched. Billy let out a startled screech of his own and tried to shield his head as he swatted at the unnaturally large winged varmint with the butt of the rifle. He managed to connect with one of its flapping wings one time, but not hard enough to disable it or knock it out of the air. The vulture continued to flit about in the air above the street, occasionally swooping in for another diving run at Billy's face.

It was the damnedest thing. Ned had never seen a vulture—or any other type of bird, for that matter—attack a man in such a repeated, purposeful way, as if the creature had a personal grudge against the deputy. He'd call it impossible, only he knew better than to classify anything as such at this point. He yelled at Billy, urging him to run and take cover in the saloon, but the man took no heed of this advice, appearing determined to best the feathered menace in head-on confrontation. Based on what Ned had seen so far, this did not seem wise. He was about to charge out into the street and grab hold of the man when a boom of gunfire from right next to him nearly made him jump out of his skin. Two shots that sounded like a cannon going off at such close range. The giant vulture landed in the street with a heavy thud and didn't move.

Billy gaped disbelievingly at the dead vulture a moment.

His head swiveled slowly toward the saloon and he raised a hand to point at his savior. "Sweet jumped-up Jesus on a handcart! Who is this sharp-shooting gorgeous angel?"

Ned glanced at Raven Decker, who was standing just a few feet to his right. She still had her gun out and pointed vaguely skyward, a wisp of smoke curling from the muzzle.

Quentin Brown chuckled. "A lady bounty hunter from another world."

Billy's face crinkled in confusion. "Come again?'

"We've got some crazy-ass shit to tell you as well," Ned told him.

"Is that right?"

Ned nodded. "Yep."

He stepped out into the street and approached the dead vulture. His brow creased as he tipped back his hat and peered closely at the perforated corpse. Other than its abnormal size, the thing looked no different from any other creature of its type native to the area. He nudged it with the toe of his boot, still amazed two bullets were enough to knock something this big out of the air. Then again, those weren't normal bullets, he knew that. They packed a bigger punch than any sidearm available in this world.

He looked at the deputy. "This wasn't a random attack, was it?"

Billy tore his gaze away from Raven and turned toward his boss. "No, sir. I don't believe it was."

Ned thought of how the man's rifle had clicked empty

LAST OF THE RAVAGERS

when he'd attempted to fire it a few moments earlier. "We heard shots. You unloaded on something in the jailhouse, didn't you?"

Billy grimaced. "That, sir, is part of the crazy-ass shit I was referring to before we were interrupted by this flying beast from hell. There was a blue thing in the cell with Riley. Some kind of weird little monster. It was . . . well, sir, it was eating the drunk sumbitch's privates."

Ned frowned, blanching at the bizarre image this description put in his head. "What?"

Raven Decker cleared her throat. "A Mog."

They all looked at her.

Raven ignored the gazes of the other men and looked right at the sheriff. "The blue meanies I was telling you about before. Remember? That's what he's talking about. The transmogrified. And where there's one, there'll surely be more."

Ned looked around, again scanning the quiet street for signs of activity and was disquieted to see no one at all out and about. A short while earlier he'd glimpsed a few people strolling the street and patronizing various local merchants. Not nearly as many as usual for what was typically a busy time of day on Main Street, but at least there'd been some hint of normality. Now, however, the town looked deserted, as if some virulent plague had wiped out the entire community.

He tried telling himself the spooky absence of people might not actually be as sinister as it seemed. The explanation might be as simple as pedestrians retreating to interior spaces after hearing multiple noisy shooting events. It was possible people were lingering behind the closed doors of businesses on both sides of the street, just biding their time until they were convinced it was safe to venture outside again.

Ned sighed.

The theory was a reasonable one, but he didn't quite

buy it, at least not as something happening on a large scale. He didn't doubt some of Snakebite's citizens were hiding behind these doors just as he'd imagined, but the emptiness of Main Street felt too heavy to believe they were there in significant numbers. He feared that other, far stranger things might account for the current state of affairs here in town.

He locked eyes with Billy. "I want to see this blue thing you shot. Let's go have a look."

The deputy's expression conveyed a distinct lack of enthusiasm for this idea, but he voiced no objection, nodding tersely instead. Raven Decker accompanied the lawmen as they started across the street. Quentin Brown remained behind, giving them a wave from the saloon's porch.

Moments later, the three of them were inside the jailhouse, crowding into the narrow hallway for a look at the slain creature, which remained where Billy had left it, face-down on the floor.

Ned gave it a hard nudge with the toe of his boot, just as he'd done with the vulture outside. As in that case, there was no doubt this thing was deceased. The back of its head was obliterated from the several rounds fired into it from Billy's rifle. In both cases, his tentativeness was an instinctive reaction to the alien nature of the dead things. He realized he hadn't fully believed everything Raven had told him until just now, if only because it was all so far outside standard perceptions of reality.

In basic appearance, the thing was as she'd described it, short and roundish with hard-shelled flesh the color of the sky on a clear day. Squatting next to it, he cringed as he gripped the thing by its shoulders and flipped it over. The feel of its alien flesh against the callused pads of his fingers stirred queasy feelings. He jerked his hand away as quickly as he could. The sight of its ruined face made him gag. It wasn't the exit wound damage that disturbed him. He'd seen enough of that in his time not to be shocked by it. What bothered him was the shape of its face and all those teeth, concentric rings of them that looked capable of shredding and devouring human limbs whole.

He looked up at Raven Decker. "This is a Mog?"

She nodded. "Yep."

"And you're sure there'll be more of them around?"

Another nod. "A *lot* more. Without a doubt. They may be lurking in hidden places, perhaps waiting for a signal from their master, but they're around. What happened here tells me similar things are probably happening to others in your town. The Mogs are restless and hungry. And they're getting tired of waiting."

Ned couldn't help thinking of the attack on Angelina the previous evening. Based on the nature of her wounds, it was a fair guess she was the town's first victim of these things. He got to his feet and went to the back to take a gander at Riley McKay. His deputy and the bounty hunter followed.

Again, the scene was just as Billy had described it. Bits of fabric were scattered all over the floor of the cell, undoubtedly shredded remnants of the dead man's trousers. What remained of the area between his legs was an appalling, bloody mess.

Ned turned away from the grotesque sight and looked at his deputy. "I need you to ride out and get together a team of the sharpest shooters you know. Or, hell, anyone at all with a gun and a trace of backbone. Track down Trey Walker and have him do the same. Send them all to the Last Chance Saloon. The sooner they can get there, the better. If anyone needs extra convincing, tell 'em their drinks are on me tonight."

Billy snorted. "Dunno how good an idea that is, sir. Some of them boys are likely to drink you into bankruptcy."

"I'll take that chance. Step to it, son."

BRYAN SMITH

The deputy snapped a military-style salute and hustled out of the building, the door banging shut an instant later.

Ned sighed. "Reckon we ought to get back over to the saloon. Let Quentin know what's on the way."

Raven smiled. "Not just yet."

She came at him fast, seizing a handful of his shirt and pulling him close. He spluttered in surprise, but before he could say anything, her tongue was inside his mouth.

TWENTY-EIGHT

THE ONE GOOD thing about being double-crossed by the reanimated saloon girl was the vanishing of the pain from his cauterized eye socket. It went from nigh unbearable regardless of how much laudanum he used to simply no longer there in the wake of his own return from the dead.

Standing before the mirror in his exam room, Doc Richardson stared at the ragged gashes across his throat and shuddered in revulsion. This was the second profound violation done to his flesh in a matter of only hours. Though there was no pain from this wound either, he could still almost feel the rusty blade of the straight razor biting into his flesh. The blade was too dull to finish the job with the first slice. Charlotte had to hold him still and rip at his jugular several more times to get it done. Each cut was a fresh lance of agony. He remembered her laughing and seeming to enjoy the way he struggled in her firm embrace.

But now that pain was gone, too, just like the pain from his ruined eye.

He hadn't been robbed entirely of sensation. His flesh wasn't numb. Pain was something he could still experience, as he'd learned by experimentally pricking the tip of a finger with a needle. Through some process unique to life rejuvenation, however, pain from wounds inflicted prior to death did not endure after revivification. He was also no longer feeling the effects of the large amounts of whiskey

177

and laudanum he'd ingested before being killed. Rarely in his adult life had he felt as terribly sober as he did now.

Richardson didn't understand any of it. He'd died after bleeding out from the severed vein in his neck. That much was irrefutable. Now he was back and he wasn't especially happy about it. Considering how much time he'd devoted to research in the area of life reanimation, the opposite should be true. Wasn't this a validation of all the things he'd believed possible for so long?

He couldn't bring himself to see it that way.

This restoration of cognizance and physical mobility did not, he believed, constitute a true return to natural life. He had no detectable pulse or heartbeat. Yet he could still think and feel things. He breathed in and out, his lungs seeming to function normally. This was likely true of other organs in his body. In the moments after reanimation, nearly all the components of his inner workings had resumed functioning. He did not, however, believe this would last, because this form of restoration was only a *semblance* of life.

In other words, he was still dead.

It stood to reason, then, that over time his organs would again cease to function, winding down once it became clear they were no longer actually needed. Dumb bodily instinct would surrender to reality. His physical form would start to deteriorate. He would start to *decay*, like any other corpse. The realization filled him with equal parts anger and sadness, but he was grateful for the removal of his pain, if nothing else. He figured he was owed some form of compensation for being so tragically misled by the devious whore.

She'd sworn no harm would come to him so long as he assisted her with her problem. He hadn't exactly trusted her, but circumstances forced him to give her the benefit of the doubt, albeit grudgingly. Her supernaturally-augmented strength meant she had the advantage over him. Any attempt at resistance or slipping away from her was met with a stern response. She dragged him out of his office and down to the hardware store, controlling him as easily as a child tossing around a rag doll.

That was disconcerting, but at no point prior to the actual moment of betrayal did he truly believe she'd kill him.

He sneered at his reflection, shaking his head.

And to think you believed yourself a genius not long ago. You're no more a genius than any drooling simpleton locked away in a sanitarium.

She killed him at the hardware store because that was where he performed the patchwork repairs on her neck wound. He packed the hole with a mixture of sawdust and clay, taking care not to overfill the space and make it even more difficult for her to swallow and talk. Once he'd finished that part of the work to his satisfaction, he used a blade to mold the external part of the mixture so it would match the curvature of her neck. The final step was covering his work with a cream-colored paint that roughly matched her skin tone. He took a grim kind of pride in the finished result, which looked nearly life-like. With the blood and tissue washed out of her long hair, it would be difficult for anyone to tell she'd suffered such a grievous wound. Of course, it was only a temporary fix at best, but Charlotte didn't seem to mind, saying it only had to last through the night.

She kissed him to show her gratitude. Or so she let him believe. In reality, the kiss was a distraction. While their lips were locked, she grabbed the rusty straight razor from the table where he'd set the implements he'd used for the repair work on her neck. This happened in the back room of the store, where the owner of the place lay dead on the floor. When Richardson's eye opened again minutes after his death, the owner's corpse was also up and moving around again. He was an even more peculiar case, because he no longer seemed in possession of his normal faculties. He was more like a puppet than a man, saying nothing and automatically obeying Charlotte's every instruction.

Grimacing now at the gruesome way the movement stretched the ripped-open flaps of flesh, Richardson lifted his chin and put his face closer to the mirror. Then he took a needle threaded with a length of suture and raised a slightly shaky hand to one of the bottom flaps. He gently poked at the skin with the needle, expecting a jab of pain, but felt nothing. He tried it again and got the same result. Interesting. While he could still feel pain elsewhere on his body, the same was not true for the wounded areas. There was some level of sensation, of pressure, but nothing else. Again, he didn't understand it, but he was grateful. No pain would make getting through this a lot easier.

He had to grip the flap of flesh between the thumb and forefinger of his other hand to slide the needle in with better precision. Now that he knew it wouldn't hurt, his hands didn't shake. He was also able to work faster than would've been possible otherwise. Sewing the ragged flaps of flesh together took around twenty minutes from that point forward. By the time he'd finished drawing the sutures tight and snipping off the ends, the zig-zag pattern of slashes across his throat no longer looked so revolting. Under dim lighting, it'd look like nothing worse than an interesting scar.

Of course, he wasn't dumb enough to rely on favorable lighting. Anyone who took more than a cursory look at him would see something wasn't right. Especially in combination with the new hoarseness in his voice. Given everything else that had happened today, it wouldn't take his friends long to figure out he'd been killed and rejuvenated. They would then quite understandably decide he was a threat. Extreme measures would follow. They were apt to dismember his body and set him ablaze behind the saloon, which was not something he desired, despite the undeniably bleak current status of his situation.

LAST OF THE RAVAGERS

He needed time to talk to them in a rational way before anything like that could happen. To convince them he was still on their side and not under the influence of Doyle. That this actually seemed true could only aid his cause. Thus far he hadn't heard the thing's voice in his head, nor was his body possessed by any outside entity. This had puzzled him at first, but he soon decided the reason was obvious. The saloon girls were simple women not blessed with great intelligence. Because he had a stronger, sharper mind, he was naturally more resistant to outside influence.

A cravat would hide the wound nicely, he decided. He was known to wear one from time to time, so its presence wasn't likely to arouse suspicion. The hoarseness might require some explanation. He supposed he could simply say he'd awakened sounding this way and vaguely attribute it to the traumas he'd experienced. Whether anyone would buy so flimsy an explanation, he had no idea. Time was running short, however, and the sooner he could win over his compatriots, the better.

After donning the cravat and a fresh change of clothes, Richardson left his office and descended to the first floor of the building. He was on his way to the locked front door when he stopped and noticed Eddie Horton's severed head resting in his barber's chair. The head's sentient eyes flicked in his direction. The thin lips curled in a sneer.

Richardson couldn't help but chuckle despite his dark mood. Even in death, the asshole barber despised him.

Hatred must be the strongest of all human emotions, the doctor mused. *It persists even after life has departed.*

Richardson walked out of the shop, closed and locked the door behind him, and descended the steps to the street. The Last Chance Saloon stood before him. Within its walls he would meet his doom or find some form of salvation. If he'd still possessed a beating heart, it would've been racing in that moment of tense anticipation.

He adjusted his cravat and started across the street.

TWENTY-NINE

FATHER SIMON FITZPATRICK was in a state of significant bother as he prepared to climb the stairs to the steeple of his church and ring the large cast iron bell. He was doing this at the behest of Mark Stratton, the mayor of Snakebite. The man arrived on his doorstep just a short while ago, looking disheveled with his shirt partially untucked and his hair not combed in the usual neat way. He'd also neglected to don a hat before leaving his house. These things suggested a great haste on the mayor's part, a suspicion borne out by the words he uttered. Words Fitzpatrick would've taken as the ravings of a madman or a person under the influence of the vile rotgut sold at the local saloons had they been spoken by anyone else.

According to the mayor, some supernatural calamity had come to their quiet little town, one of potentially apocalyptic proportions. Not in the global sense, of course. The man wasn't claiming Jesus had returned. The threat he described sounded vaguely pagan in nature, but much about the specifics didn't quite fit with even that heretical belief system. A lot of what Stratton had to say sounded frankly nonsensical to the priest's ears, but the man was clearly taking it all quite seriously. He appeared to sincerely believe it could spell the demise of everyone in Snakebite.

From what Fitzpatrick could gather, nearly everything he said was information relayed to him secondhand. A man on horseback—one of the town's deputies, apparently—came to his house and blurted it all out before riding away to round up a posse of some sort. This did nothing to convince the priest of the veracity of the information. Stratton added he'd seen proof of one of the wildest of the bizarre claims with his own eyes. According to him, an elderly lady known to have perished of natural causes the previous day was now up and walking around with a vacant look in her eyes. This astonishing thing purportedly occurred at Stratton's ranch, where the lady had been employed as a cook. Anger stirred inside Fitzpatrick upon hearing this tale. It was a blatant mockery of the resurrection miracle. He attempted to rebuke the mayor, but the man was having none of it, being in an adamant and forceful mood.

Before leaving, the mayor made Fitzpatrick promise to ring the church bell, a gesture he hoped would draw as many of the faithful out of their places of dwelling as possible. The tolling of the bell should remain constant for a sustained period of time, long enough to get the message across that something requiring urgent attention was happening. The mayor hoped the priest could convince the members of his flock to remain inside the church until it became clear the danger had either passed or until all hope was lost. He did not seem at all certain of a positive outcome, but he hoped the sanctity of a holy place would protect those who believed, which was at least half the population of Snakebite.

"And what of those who don't believe?" the priest asked him, unable to keep an edge of scorn from his voice. "How will you protect them?"

Stratton grimaced and shook his head. "They will have to fend for themselves. There's no time to call a meeting at the town hall or get word out to everybody by other means. But ring that bell, Father. Let's save as many souls as we can tonight."

And with those gloomy words, he departed in haste.

Father Fitzpatrick believed it was all balderdash. Every unhinged, blasphemous word of it. At least all the fantastical parts. Despite that, he would err on the side of caution and do as the man requested. It was possible something bad *was* coming to Snakebite. A gang of marauding outlaws or native savages. Such things were not unheard of in the west, though often the myths surrounding these very real dangers were blown out of proportion. An earthly threat that could not easily be defeated could come to seem *un*earthly to the uneducated or superstitious. He believed that was happening here, at least to some extent. If a gang of bandits, for instance, was riding into town, perhaps some lives *could* be saved by summoning the faithful.

He'd taken his first step up the stairs when the front door creaked open behind him again. Believing the mayor had returned to spew more insanity, he took his foot off the step and turned around with an uncharacteristic curse right at the edge of his tongue. The curse went unspoken when he saw who was actually standing framed in the bright sunlight visible through the doorway.

He frowned and moved away from the staircase. "Mrs. McKinley? Have you come seeking shelter from the, um . . . " He sighed, unable to bring himself to give voice to the nonsense uttered by the mayor. "What brings you here today?"

Eleanor McKinley smiled as she started walking slowly down the aisle between the pews. She wore a plain black dress of mourning, a somewhat immodest one with a hem that reached just below the knee. There was a raggedness to the hem, as if part of it had hastily been torn or cut away. As she came closer, the priest noticed she was barefoot. By the time she was halfway down the aisle, she still had not spoken a word. It was at that point the priest first felt a twinge of wariness, perceiving what struck him as a smug quality in her smile. This was an ungenerous impression, one that would normally spark a sense of shame, but that was not the case this time. With each step closer she took, he felt more certain something was seriously off about her.

"Are Thomas and the children with you today, Mrs. McKinley?"

Eleanor was a solid Christian woman. Not once in his memory had her family ever missed any of the regular services. It was inconceivable to imagine her allied in any way with the dark forces allegedly overtaking Snakebite. Surely not in any willing way, at least. In the unlikely event Stratton was correct about everything, however, it was possible she was being used as an unwitting pawn by the unearthly evil supposedly in their midst.

She was nearly to the bottom of the aisle by the time she finally spoke. "No, Father, my husband and children are not with me today. Would you like to know why?"

The priest didn't know what to say. Given her strange demeanor, he was no longer sure he wanted that information. That sense of wrongness continued to increase as she drew closer. She exuded a palpable sense of malevolent energy and corruption. It radiated from her skin like heat from the sun, inducing a sensation like thousands of worms crawling over his flesh. A queasy feeling stirred within him and sent bile rushing into his throat. For a moment, he felt dizzy and on the verge of fainting. Perspiration formed on his brow and leaked into his eyes, making him squint.

Eleanor laughed when he took an instinctive, staggering step backward. There was mockery in the sound. Coming from a woman who'd always been so unfailingly polite and deferential in the presence of a man of the cloth, it was an unnerving thing to hear. He now feared he'd been wrong to think she could not willingly be aligned with evil forces. For all he knew, the potential for it might have lurked inside her all along, just waiting for something to summon her darkness to the surface.

She was now in the open space between the pews and the chancel and still coming closer. "You don't look well, Father. Would you like to lie down somewhere?"

More mockery.

The note of faux-concern she'd put in her voice in no way concealed the underlying contempt she felt for him.

Now she was no more than six feet away.

Father Fitzpatrick took a few more backward steps. "Stay away from me, you serpent."

Eleanor pulled the flimsy black dress off over her head and allowed it to slip from her fingertips to the floor. "I wonder, Father, have you always stayed true to your vow of celibacy? Have you never known the touch of a woman?"

The priest felt his mouth go dry at the sight of her naked form. He'd suspected she wore no undergarments beneath the dress, an assumption now revealed as truth. Despite her insinuation, he'd never strayed from his celibacy vow, not once in his entire career. Occasionally it was necessary to masturbate to relieve the unbearable pressure that built up as a regrettable consequence of his body's natural processes, but he liked to believe God forgave him for that. Technically, it wasn't allowed, but he was only human and it wasn't possible to go through life without an outlet of some sort. He was rigidly observant in every other way and had always been a faithful, diligent servant of the Lord.

Now he found he couldn't move as she came closer still. Only by sheer accident had he ever caught a partial, fleeting glimpse of a disrobed woman. To have one stand so boldly before him overwhelmed him in ways he hadn't anticipated. This was no wrinkled old nun at the seminary. Eleanor McKinley was voluptuous and perfectly formed in all ways, seething with vitality and seeming to glow from within like some pagan temptress. He was so entranced by her he didn't realize she'd come within touching range until she took his hand and placed it on one of her perfect breasts.

LAST OF THE RAVAGERS

Father Fitzpatrick whimpered.

His knees shook.

His hand remained on her breast as she leaned into him and slipped a hand inside his pants, making him gasp and whimper again as her fingers curled around his tumescent penis. She gave him a hard squeeze and he leaned against her, his face falling into the crook of her neck. His helpless tears leaked onto her warm skin. Whether they were tears of regret and fear or of helpless, relieved joy, he could not say. Perhaps they were both.

She turned her head and put her mouth against his ear, nipping at the lobe and making him shudder. "My family isn't here because they're dead. Slaughtered. I danced in their blood and rejoiced." She nipped at his earlobe again and moved her hand up and down the length of his shaft. "What do you think of that, Father?"

There was no mockery in her voice this time. No false notes. He was certain she was telling the absolute truth. Her family was gone and she was overjoyed about it. He couldn't fathom how something so terrible had come to pass and couldn't bring himself to verbalize the condemnation she so clearly deserved, because that part of him existed only beneath the surface for now. He was held in sway as she continued her masterful manipulation of his body, fully in thrall to passions denied for decades.

She swirled her tongue inside his ear, making his knees buckle slightly. "You were heading up to the steeple when I showed up, weren't you?"

He shivered and grabbed hold of her to keep himself upright. "Yes. Y-yes." He swallowed with tremendous difficulty. "Th-that's right."

She made a sound of pleasure and writhed against him, maintaining her firm hold on his cock the whole time. "As I thought. No doubt to ring the bell and summon the faithful in order to shield them under God's roof. Am I right?"

He sniffled and nodded his head in the crook of her neck. "I don't have to do it. I won't if you don't want me to."

She chuckled. "Quite the contrary, Father. I *want* them summoned. We need them, you see. To join our army of the dead. You'll be one of our unholy soldiers, too, Father." Her teeth clamped down on his earlobe. "Right after I do . . . this."

He screamed as she bit through his earlobe, wrenching it away from the rest of his ear with one savage twist of her head. That pain was bad, but it was nothing compared to what followed. He frantically tried twisting out of her embrace, but she effortlessly held him in place. Her hand slid to the bottom of his now slick shaft, the increased pressure of her grip becoming painful and then agonizing. Enfolding his balls and the base of his penis in her hand, she began to pull the genitalia away from the rest of his body. He screamed again and struggled even harder to break free of her embrace, again to no avail. As she did this, she made orgasmic noises and lapped at the blood leaking from his mutilated ear. Then she tore off his cock and yanked it out of his pants, triumphantly holding it aloft.

She laughed as he fell to the floor and rolled onto his side, screaming and clutching at the rapidly darkening front of his pants, kicking his legs like a wailing infant in a crib. Moments later, he rolled onto his stomach and tried crawling away from her, as if that would do any good. Laughing again, she flipped him over and straddled him, forcing his mouth open as she inserted the long, bloody organ all the way inside his oral cavity. Next she held his mouth closed while he choked on his cock. As his struggles began to wind down, she slipped a finger inside one of his eye sockets and ripped out the eyeball. She tilted her head back, opened her mouth wide, and dropped the blood-dripping orb inside it, moaning again as it slid slowly down her throat.

Delicious, as always.

Then she went up to the steeple to ring the bell.

THIRTY

AFTER ABOUT AN HOUR of rousting likely candidates for the sheriff's gang of sharpshooters out of their homes and rented rooms, Billy arrived at the abode of fellow deputy Trey Walker. Walker and his woman lived in a ramshackle little house on the outskirts of town. In Billy's opinion, describing the man's dwelling as a "house" was overly generous. There was a precarious lean to the structure and much of the cheap lumber used in its construction was badly warped. A number of planks had come loose from the rickety frame, their ends curling outward. He was reminded of some of the rundown country shacks he used to see in the woods back home in Georgia. The place barely looked fit for human habitation.

There was no sign of Trey as Billy brought his horse to a halt near the front of the house, but Eva Rockingham, his live-in companion, sat slouching in a chair next to the partially open door. She had her head tilted back with her eyes closed and her face turned toward the sky.

The woman gave no indication of having heard his approach. Her mouth was open and her arms were dangling by her sides. There were flecks of drool at the corners of her mouth. This was not unusual for Eva. She'd long been engaged with a torrid love affair, but it wasn't with Trey. Opium was the thing she adored most in this world. She was attired in the scanty manner of a saloon girl, in torn stockings and undergarments. Formerly employed as one of Miss Agatha's girls at the Last Chance, this was also not surprising.

Billy loudly cleared his throat. "Eva!"

No response. She didn't even stir.

Shaking his head in disgust, the deputy climbed off his horse and approached the unconscious woman. He gave her a solid shake and stepped back as she snorted and finally came awake. She looked around in bleary-eyed confusion a moment before her gaze settled on his face.

She sat up straighter and scowled. "What do you want, Billy?"

"Is Trey here?"

She looked around blearily again, as if searching for him. Then she leveled that sleepy scowl at the deputy and said, "Don't look like it. What do you want with him?"

Billy sighed.

This was a perfect example of why he never liked dealing with Eva. She was reflexively contrary and cantankerous by nature, never in need of a legitimate reason to argue and generally be a pain in the ass. He was grateful for rarely having to interact with her, but on this occasion it couldn't be avoided.

"There's an emergency in town. Sheriff sent me out to fetch him."

Scowl still in place, Eva looked around again until she found an uncorked jug of what was probably whiskey mixed with something much stronger. It was on the ground by the chair. She picked it up and drank deeply from it before setting it down again. "This is his day off. You and the sheriff need to handle whatever emergency you're having on your own."

Billy shook his head. "No can do. This here business is of a mandatory nature. Where is he?"

Eva gave him a long, silent stare before leaning back in the creaky chair. She tugged up the hem of her negligee and spread her legs wide, revealing an uncovered pubic thatch. "Like what you see?"

Billy sighed. "Do you not have any self-respect?"

She smiled for the first time. "Not a bit. Come inside a minute and give me a ride. A good hard one. Then maybe I'll tell you where Trey is."

"Lady, if you don't tell me where that no-account sumbitch is right now, I'll pick you up and shake the information out of you." He gave her the hardest, flintiest look he could manage to show how serious he was. "I mean it."

She laughed. "I bet you do, but you're wrong if you think that scares me. Come on, Billy. Toss me around and give it to me rough. That's how I like it."

Billy sneered. "You should be ashamed of yourself. Does Trey know you offer up the goods to anyone who comes around?"

Eva reached for the jug again and set it on the edge of the chair between her spread legs. There was no trace of wantonness in her flat expression now. "Trust me, he don't care. Not that I give one shit what Trey thinks about anything. You're really not gonna fuck me?"

"No, ma'am."

She grunted and sat up a little straighter, her demeanor changing in a way that suggested she'd tired of toying with him. "Trey's gone to Hell."

Billy winced. "Aw, shit."

She laughed and tipped the jug at him in a mock toast as he turned away from her and climbed back up on his horse. "Have fun with those reprobates, Billy. Come back around if you ever change your mind, you hear? I'll give up the goods for you any time, honey."

She was still laughing as Billy got his horse turned around and rode away at high speed.

191

Hell was the name of one of the other saloons in Snakebite. The building it was housed in wasn't much larger than the pathetic hovel Trey called home and looked only slightly less ramshackle. The name of the establishment was painted in large red letters on a sign above the door. To the left of the name was a depiction of a horned devil with a long, pointed tail. Located at one end of the town's least prosperous street, where several buildings stood empty, the place was a dump. There was no piano or upstairs brothel. No upstairs at all, in fact. There was also no door at the entrance, because Hell never closed.

Hell had a bad reputation. One of the worst in the entire Arizona territory, in fact. Stories that might or might not have been tall tales about the notorious watering hole circulated throughout the region, often passed on by visitors to Snakebite who'd never actually had the guts to venture inside. Billy didn't lack for guts, but he only came around when he was left with no other choice. On occasion his work as a lawman brought him here when certain questions needed asking of certain lowdown individuals.

Only the worst of the worst drank here. At any given time, odds were good multiple persons wanted for heinous deeds committed elsewhere were seated on barstools under Hell's leaky roof. Bounty hunters in the region knew this and would sometimes stake out the place, waiting for wanted men to come staggering outside. Sometimes the tactic worked, but once in a while a bounty hunter wound up dead in the street, shot full of holes in front of no witnesses. None willing to come forward, anyway.

Billy hitched his horse to a post out front and walked through Hell's open doorway. He stopped once he was about five feet inside and stood there with a hand on Big Boomer's holstered grip. "Trey Walker!"

LAST OF THE RAVAGERS

The soft rumble of conversation came to an abrupt halt as about a dozen heads turned his way. A haze of tobacco smoke hung heavy in the stale, hot air as Billy surveyed the unfriendly faces. Some he recognized as belonging to former regulars at the Last Chance Saloon. In most cases, these were men banned from Quentin Brown's establishment after one too many violent incidents. Several others present weren't familiar to him at all. The ones he didn't know all had that same hard-bitten look, along with the stench that came from too many months spent in the open desert or riding the trail. He had no doubt the majority of the strangers were bandits and killers.

The lighting in the place was dim, much of it ambient illumination seeping in through the open doorway and gaps in the wood planks that formed the walls and ceiling of Hell. There were lanterns, but they wouldn't be lit until after nightfall, at which point the saloon would become an exponentially even more inadvisable place to visit. The bar wasn't even half the length of the bar at Brown's place, but each of the creaky stools had a butt sitting on it. Men playing cards filled the chairs arranged around two small tables. A few other patrons lounged in chairs set against the back wall.

Trey Walker was one of the men in the back. Another person knelt in front of him, gobbling his knob. Squinting into the shadowy recesses of the place, Billy began to discern disquieting aspects of the other person, who was of enormous girth and clad in a dress far too small for her form. Drooping breasts proportionate in size to the large frame spilled out of the top of the dress. Much of the exposed flesh was lavishly illustrated. After another few seconds of squinting, he realized he'd seen this person before. The cock gobbler was Rosie, the bearded lady from the traveling sideshow that'd passed through town on the way to Tucson about a month ago. For some reason, she'd stayed behind after the sideshow left town, apparently to work as a barroom whore in Hell. Billy could imagine no good reason why she'd want to do that and suspected some level of coercion had been involved. He hated it for her, but he had bigger concerns right now.

One of the men staring at him let out a loud fart.

No one laughed.

Billy raised his voice and called out to the deputy again. *"Trey Walker!"*

The town's other part time lawman opened his eyes and took note of Billy for the first time. He groaned in aggravation and gave the bearded lady a hard shove, causing her to tumble away from him to the floor. Tucking his cock back inside his trousers, he got to his feet and lurched his way over to the bar, signaling the man behind it for a drink. The barkeep—who looked every bit as unfriendly as everyone else in Hell—poured what looked like black sludge into a glass and set it on the bar for him.

Trey knocked back the rotgut in one go, thumped the glass on the bar, and demanded a refill. "What do you want with me, Billy?" The man's head wobbled slightly as it swiveled toward him. "I don't like being harassed on my day off."

Billy sneered. "I recommend you don't have that next glass of coffin varnish. Ned sent me to fetch you. We've got an emergency-type situation on our hands. You're needed at the Last Chance Saloon as of right now."

One of the card players snorted derisively. "I wouldn't piss on that place if it was on fire."

This prompted the first laughter Billy had heard since entering the place, but it wasn't a good-humored sound. It was rife with similar notes of derision as well as a palpable degree of potent anger from those no longer allowed to darken the doors of the Last Chance. This was a resentful bunch not particularly inclined to care about things like civic duty, not even when it was in their best interests to do so. Probably some of them were good shooters, but asking for help here was pointless. Expecting Trey to help was also looking like a lost cause. The sumbitch appeared just as impaired as his addict girlfriend. Or whatever Eva actually was to him. After his visit here today, Billy was no longer sure on that count.

Billy wavered for a moment on the verge of backing out of Hell and continuing the recruitment effort on his own for a bit longer, but he decided to take one last shot at convincing Trey to leave with him. "That tin star pinned to your shirt means you have certain obligations, sonny boy. Pull yourself together and do your job."

Trey picked up the refilled glass of rotgut and again tossed back its contents in one go. Instead of setting the empty glass on the bar again, he wheeled about and slingshotted it at Billy, who lurched out of the way just in time to avoid being conked in the noggin. He then ripped the badge from his shirt and tossed it on the ground. "I quit."

Accepting now that the situation was hopeless, Billy figured it'd be best at this point to leave without another word, but a flicker of spite overrode the wiser impulse. "Reckon I see now why your woman was throwing herself at me when I stopped by your place."

Trey had turned away from him, but now his head rotated slowly back in his direction. "What'd you say?"

Billy smirked. "You heard me, hoss."

In the midst of the tension building between them, no one took note of Rosie getting to her feet and lumbering woozily over to the bar. If anyone *did* notice, they paid her little mind at all. This didn't surprise Billy. She probably barely registered as human to the patrons of Hell. Trey didn't notice her until he reached for the gun holstered at his hip and found it wasn't there.

"What the—"

His next words died in his throat when he turned about and saw the muzzle of his own gun pointed at his face.

Rosie squeezed the trigger and a loud bang made everyone seated at the bar flinch. The bullet punched straight through the center of Trey's forehead. He fell against the bar a moment before dropping heavily to the ground. In the same moment came the distinct sound of multiple pistols being yanked free of their leather holsters. Most of them were then aimed at Rosie as she swung her arm around and shot the man behind the bar in the face. An eruption of gunfire followed, most of it directed at the avenging circus lady, who'd apparently finally had enough of being roughed up by Hell's scummy clientele. She was hit numerous times but managed to remain upright several moments longer as she continued to wobble about and fire Trey's gun until all its chambers were empty. A lot of bodies hit the floor as the smell of gunpowder became more pungent than the stench of trail-filthy bandits.

A sneaky little bastard at one of the card tables pulled his weapon and aimed it Billy's way instead of at the much larger target presented by Rosie. He was fortunate Rosie happened to lumber into the path of the first bullet the little man fired, because until then the bastard had him dead to rights. Instinct kicked in after that, causing him to lurch to the side as he pulled Big Boomer free and started firing. As soon as Rosie finally dropped to the floor, he got his six-shooter pointed in the right direction and shot the sneaky sumbitch right through one of his flinty little eyes.

He kept firing as he backed out of the place.

Working as fast as he could, he got his horse unhitched from the post outside, hopped up in the saddle, and kicked the whinnying beast in the flank, riding away from the scene of slaughter at high speed.

Once the sound of gunfire died away, all was quiet inside the place called Hell save for the moaning of the wounded. Then even that faded. One man hit only in the belly got out and crawled into the middle of the street before breathing his last. No one else survived, the rest of

LAST OF THE RAVAGERS

the wounded expiring within minutes of the last shot being fired. Billy was almost all the way back to the Last Chance Saloon by the time some of the dead began to stir.

THIRTY-ONE

THE FRENZIED BOUT of lovemaking with Raven Decker was like no other carnal interlude in Ned Kilmister's life up to that point. Having traveled a fair bit in his younger days, he was a man of experience who'd bedded enough women to believe he had a good idea of the range of things possible in the sexual arena. He now understood how naive a notion this had been. The interlude began at her instigation for one thing, which in itself was unusual. What really distinguished the experience, however, was the way she thoroughly took charge and guided things at every step along the way. It was all about satisfying her desires, with anything he might've wished for existing only on a secondary level.

On the whole, he had no complaints, even if he was left feeling slightly off-balance and disoriented in the aftermath. It wasn't just her unusual degree of assertiveness that accounted for the feeling. He was older now and a good while had passed since he'd last availed himself of the services of one of Quentin's saloon girls. Might've been as much as a year ago or even longer. And then here came Raven, crashing into his life like a tidal wave and putting an end to the dry spell in the most memorable way imaginable. Even now, many minutes after the end of their frenzied coupling, his heart was hammering away at a far faster than normal rate

She sat on the cot in the spare cell with her back

against the wall, still naked as she puffed away at one of his stogies and regarded him with a look of amusement. "What's the matter, Ned?"

He looked at her from his position on the floor, where he sat with his back against the iron bars separating the two cells. "What do you mean?"

She chuckled. "You look sort of shell-shocked."

He nodded. "I reckon that's a fair description. I'm not accustomed to being . . . *handled* that way." He flipped a hand at her in a dismissive way. "Took me by surprise is all."

Raven smirked as she exhaled a stream of smoke. "What a repressed world this is. Where I come from, women are allowed to be just as passionate and impulsive as men. When I want something, I take it. So I took you. And I'll tell you something else—I knew I'd do it at some point the second I laid eyes on you."

Now it was Ned's turn to smirk as he puffed himself up a little. "Well, hell. I never knew I was that damn handsome."

She laughed. "Don't get too full of yourself, old man. You ain't bad-looking, that's for sure, but this was really more about what we're facing tonight. A tension reliever ahead of the big storm."

Ned's expression darkened, his shoulders sagging as he put the back of his head against the bars. "Tell me the truth. How likely is it we all die tonight?"

She stubbed the stogie out on the wall and shrugged. "Could go either way."

Ned grimaced. "That's reassuring."

"You asked me to be honest."

Ned sighed. "That I did. And I'd only want the unvarnished reality." He grunted, managing a small smile. "Though I must say, if I've really gotta die tonight, I'm glad we did what we did here."

Raven moved to the edge of the cot and started

gathering up her clothes. "That your way of thanking me for fucking your brains out?"

He snorted. "I guess it is."

She started hurriedly pulling on her buckskins. "Get dressed, Ned. It's time we got back to the saloon."

Getting to his feet with a groan and a creaking of bones, Ned searched the floor for his garments, which were scattered all about. As he first pulled on his drawers, he glanced into the neighboring cell and winced upon seeing the obscene ruination of Riley McKay's privates. Now that he was no longer in the grip of helpless passion, he felt slightly sick at having engaged in sexual congress right next to a mutilated corpse. If Raven harbored any similar compunctions, she showed no signs of it whatsoever. It was just more evidence of how diffcrent she was from any other woman he'd ever met. Whether that was a good thing or not overall, he couldn't honestly say. In some ways, yes, it absolutely was a good thing. In a few other ways, he wasn't sure. If at the end of the night he and his friends were still alive and the man or thing called Doyle was dead, his mixed feelings wouldn't matter one damn bit.

Once they were fully dressed, Ned grabbed some extra ammunition from a cabinet in the outer room. He locked the place up as they stepped out onto the porch. Turning around, he noticed the sun was much lower in the sky now. Nightfall was only a couple hours away, at best.

As they started across the street, he noticed two men lounging on the saloon's long porch. One sat on a bench, while the other leaned against a pillar as he smoked a hand-rolled cigarette. The one on the bench was Dan Cunningham and the other was Steve Dickinson. Both men were cattle handlers at the ranch owned by Mark Stratton. The mayor's ranch was easily the largest such property in the area. Dan and Steve were good men who never got up to any serious trouble. Both enjoyed a drink as much as anyone else but could hold their liquor better than most.

LAST OF THE RAVAGERS

Because Stratton employed so many men at the ranch, they had their own drinking establishment out there, a place called The Long Pig Saloon, the existence of which accounted for why Dan and Steve were rarely seen hanging out at the Last Chance.

"Evening, gents," Ned said, as he and Raven neared the porch.

Steve Dickinson tipped his hat at them as he puffed on his cigarette. "Evening, Ned." He glanced at Raven, smiling. "Ma'am."

Raven acknowledged his greeting with a nod, but said nothing.

Ned glanced at the pistols holstered at each of the man's hips. "Billy send you fellas out here?"

Dan Cunningham spoke up from the bench, hoisting the mug of beer gripped in one of his big hands. "He sure did. Said drinks were on you tonight." He chuckled. "*All* of them."

Ned nodded. "Can confirm. I hope he told you more than that, because things might get a little dicey here before long."

Dickinson grunted, exhaling more smoke. "Aye. He told what sounded like a tall tale, but he was dead serious. You know Billy. Man's a bit of a jokester, but he's all business when it counts. Could tell we needed to be here and do our part."

Cunningham nodded after taking another big gulp of beer. "Only a coward would run for the hills at a time like this."

Hearing the resoluteness in their voices gave Ned a much-needed morale boost. If the rest of the men Billy sent his way were half as gung-ho, they'd be in good shape. "We certainly appreciate you being here, fellas. We'll need all the help we can get."

As he uttered those last few words, the tolling of a church bell began to ring out from another part of town.

The sound didn't stop after a few clangs of the bell, going on and on as Ned and Raven turned their heads and stared off into the distance. They did this even though the town's only church with a belltower wasn't visible from where they stood.

After listening to the sound a bit longer, Ned exchanged frowning glances with Raven and the men lounging on the porch. "Did I lose track of the days again? It ain't Sunday yet, is it?"

Dickinson shook his head. "Not until tomorrow. Anyway, ain't no big mystery. Stratton went rushing off to talk with Father Fitzpatrick a while ago. Wanted him to summon the faithful in hopes they'll find adequate protection under God's roof."

Ned gave this a grim-faced nod, but made no comment.

He and Raven went on into the saloon.

THIRTY-TWO

THE DEAD STARTED showing up outside the saloon as the sun descended toward the horizon and twilight time began. As the rays of the sun began to fade, so did the suffocating heat. Soon the evening air in Snakebite began to feel almost refreshingly cool by comparison. This brought with it a marginal degree of relief for those still among the living, but that feeling would soon be offset by far more troublesome developments.

As the first of the dead began to gather in the street, they were not immediately perceived as threats, because there were just a few of them and they were not readily identifiable as dead. There were no visible wounds amongst any of the early arrivals, at least none that were easy to see in the encroaching semi-darkness. Also delaying any sense of alarm was the familiarity of the faces, which was evident even in the deepening shadows on the other side of the street. These were not strangers to Snakebite. They were people who lived in and around the town and worked hard to scratch out a living in a place where doing so wasn't easy. Trusted and mostly well-liked people the men and women inside the Last Chance Saloon saw almost every day. They were also talking quietly among themselves and few gathered at the saloon that day had ever been in the presence of dead folks capable of speech. The men lounging on the saloon's porch simply assumed the handful of townsfolk lingering in the street would eventually come inside and belly up to the bar for a drink.

That did not happen.

Instead, their murmured conversation soon came to an end, at which point they all turned and stared silently at the saloon from the opposite side of the street. By then they were more than a half-dozen in number. They all had similarly unnerving blank-faced expressions.

One of the men on the porch belched and said, "Someone go on in and get Ned out here. This shit don't look right."

Another man grabbed his repeating rifle from where it leaned against the porch rail and hurriedly started feeding shells into it through the side port. "You can say that again. This here's about the creepiest shit I ever did see."

The comment provoked mumbles of agreement.

Someone pointed down the street. "Look! There's more coming. Shit, a *bunch* more. What the hell have we gotten ourselves into, boys?"

No one had an answer for that.

Not one they were willing to speak out loud, anyway.

Steve Dickinson dropped a half-smoked cigarette on the porch and snuffed it out with the heel of his boot.

Then he went inside to talk to Ned.

After being apprised of the developing situation, Ned went out to the porch to have a look-see for himself. Raven joined him there seconds later, sidling up next to him and taking hold of his hand long enough to give it a nice squeeze before releasing it again. The gesture surprised him, conveying a capacity for tenderness he hadn't imagined she possessed. Whether it was meant to reassure him or calm her own nerves, he couldn't say.

LAST OF THE RAVAGERS

Also stepping outside with them were Billy Conway and Doc Richardson. In a typical display of bravado, Billy became the first among the saloon defenders to attempt communication with the crowd of silent observers. It was a boisterous, shouted demand to know what they were up to. When that yielded no results, he switched to creative insults regarding their intelligence or lack thereof. Doc Richardson, by contrast, remained unusually quiet, as he had all evening so far. He appeared visibly disturbed—even more so than the rest of them—and almost immediately went back inside.

As Ned watched with a growing sense of disquiet, a few more new arrivals waded into the midst of the group on the other side of the street. Like the others, they then turned and stared blankly at the saloon. They struck Ned as being like soldiers or perhaps religious congregants awaiting some signal from their leader. That was unsettling, but most of them appeared unarmed. The group included both men and women at this point. He did spy pistols strapped to the hips of two of the men, but that wasn't unusual in a town where many openly wore guns when venturing out in public.

One of Stratton's men loudly cleared his throat. "This is downright eerie. Should we maybe just start blastin' these fools before the whole danged street is filled with them?"

Ned peered into the familiar but shadowy faces standing opposite the saloon and had no good answer for that. He saw not enemies but friends and neighbors. People who'd stop and chat with him as he strolled the streets every day. But that was the soft part of him reacting. The kind-hearted part hidden by the gruff exterior of a lawman. He realized with sorrow any hope of surviving the night would hinge on ignoring those instincts.

The same man spoke up again. "Oh, shit. Look at that one! She's bare-ass naked!"

He pointed off to the left.

Ned glanced that way and saw the shadowy, slender form of a woman gaining clarity with each lurching step she took down the street. The truth of the words hollered by Stratton's man also became clearer. She was indeed absent even a stitch of clothing, but the display of public nudity was far less distressing than other, more lurid aspects of her appearance. Her flesh was moonlight-pale, but splattered crimson in many places. Where her eyes should be were two black holes. Crimson streaks on her face made her appear as if she were weeping blood. There was also a hole in the hollow of her throat, a wound clearly made with a blade of significant size. Her nude form offered no clues regarding her identity, as most of the good Christian women in Snakebite tended to wear clothing that obscured shape. Once she was significantly closer, Ned discerned hints of familiarity in the structure of her facial features, but he still couldn't quite place her, the empty eye sockets and blood throwing off his perceptions.

One thing he knew for certain was the unfortunate woman was not among the living, at least not in the traditional sense. Someone had killed her and now she was up walking around again, just like Angelina earlier in the day. Ned amended that thought an instant later. Not *just like* Angelina. This walking corpse was not nearly as animated, her gait slow and lumbering, her mouth hanging open in a way that made her look like an imbecile.

Ned sent one of Stratton's men inside to fetch a lantern. The darkness was getting deeper. The man returned just moments later with the requested item. Ned took it from him and descended the steps to the street. Holding the lantern aloft, he strode purposefully a short ways in the direction of the approaching crowd, stopping about ten feet beyond the end of the porch. It was close to full dark now and he had to squint to get a better sense of their numbers. What he saw made his breath catch in his throat. There were far more of them than he imagined. He caught flickering glimpses of numerous faces he recognized. Some looked almost normal despite their blank expressions, while others had absorbed severe and extensive physical damage. One of the faces belonged to Father Fitzpatrick. The priest's chin was covered in blood and his face looked bloated, as if a large piece of meat was lodged inside his mouth.

A sick feeling twisted inside Ned as he recalled the tolling of the church bell earlier and began to realize what must have happened. The faithful had responded to the call, only to wind up massacred at the church. Others here might have perished individually in their homes or places of business, but he had no doubt the bulk of them were devout members of Fitzpatrick's congregation. Only someone truly diabolical and irredeemably evil to the core would orchestrate that kind of mass slaughter of innocents. It was a clever strategy, building an army of the dead in one fell swoop. Napoleon himself might have admired the ingenuity of the creature Raven called Doyle.

Someone called out to him from the porch of the saloon. Only then did he realize some of Doyle's reanimated acolytes were passing by him to either side, almost within grabbing range. He'd been too wrapped up in morbid fascination for this to fully register until then. The shouts made him more cognizant of the encroaching danger, but he did not immediately retreat to the relative safety of the porch.

Still holding the lantern aloft, he began to make out something else unusual in the midst of the oncoming crowd. In the center of the street about thirty feet distant was a tightly-grouped contingent of the dead. They were working together to hold aloft another person. The person was in an almost languid seated position, appearing comfortable atop the numerous upraised palms. At first Ned tensed, thinking the person being carried might be

Doyle, the crowd bearing him forward like a conquering king coming to confront the last stronghold of a soon to be vanquished enemy. As the tight group drew closer, however, he realized this was wrong. The passenger riding all those upraised palms was another naked woman.

Ned gasped in fright as someone grabbed him from behind. He shook himself loose and spun about swinging the lantern, thinking he was being attacked by one of the walking corpses, but it was only Raven. She managed to jump back just in time to dodge the lantern. Words of apology went unspoken as she grabbed him and hauled him out of the way. In the same motion, she drew her oversized pistol with her other hand and fired at the walking dead man who—unbeknownst to Ned—had come up right behind him with a raised axe. Her gun boomed in its heavily percussive way and a bullet in the face dropped the man to the street. He did not get up again, which Ned found curious. In his experience with the rejuvenated dead so far, it took a lot more than just one bullet to put them down. Of course, the bullets in Raven's gun were not of any normal variety.

He did not resist as she dragged him back to the porch, which was more crowded by then, packed with men who'd come out of the bar to see what the commotion was about. A few were stray regular customers who'd wandered in as evening approached without knowing anything was amiss. Among the others were more of Stratton's men and some of the other sharpshooters Billy had recruited before abruptly returning from his mission. As the crowd in the street became more densely packed, one of them hopped down from the porch, unhitched his horse, and rode away.

Ned sighed. "Anyone else feel like deserting?"

Some tense moments elapsed. The men on the porch said nothing, but a few exchanged nervous glances. Just when it looked as if there would be no more deserters, Dan Cunningham stepped off the porch and headed for the hitching rail. Another of Stratton's men drew his pistol and aimed at the back of Cunningham's head.

Ned yelled at him to lower his weapon. "Let the yellow-belly go. We need men with guts for this fight, not cowards."

The man nodded and holstered his pistol.

His face twisted in a look of disgust, Ned watched Cunningham mount his horse and ride away. In doing so, the man took pains to avoid the many looks of condemnation directed his way. All the man's big talk earlier about not being a coward and doing the right thing had been revealed as only talk. Ned sincerely hoped the rest of these men were made of sterner stuff.

Despite the rapidly growing size of the crowd, the portion of it that was right outside the saloon remained on the opposite side of the street, maintaining an open space in front of the porch. Ned sensed there was a purpose to this, a hunch proven correct moments later when the naked dead woman with no eyes lumbered into the middle of the open space and dropped to her hands and knees about ten feet from the edge of the porch.

Billy leaned close to Ned and whispered, "I've seen some weird shit when messed up on one thing or other, but this takes the damn cake." He snorted. "Hell, it takes the cake, bakes another goddamn cake, and takes that, too."

Ned had to concur.

The procession carrying the other naked woman arrived at the edge of the crowd. After she was gently lowered to the ground, she also ventured into the open space. Instead of also dropping to her hands and knees, however, she stepped up on the kneeling woman's back, using her as a human soapbox as she stood atop her and faced the men on the porch. She stood with her hands on her hips and with her chest proudly outthrust. A mischievous smile twisted her mouth as she surveyed the bewildered and frightened faces watching her.

"Brave defenders of our fair town, heed well what I have to say." The woman spoke at an elevated volume, putting her lungs into it in a way that made her words reverberate in the street. "If you wish to live to see another day, throw your weapons into the street and surrender immediately."

Ned recognized the woman now. She was Eleanor McKinley, mother of three young children and wife to Tom McKinley. They were widely regarded as one of Snakebite's most wholesome, god-fearing families. A quick scan of the outer fringes of the large crowd revealed no signs of her husband or kids. Intuition told him they'd met with misfortune. He was having a hard time reconciling his memory of the demure woman he'd known with the blood-spattered naked lunatic addressing them now. It was as if she'd undergone some demonic transformation.

After loudly clearing his throat, he raised his own voice in response. "I don't think we'll be doing that. With respect, Eleanor, what has happened to you? Where is your family?"

She laughed. "They have been sacrificed in the name of your new master. I never loved any of them, anyway. The children were loathsome parasites. My husband was a worthless fool barely fit to be called a man at all. I reveled in their deaths. Danced in their blood. And if your men don't surrender, sheriff, I'll do the same with all of you."

Ned's brow creased. "Uh-huh. I see. Would this so-called new master person be the man called Doyle?"

Eleanor's expression sharpened. "You are not worthy to speak his name, Ned. He is not a man. He is a god."

This earned snickers from a few of Stratton's men.

The sound of their amusement prompted a smirk from Ned. "A god, eh? Well, where is he? Perched on his heavenly throne, perhaps, waiting to see how things play out before showing his cowardly face in public?"

A corner of Eleanor's mouth quivered, a sign she was

LAST OF THE RAVAGERS

teetering on the brink of an enraged outburst. Her nostrils flared and her hands clenched as she spent some moments striving to remain calm.

At last, she let out a long breath and smiled again. "You will pay for your disrespect, sheriff. I'll personally oversee your days of torture and laugh in your face as you beg for mercy. I'll tear your cock off and feed it to you inch by inch. I'll pluck out your eyes and devour them. I'll slit your throat and drink every last sour drop of your worthless blood. I'll crack open your fucking skull and eat your brains, thus absorbing everything you've ever learned or thought, and I'll laugh at all your pathetic little secrets"

A few silent moments ticked by as she trailed off, apparently awaiting a response.

Then Billy snorted derisive laughter. "Oh, is that all? We thought there'd be some *serious* consequences."

More snickers from others gathered on the porch followed this remark, including a few that were almost delirious giggles.

Eleanor unleashed an ear-piercing screech of rage followed by a screamed single word: "*Silence!*"

The volume of her voice was shockingly loud, filling the street with a percussive force that struck Ned as artificially enhanced. He didn't know how that was possible unless she truly had been transformed by some magical or supernatural means. Whatever the case, the outburst produced the result she desired. Even Billy fell silent as they all stood there and waited to see what she would say or do next.

Entire minutes passed.

Razor-sharp tension built up during the silence. The potential for bloodshed and calamity was a palpable thing, hanging in the air like poison.

Then Eleanor's expression softened and the corners of her mouth curved upward in a smug smile. "Yes. You're all beginning to feel it. The power I have now. I can see it in

211

your terrified eyes." She laughed. "Come to me now, Ned, on your hands and knees. Humble yourself before me. Hang your head and grovel like the coward you are at heart. Do that and I may yet let some of your people live."

Ned frowned. "But not me?"

She shook her head. "You've doomed yourself with your insolence. But you can still save some of the people you're sworn to protect. Come to me, Ned. I want to see you crawl. I want you to kiss my feet and beg for my forgiveness. If you refuse, be certain of this. You cannot hope to stand against us. My new husband, our conquering king, has built an invincible army of the dead. We will swarm and overwhelm you. You'll all die screaming and for nothing." She took a moment to look each man on the porch in the face. "Surrender is your only chance."

Ned's frown deepened. "Conquering king?"

She smiled. "Doyle. My husband. The last of the Ravagers. Lord of the Dead and master of all things."

Ned grunted. "And what exactly does he want of us? Beyond abject surrender, I mean. There must be something."

She nodded. "Of course. He requires a bountiful harvest of souls. A process that is well underway, as you can see." She spread her arms in a gesture meant to encompass the entire crowd. "But there is something even more important. Among you is a stranger. A woman never before seen in these parts. You have no reason to trust anything she says."

Ned glanced at Raven, who was staring fiercely straight ahead. She appeared unaware of his scrutiny. What Eleanor was saying wasn't entirely untrue. He knew next to nothing about Raven. It was possible she might be lying about some things or exaggerating other things, just as it was possible any stranger in town might attempt some level of deceit. But his gut was still telling him she could be trusted. Probably.

LAST OF THE RAVAGERS

"Hand this woman and all her possessions over now," Eleanor continued, smirking again. "Do this and I may yet let a few of you live and serve as my slaves. These lucky few may even learn—"

"Aw, goddammit," Billy cut in, shaking his head. "How much more of this horseshit do we have to listen to? Can someone please just shoot this bitch now?"

Before anyone else could say anything or otherwise react, Raven drew her oversized pistol from its holster and aimed it at Doyle's emissary.

Eleanor tossed her head back and laughed with gusto, shifting her feet in a way that caused the woman she was using as a perch to sag slightly. Her arms were shaking from the effort needed to hold her mistress aloft. Somehow, however, she managed to keep from collapsing.

"Foolish woman," Eleanor said, laughing again. "Your gun can't hurt me. The power bestowed upon me by your new master will deflect your bullets, bend the arc of space and time and—"

Raven squeezed the trigger of her gun and another of those big booms filled the street. The bullet smashed into the center of Eleanor's face, punching a large hole through it and sending a rain of blood and brains arcing high into the air. Several people at the front of the crowd behind her got splashed with it. Her body flew off the back of the eyeless woman and landed in the street with a thud.

There was a tense moment of frozen silence.

Then the eyeless woman, still on her hands and knees, let out a loud moan of anguish. She scrambled around and felt her way over to Eleanor's unmoving corpse. Unlike the others, she showed no immediate signs of rising any time soon. The eyeless woman fell atop her and again wailed in inconsolable anguish.

From out of nowhere, a heavy wind rose up and began to gust through the street. The gust rapidly increased in intensity, stirring up dust and sending a stray plank of old wood flapping through the air. There was another sound beneath the whistling of the rising wind, a primal howl of fury that raised goosebumps and set Ned's heart to fluttering.

Raven grabbed hold of his arm and started dragging him backward toward the swinging batwing doors. "Time to batten down the hatches. Everyone back inside. *Now!*"

The men on the porch needed no additional prompting.

There was a logjam at the door as everyone hurried back inside the Last Chance Saloon. Moments later, the inner door was slammed shut and locked, but for many it felt like an all-too-flimsy barrier against the undead army that was already starting to advance.

THIRTY-THREE

THE SALOON HAD two windows facing the street, one to either side of the now locked and closed inner door. They were the most obvious vulnerable chinks in their defensive armor. Because Raven had provided advance warning of an assault, some level of preparation had occurred. Inside the saloon was a pile of lumber, some hammers, and a bucket of nails, items procured from the hardware store by some of the men who'd responded to the sheriff's call to arms. They found it necessary to break into the store upon finding it closed earlier than usual. Once inside, it wasn't long before they discovered evidence of violence in the back room. There was an awful lot of blood spatter, enough to suggest someone had died, but there were no bodies present and no time to investigate anyway.

Unfortunately, a prior lack of urgency among many of the men meant much of the lumber was still piled up on the floor. Few had suspected events would unfold in such a dire way so quickly. The men had joked and told stories, treating the occasion more like a party than a time that would've been better spent preparing for battle. This was undoubtedly because up until just now none of them had personally witnessed any of the bizarre and unsettling things Ned and his cohorts had been dealing with all day.

Suddenly, however, lack of urgency was no longer an issue as a mad scramble broke out inside the saloon, with several men grabbing pieces of lumber, hammers, and nails. They then ran to the windows, where they jostled with each other for position as they hurriedly attempted to hammer the planks into place. There was a lot of agitated cursing as in their haste they frequently jabbed themselves with the long nails and occasionally smashed the heads of hammers against their fingers. Despite their frenzy and the unorchestrated nature of the work being done, they nonetheless managed to get quite a few planks hammered into place in surprisingly short order.

Not fast enough, however, to prevent a partial breach by the advancing mob outside. There was a shattering of glass as multiple hands punched through the windows, reaching through the gaps between planks and grasping at the men on the other side. Some of the men not hammering at the planks drew their weapons and slipped them through the gaps, firing at the people outside. The sound of gunfire went on and on as it became necessary to reload and resume shooting at the angry-sounding mob. The air quickly thickened with the smell of gunpowder. Some of those grasping hands tried tearing at the freshly erected planks, prompting the men with hammers in their hands rather than guns to smash away at them.

For a time things looked bleak for those inside the saloon. The men at the windows appeared on the verge of being overwhelmed, but they kept at it with impressive tenacity and courage, showing why Billy had picked them when he went looking for men to defend the saloon. Finally, after a time that seemed like an eternity—but probably wasn't much more than ten minutes—they began to gain the edge. The alarming number of gaps between planks dwindled until at last none remained, but the work didn't end there. Many of the remaining pieces of lumber got nailed across the door as reinforcement. Only when there was no lumber left did the work stop.

The exhausted men stepped back, sweating and

LAST OF THE RAVAGERS

panting as they and the others who'd merely observed watched the boarded-up entrance and windows vibrate from the pounding they were taking. They'd bought themselves some time, but no one expected that barrier to last forever.

In a few more minutes, however, it became clear it would hold long enough to allow them all to gather their wits and decide what to do next. Quentin Brown slipped behind the bar and began pouring drinks for all who wanted them, which unsurprisingly was nearly everyone.

Among those who had not worked to fortify the saloon was Doc Richardson. He was not as physically capable as these younger, stronger men, but the real reason he refrained was because he knew Doyle would punish him for participating. The creature had already punished him a few times for trying to resist his will, triggering severe flashes of pain that felt like being repeatedly stabbed in the abdomen. Other times Doyle made his brain feel like it was on fire, a boiling mass of scalding lava inside his head. The sensation made him want to crack his skull open and let the molten tissue leak out, but the monster wouldn't even let him do that. The worst thing of all was how he could hear the thing's mocking laughter inside his head.

All had seemed well for that first hour after venturing into the Last Chance Saloon. There was no hint of anything similar to what had happened to Charlotte and Angelina happening to him. He retained full mental autonomy, untainted by outside influences. Enough time passed for him to become comfortable and more firmly convinced that he would not fall under Doyle's control. Yes, he was technically dead, in a sense, but he remained in possession of his basic humanity.

This belief was revealed as pure delusion as Doyle's

BRYAN SMITH

army of the dead began to gather outside. When so many of the men went out to the porch to see what was happening, the so-called Lord of the Dead seized the opportunity to finally announce his presence inside Richardson's mind. The doctor almost wept upon first hearing the thing's insinuating voice, knowing right away it meant he wasn't nearly as strong-willed as he'd hoped. His futile and feeble attempts at resistance happened while the woman in the street addressed the saloon's defenders.

Resistance was no longer an option.

He never wanted to feel anything like that brain-fire again.

Before the night was over, he would be forced to betray his friends. At least one would have to die at his hands. Doyle also expected him to make an attempt on the woman bounty hunter's life. The creature advised him the attempt was almost certain to fail, which was why it was absolutely imperative that he at least kill Ned Kilmister beforehand.

Richardson didn't want to do it.

Ned had always been the closest thing he'd ever had to a real friend in this town on the edge of nowhere. Being tasked with the man's murder was an affront to everything he'd ever believed in or cared about. There was also the grim reality of what would become of him after committing the murder. The men in the bar would avenge Ned, of that he was certain. He'd be hacked to pieces with Quentin's machete or stomped into mush.

What he wanted didn't matter.

He would do it, consequences be damned. Doyle had assured him he would be resurrected come sunrise tomorrow regardless of what happened here tonight. After being resurrected, he would serve forever as one of the creature's many enslaved souls, becoming transmogrified. The prospect of that kind of existence didn't hold much appeal, but it was better than not existing at all.

Richardson stood at the end of the bar and watched the

rest of them drink, a mixture of shame and resentment rising within him. He'd love nothing better right now than to get howlingly drunk, but he'd learned that wasn't a good idea after a glass of whiskey earlier. Unbeknownst to him until then, it seemed Charlotte must've nicked his esophagus with her razor, and evidently the stitches in his throat were not drawn tightly enough to prevent leakage. Some of the whisky had dribbled out and stained his cravat, making him thankful it was dark in color.

He touched the pocket of his coat, feeling the shape and weight of the knife inside.

Not much longer now, he thought. *Soon I'll be beyond redemption forever.*

After downing two glasses of whiskey in as many minutes, Ned signaled for a bottle and Quentin handed it over with a harried look on his face. The instant the bottle was out of his hand, the barkeep moved on to filling a line of empty glasses gripped by the men crowded up against the bar. Judging by their troubled, haunted expressions, it seemed likely no amount of liquor could adequately calm their nerves for the struggle still ahead. Soaking up booze wouldn't help them shoot any straighter, either, but they were all too rattled by the things they'd seen to give much of a damn. Alcohol in significant quantities was the only remedy any of them cared about and Ned wasn't about to admonish them for it, not with a bottle of his own in hand.

He moved away from the bar and approached Raven, who was standing apart from the rest of them, leaning against one of the side walls near the unattended piano. Ned doubted she or anyone else would be sitting down to plink out any tunes tonight, what with the party atmosphere that had prevailed earlier being only a memory now. The only music that might be appropriate at this point was a funeral dirge.

Ned offered her the bottle and she declined with a single shake of her head, staring straight ahead in a vague way, without appearing to focus on anyone or anything inside the saloon. Looking around, Ned noted how a number of the men kept glancing over at her before quickly looking away. These were men who, under normal circumstances, wouldn't be able to stay away from her. He knew this because that was just how they were in the presence of any halfway attractive lady, let alone one as strikingly beautiful as Raven. He'd seen it plenty of times, but they were keeping their distance. She'd slain the representative of their enemy, which should've endeared her to them, but instead they seemed nervous in her presence.

Not just nervous. *Afraid.*

Ned took a quick swig of whiskey and cleared his throat. "You said a while ago you had some kind of surprise in store for Doyle." He glanced over at the boarded-up windows and door, grimacing at the way the wall continued to vibrate, as if the earth itself was shaking. His gaze flicked back to Raven, who was still staring straight ahead, the look on her face thoughtful rather than fearful. "Is that really true?"

He heard fear tinged with a shaky hopefulness as he asked the question.

She looked at him. "Oh, yes."

The look on her face was hard to read. She was in a serious mood, no doubt, but she still did not appear particularly troubled. Then again, that could easily be a false perception. He had no idea what was actually going on in her head. Despite the intimate interlude they'd shared earlier, she was still nearly as much of a stranger to him as she was to the rest of these men.

Ned grunted. "And he's afraid of you. That's why he won't just walk in here."

She shrugged. "It's not as simple as that." A small smile ghosted the edges of her mouth. "Few things are, you know."

Ned's brow furrowed as he thought about that a moment. Her cryptic response was far from reassuring, as well as being a lot less illuminating than he'd like. He directed another quick glance at the boarded-up entrance, hearing the growing fury of the wind outside. Things other than the pounding hands of the dead battered the exterior of the saloon, stray objects picked up by the wind and thrown through the streets. One especially loud crash from upstairs made everyone gasp and flinch. Several of Miss Agatha's girls came streaming down the staircase from the second floor after that, some shrieking while others blathered about a horse that had come crashing through one of the windows up there. Apparently it was still alive and partly lodged inside the window. An instant later, Ned's ears picked up a sound of distressed neighing.

Shit. That poor animal.

Ned looked at Raven. "Seems to me now might be a good time to break out that infinity thing, being as how you said he could be defeated with it." He eyed her bedroll, which was on the floor at her feet. While it was undoubtedly packed with a number of essential items, it didn't look large enough to contain anything as powerful as the thing she'd described. "Where is it, exactly?"

She surprised him by laughing softly as she shook her head. "You are in no way prepared to hear this,, but I promise you it is the absolute truth. The Last Chance Saloon itself *is* the Infinity Engine."

Ned opened his mouth to respond, but found himself temporarily at a loss for words. He stared at Raven in puzzled, silent confusion a moment longer as the commotion inside the saloon became increasingly more frantic. A few men raced up the stairs to have a look at the stuck horse while others attempted to calm hysterical saloon girls. One man chose to use the general state of chaos as an excuse to aggressively grope one of the girls. Another girl saw it happening and cracked a bottle over his head, sending him unconscious to the floor. Both women then proceeded to stomp the man repeatedly on his head. No one bothered to stop them. Meanwhile, the battering of the building increased in intensity, the entire structure seeming to sway.

"I don't understand," Ned said at last, squinting at her as the boards shifted beneath his feet. "The Last Chance is just a building. A saloon. An ordinary place. What you're saying makes no sense."

Raven smiled. "It only seems that way because you lack the context and knowledge to understand. Here, in this timeline and in this version of this world, this building functions as a saloon. And, yes, it looks like one, but you're only seeing the outer layer draped over the framework of a far more complex structure, parts of which aren't even visible to the human eye. The outer layer you perceive can absorb physical damage. Windows can be shattered. Doors can be smashed open. But the underlying framework cannot be destroyed." She laughed again at his bewildered, uncomprehending expression. "Come now, Ned. I told you earlier—tonight's showdown isn't happening here by random chance."

Ned grunted. "You've kept things from me, though. *Lied* to me."

Raven's smile faded. "Of course I kept things from you. You wouldn't have understood. But I never outright lied. And you wouldn't have gone along with any of this if you'd known the full truth."

Ned's guts clenched. "Which is?"

She sighed. "The edifice you know as the Last Chance Saloon was built upon a convergence of natural energy lines, a juncture of rare, raw power. From within these walls, literally anything is possible with the right knowledge. Instant travel within countless millions of alternate realities, with an ease far beyond even my current capabilities. Travel through time. And only in a place like this can a thing like Doyle be killed. All that's needed is the fuel necessary to overdrive the engine."

For the first time since their initial meeting, Ned felt wary in Raven's presence. He glanced around. No one was watching them or eavesdropping on their conversation. Well, there was *one* person with his eye on them. Doc Richardson looked like he was trying to make his way over here, but he was moving slowly, as if having some form of physical difficulty. Not surprising, given everything the man had been through today.

Ned met Raven's gaze again. "What sort of fuel?"

Her face was a blank canvas now, no trace of emotion. "The Infinity Engine's energy core is being overdriven as we speak, by draining the souls of the dead and dying in this town, as well as from the souls of all the men and women in this room who will soon also perish. Vanquishing monsters invariably requires a great sacrifice, Ned. In order to destroy this particular monster, your town has to die."

"You," Ned croaked, barely able to push the word out through the lump in his throat. He swallowed hard and tried again to give voice to the rage rising up inside him. "Evil has come to this town. That much is true. But it's you, isn't it? You're the evil one. Not Doyle."

Raven shook her head, her expression turning weary. "I'm not evil, Ned, not in the greater scheme of things. I'm sorry you feel that way, but I won't apologize for anything I've done. And you're wrong. Doyle *is* evil. He's murdered entire worlds in the name of eluding justice. Given the chance, he'll annihilate many more worlds. A few thousand must die tonight to save billions more in the future. It's a terrible but necessary thing. Surely you must see that."

Ned sneered. "This is my town you're talking about,

lady. My friends. My neighbors. The place I've called home for a lot of years now. To hear you say it, all that means not one goddamn thing. We're insignificant. Well, pardon me if I happen to disagree."

He took out his gun and pointed it at her face.

Her expression hardened. "What do you think you're doing, Ned?"

He indicated the entrance with a tilt of his chin. "That howling wind out there. These vibrations. That's the engine causing all that, isn't it?"

She nodded. "It generates a massive disturbance in the space-time continuum when overdriven."

Ned cocked the hammer of his Peacemaker. "Shut the goddamn thing off."

Raven shook her head. "I can't. Not until the cycle is complete."

Ned had no idea what she meant by that and was about to say so when a gunshot rang out from close range.

Russ Harper was still shut away in his room upstairs when all the noise started up outside. Whatever the nature of the disturbance, it sounded positively cataclysmic. Under ordinary circumstances, he might feel compelled to leave the room and investigate, but he had a delicate situation on his hands. The bed was jammed up against the door to prevent anyone from getting inside, although so far no one had tried, which was really surprising given the amount of crashing around that happened after Charlotte seemingly turned into some kind of demon and tried to kill him.

The bitch stabbed him almost as soon as they were alone in his room earlier, and for a fleeting, terrible moment it looked like he'd be biting the dust right there and then. Fortunately for him, something primal in his brain kicked into action the instant the pain lit up his nerve-endings. He grabbed her by the wrist before she could retract the knife, and with his free hand he punched her in the face with all the strength he could muster. An odd thing happened when that punch connected. Her head snapped backward and stayed there, tilted at an unnatural angle. At the same time, some type of gooey, gloppy substance popped out of the back of her neck and landed with a splat on the floor. She started clawing at the back of her head with one hand while the other maintained its grip on the knife lodged in his abdomen. A lot of hissing and hacking sounds started coming out of her throat. It was all very strange, but Russ knew his survival depended on pressing whatever advantage he'd just gained, so he wound up and punched her again.

This time his fist connected with the tip of her chin. He let go of her wrist and her hand came away from the knife's handle as she went flying backward. The knife was still lodged inside him as she crashed against the bed and immediately bounced back up again. Crashing against the bed had the effect of popping her head forward again, as he saw when she came rushing at him with a crazed look in her demoness eyes. The head, however, did not look stable in its perch atop her shoulders, wobbling about as she ran forward with her arms outstretched.

Before she could reach him, he plucked the blade from his flesh and jabbed it into one of her eyes. She made a sound like a partially muffled screech, its volume apparently inhibited by damage inside her throat. She grabbed onto him and he held onto the knife in her eye as they violently danced about the room in a mad parody of a ballroom dance. This continued until he managed to slam her against one of the walls and drive the knife deeper into her eyeball, eliciting another guttural screech punctuated by a series of strange clicking sounds. She clawed at him, scratching his face and drawing blood as he worked to extricate the large, serrated blade from her ocular tissue.

A chunk of the eyeball adhered to the blade when he finally managed to twist it free.

He immediately tried to stab her again—this time in the throat, as that was clearly an even more vulnerable area than it would normally be—but she managed to get her hands braced against his chest and shoved him away. The maneuver sent him hurtling across the room, causing him to collide with the little side table next to the bed. Evidently not an especially sturdy piece of furniture, the table crumpled beneath him and he dropped with it to the floor. He slid off the pile of debris and rolled onto his back in time to see Charlotte coming at him again, launching herself at him like a woman leaping off a cliff into a lake. There was no time to roll out of the way, but he was able to get the blade turned upward in time for her to fall upon it, impaling herself. She screeched gutturally again and tried to bite his throat. Her teeth pierced his flesh, but he wrenched his head away before she could tear open his jugular vein.

She laughed in a croaky graveyard way. "Give up and die, Russ."

He sneered. "Never."

This was only outward bravado, defiant reflex. In truth, he feared he was close to defeat. She possessed an unnatural level of strength for a woman of her size and build. It was like wrestling with a bear with nice tits. He still didn't quite comprehend exactly what was happening, except that there was definitely something extra-normal about it. At a loss for what else to do, he gave the knife stuck in her guts a savage twist. Her body convulsed as she screeched in pain, allowing him the leverage he needed to shove her off of him.

He scrambled away from her and took a frantic look around before spying his bedroll. Grabbing it, he lurched to his feet and dropped it on the bed. Once he had it spread open, he was quickly able to locate the item he wanted. His hand closed around the handle of the hatchet just as he heard Charlotte get to her feet again.

"You hurt me," that guttural voice said, sounding more enraged and venomous than ever. "You're going to pay for that."

He turned around and swung the hatchet. The timing was perfect as the heavy blade chopped through her neck a fraction of a second before she could reach him. Decapitating her only took the one hack thanks to the already damaged condition of her neck. Her head tumbled away from her body and he fully expected that to be the end of it, but this was quickly revealed as an erroneous assumption.

The headless body kept coming at him and soon had its hands wrapped tightly around his throat. He gurgled in surprise as he frantically started swinging the hatchet again. Within seconds, he'd separated one of her arms from her body, but the hand remained clamped to his throat, fingers pressing tighter and tighter. He wasn't able to start prying it loose until he'd also hacked off the other arm, at which point he dropped the hatchet and staggered about the room. Clamping his hands around the wrists of Charlotte's dismembered arms, he flung himself about and bounced off the walls multiple times before he was finally able to tear the hands free.

After tossing the arms away, he paused for a moment to suck in several deep, ragged breaths. Standing with his hands braced on his legs, he happened to notice the blood leaking from the wound in his abdomen.

Gonna have to do something about that.

Then he glanced up and saw the headless, armless torso coming at him.

He groaned.

Goddammit.

He dodged a kick as he dashed past what was left of Charlotte and scooped the hatchet off the floor. It was time to stop messing around and eliminate this threat once and for all. He went into a frenzied state, hacking and hacking away at the saloon girl turned monster until her body was in a lot of pieces on the floor and finally incapable of assaulting him in any manner. The weird thing was how the many pieces of her were all still animated, twitching and writhing about ineffectually. There was no way any living person or creature could take that much damage and survive. He could only conclude she wasn't alive but instead was in a state of undeath. Or perhaps she'd died earlier and had somehow been reanimated. The latter possibility made him think of Mary Shelley's *Frankenstein*, which had long been one of his favorite novels.

In the aftermath of the struggle, he found himself feeling fatigued almost to the point of passing out. His eyelids drooped and his head felt heavy. Realizing unconsciousness was looming whether he liked it or not, he hauled the bed across the room and jammed it against the door. His hope was this would prevent anyone from walking in and seeing the mess he'd made of Charlotte while he was passed out. Once this was accomplished, he fell upon the bed, positioning a pillow beneath his abdominal wound in the last seconds before the world went black.

Hours had passed by the time he awakened. A glimpse of the dark sky visible through the window in his room made that obvious. It wasn't full dark yet, but it was getting close. The pillow was stuck to his abdomen as he pushed himself up from the bed. Grimacing as he peeled it away, he was grateful to see he was no longer bleeding freely from the knife wound. The pillow was soaked with blood. Looking at it, he realized how fortunate he was to have gotten it pressed up against the wound before drifting away. Also fortunate was how the blade seemed somehow not to have nicked anything vital, which he figured was pretty goddamn miraculous.

LAST OF THE RAVAGERS

Until, that is, Doyle started speaking in his head, filling him in on some things, such as how he was dead now, having bled out from the abdominal wound. The first intrusion of the voice was a shock, as was the revelation of his death. Also shocking was learning he now existed helplessly in thrall to Doyle, the Lord of the Dead.

Doyle gave Russ a mission.

One he best not fail if he didn't wish to spend eternity in hellish torment.

Russ retrieved the knife that'd been used to kill him. He then pulled the bed away from the door and stepped out into the hallway, one end of which was embroiled in chaos. A knot of onlookers stood outside a room a few doors down to his right, jostling for a better look at what was happening inside. He heard the distressed whinnying of a horse in pain, a sound that brought with it a pang of sorrow. Hearing any animal in pain was a terrible thing. Seconds after exiting his room, he heard multiple booms from a shotgun. The whinnying became even more distressed after the first boom but ceased thereafter. He could make no sense of what was happening down there, but it was none of his concern.

He had a mission to fulfill.

He turned away from the scene of chaos and hurried down the shorter hallway branch, descending the staircase there to the brothel's back door. Some heavy pieces of furniture were jammed up against it, presumably as a hurriedly assembled barricade. Two men with rifles stood near the pile of furniture, serving as defense backup should the barrier be breached. The guards made the crucial error of assuming he was on their side since he'd come to them from within the saloon. That changed when he got close enough that they could see the blood all over him, but by then it was too late. He launched himself at them before they could bring their weapons to bear, stabbing both men numerous times with only a single errant shot being fired.

BRYAN SMITH

The dead men reanimated minutes later, awakening to find themselves controlled by Doyle. Working together, Russ and the ex-guards hauled the heavy furniture pieces away from the back door.. Then Russ opened the door and let in a stream of Doyle's little blue friends.

THIRTY-FOUR

THE GUNSHOT WAS fired from only a few feet away, so overwhelming loud at that range it made Ned feel as if he'd been hit square in the back with a sledgehammer. He lurched forward and fell into Raven's arms. She grabbed hold of him to keep him upright and just for an instant he felt like he was back in that cell with her. He looked into her breathtakingly beautiful blue eyes and felt a powerful echo of that same passion. Then he flinched again as a second close-range shot rang out, followed immediately by yet another, that big sound hammering painfully at his ears.

Raven gripped him tighter each time the gun roared and for a few strangely disconnected moments it was almost possible to forget she'd just confessed to orchestrating slaughter on a mass scale. Another part of him spent those same moments waiting to feel pain from the gunshots. He was certain he'd been hit, but the expected lash of searing agony never came. A brief moment of physical self-assessment followed. As best he could tell, no bullets had perforated his flesh. In another few seconds, he became aware of other sounds beyond the ringing in his ears.

Sounds of frantic struggle.

Ned disengaged himself from Raven and turned around to see Billy Conway and Steve Dickinson wrestling with Doc Richardson. A knife was gripped in one of the doctor's hands. Its blade was stained bright red with blood. Dickinson had a slash wound across one of his cheeks and Billy had a shallower cut along his jawline. These wounds, however, were insignificant and superficial in comparison to Richardson, who appeared to have been shot multiple times, including once in the jaw. Currently the bloody blade was pointed straight up in the air as both men struggled to get the manic doctor under control and pry the weapon loose. Billy's pistol—with the "Big Boomer" scrollwork along the barrel—was on the floor, either having been knocked loose or dropped in favor of an attempt at physical containment. The younger men were having a much harder time subduing the middle-aged physician than Ned would've expected. Richardson, in fact, looked on the verge of shaking himself loose.

The doctor's violent outburst left Ned dumbfounded. It seemed to have come out of nowhere. Not only that, but a man who'd been through the type of severe physical trauma he'd endured today shouldn't be capable of putting up this much of a fight. He sure as hell shouldn't still be on his feet after being shot so many times. Ned just couldn't figure it out.

Until it all abruptly snapped together in his head.

He groaned.

Aw, shit. Goddammit, Doc.

Ned felt a hand on his shoulder. He was about to glance backward when Raven roughly moved him out of her way and aimed the big barrel of her gun at Albert Richardson's face. Fire leapt from the big muzzle of the strange gun as it sent one of those oversized rounds hurtling right at Doc's forehead. The bullet punched through his brow at dead center and blew out the back of his head. A handful of people standing several feet away gasped in shock and disgust as they were hit by a wave of blood and brain matter.

Doc dropped to the floor and didn't move.

LAST OF THE RAVAGERS

Everybody stood around in silent shock for a moment. Outside, the wind continued to roar and batter the building, which was vibrating so hard now it felt in imminent danger of flying apart, despite what Raven had said about the indestructibility of the underlying structure.

Billy stared at Raven in a look of open-mouthed amazement. Then he shook his head and said, "Where do I get me some of them magic goddamn bullets? Mine didn't work worth a lick."

Before she could respond, the door at the top of the staircase burst open, instantly drawing everyone's attention in that direction. Screams rang out as a few men bearing firearms and other weapons came thundering down the stairs accompanied by a parade of the little blue creatures with the stout bodies and weird heads. Many of the creatures didn't wait to reach the bottom of the stairs before attacking the people in the saloon, instead flinging themselves over the bannister into the crowd. More screams filled the air as the creatures opened their mouths wide, revealing the many rings of rotating, whirring, gnashing fangs.

Those fangs tore into vulnerable human flesh with brutal, unstoppable efficiency, that awful grinding sound becoming almost as loud as the accompanying screams. Flesh was shredded. Limbs torn loose and tossed across the room. Numerous instantaneous disembowelments happened, with strands of guts soon draped over seemingly everything like gory Christmas decorations. Gunfire rang out as the armed men in the saloon fought back with everything they had, wounding and perhaps even killing a few of the blue bastards before it became clear the situation was hopeless.

There were just too many of them.

As the melee unfolded, Raven dragged Ned in the direction of the bar, with Billy following along behind them. He tried resisting at first, believing he should stand

and fight with the few surviving men and women of Snakebite, but he soon saw it was pointless. There'd be no saving any of these people, a realization as bitter as any he'd ever experienced, but denying it was impossible. They slipped behind the bar, where they found Quentin Brown hunkered down on the floor. In one hand, he held a pistol that was an exact duplicate of the one owned by Raven. Gripped in his other hand was the iron ring for opening the cellar door. One of the blue creatures was lying still under the bar, with the back of its head blown open. Wisps of smoke were still wafting from the muzzle of Quentin's gun.

Ned frowned when he saw it. "Where'd you get that?"

"Never mind where he got it," Raven said, scooting closer to the cellar door while keeping her head below the level of the bar. "I'll explain in a few minutes, if we're still alive by then."

A liquor bottle came sailing over the top of the bar and shattered against the wall behind them, raining glass shards and foul-smelling cheap liquor down upon them. This set off a chain reaction of more exploding bottles and soon the inside of the saloon began to smell like a distillery in addition to smelling like an abattoir. Those few remaining citizens of Snakebite still alive were either out of bullets or couldn't take the time to reload without getting devoured, thus they resorted to grabbing and fighting with whatever was in reach.

Quentin pulled on the iron ring and the cellar door creaked as he lifted it up. Raven was the first to drop through the rectangular opening in the floor, her boots thumping down the wooden stairs in the darkness below. Billy was the first to follow when Ned hesitated, disappearing into the darkness within seconds.

Ned looked Quentin in the eye. "Who are you, really?"

The barkeep's expression was grim but tinged with sympathy. "I'm who I've always been. Your friend. I'm also the Overseer."

LAST OF THE RAVAGERS

"The what?"

Quentin shook his head. "No time. Down you go."

Bracing the door open with a shoulder, he grabbed Ned and shoved him through the opening. Once through it, he hit the staircase without first gaining proper footing and tumbled painfully downward. At the same time, Quentin raised his gun and fired at two of the blue things as they came over the top of the bar. One bullet found its mark and the creature's head exploded like a bag of blue paint. The other hissed and flashed its front row of fangs as it leapt at him.

Quentin Brown dropped into the floor opening, allowing the door to flap shut overhead.

The last of the Ravagers stood at the far end of Main Street. He wore a long duster over his clothes and had a wide-brimmed hat pulled down low over his eyes. Dust and debris swirled around him as the hurricane-force winds ripped the town apart. A wagon wheel came flying straight at his head, but it struck the invisible protective bubble he'd woven around himself and went sailing off in another direction. The bubble would move with him whenever he was ready to start walking down the street toward the Last Chance Saloon. It would, unfortunately, cease to exist once he was inside the saloon itself, his magic weakened by being so close to the core of the Infinity Engine. By then, at least, the bubble would've served its purpose of sheltering him from the maelstrom.

There was still a chance he might choose not to approach the saloon at all and instead hop into some other reality, thereby delaying the inevitable moment of reckoning with Raven Decker a while longer. For a year or a hundred years, perhaps. He could put it off for a thousand years or longer if he wished, though that would require great diligence on his part, because Raven would never cease tracking him across the realms.

She was an infamous figure in certain obscure circles, a relentless and tenacious hunter of Ravagers. She'd personally ended the lives of so many powerful necromancers, taking that power for herself when she consumed their souls. In the interest of staying roughly on the same level as Raven, he embarked on a quest to kill as many of his own kind as he could. The society of dark wizards soon caught on to his game and started hunting him as well. This went on for countless centuries, until he was the only remaining Ravager. He hated Raven for the way she'd forced him into aiding in the destruction of his people, but he feared her as well. She was the only living creature who might feasibly kill him under the right conditions, and he had no interest in a direct confrontation with her unless he felt absolutely certain of emerging victorious.

Thus far that had not happened.

Nor did he feel any such certainty now. Jumping out of this world would undoubtedly be the prudent thing to do.. What stayed his hand was knowing this might be the best shot he'd ever get at eliminating her. The thing that made this moment of near confrontation so different from all the others was the presence of the Infinity Engine.

He'd spent a large part of his unfathomably long life doubting it even existed, but now he knew otherwise. It was here in this nothing little village in one of the most miserably backward and unremarkable realities he'd ever visited, in the middle of a desert where only the foolhardiest of mortals would choose to live. In a way, the location was amusing. The engine's ancient builders must've had quite the sense of humor, putting it in such a forbidding environment.

If he could somehow eliminate Raven and seize control of the most powerful machine ever assembled, there would be no limit to what he could do. Assuming the old stories passed on by his teachers so long ago were true, he who controlled the Infinity Engine would control existence itself. He could make or unmake worlds. Enslave billions or wipe away entire layers of reality. Bend the arc of history on any world in any direction he chose, a theoretical pursuit he suspected he'd find vastly entertaining. A parlor game of the gods.

Another possibility, however, held a much greater allure. Again, if what he'd been taught was correct, in theory one could harness the power of the Infinity Engine to scrub away all traces of a person's existence across all layers of reality. He could entirely *unmake* Raven Decker. It would be as if she'd never lived at all. Even alternate versions of Raven in other realities—ones that never became hunters or acquired anything like the power she possessed—would be removed, forever eliminating the chance of another rising to take the place of the primary Raven.

It was so tempting to start walking down the street and just have it out with her, engage in one last apocalyptic battle with all the magical resources at their fingertips. Yes, she was fearsomely powerful, but so was he. There was a chance he could best her in such a contest. A *good* chance. But that lack of absolute guarantee remained daunting. He didn't want to lose. Didn't want to vanish into the void forever.

He didn't want to be *unmade*.

As the self-styled Lord of the Dead, he remained attuned to the souls of those whose lives he or his minions had killed here. A short while ago, there'd been so many, but their number was dwindling. Some were carried away and smashed to pieces by the furious wind. Others were perishing in the battle taking place inside the Last Chance Saloon. Some freshly acquired souls would frequently replace ones he'd lost, but then they were extinguished as well, devoured by the overdriven core of the engine. He felt Russ Harper blink out of existence after killing almost a dozen men and women. The loss of the man didn't trouble Doyle. Only one of tonight's losses bothered him in the least. He'd taken such great pride in corrupting Eleanor McKinley so thoroughly. The best part was he'd barely had to try. A monster had lurked inside her all along, waiting and hoping for the right excuse to be set free. Her abrupt end was regrettable, but there was nothing to be done about it now. Well . . . almost nothing.

With the Infinity Engine, he could bring her back.

They could rule all of existence together for eternity, luxuriating in unparalleled extremes of decadence and depravity.

It would be glorious.

Unfortunately, he could still feel Raven out there somewhere. They were attuned to each other in another way, a psychic link forged by devouring the souls of so many powerful necromancers. It was why he was always on the run, and why he always tried to stay several steps ahead of her. She'd caught up with him, though, and he felt every atom of his corporeal form vibrate with terror just from being so close to her.

He was so tired of being chased.

But he didn't want to die.

With a pang of regret, he began to summon the magic necessary to jump across the realms. He held his hands out with his fingers extended, drawing in energy from the elements. The fabric of this reality began to soften, but then he became aware of something astonishing.

Of something he could no longer feel.

He clenched his hands into tight fists and ceased summoning the magic.

Concentrating with every fiber of his being, he reached out into the world around him and tried to feel her out there, but she was gone.

LAST OF THE RAVAGERS

Raven was gone, her spark extinguished.

He knew from much past experience they could not shield that spark from each other at such close range, which could only mean she'd died or jumped to another realm. The latter seemed unlikely. Raven Decker did not run from fights. Her death seemed incredible and unlikely, but there was no trace of her. He supposed she might've expired in battle with his minions. The possibility was hard to fathom given how strong she was, but perhaps she'd let her guard down at the wrong moment. She was flesh and blood, after all, technically a mortal despite a life prolonged across centuries by magic. So it was possible.

She might really be dead.

Doyle lingered in indecision at the far end of Main Street a while longer.

Then, knowing he might never have a chance like this again, he started walking.

Ned stirred at the bottom of the staircase after blacking out a few moments. He was in a lot of pain as he sat up groaning, but in a few moments he realized he was basically okay on a physical level. He was banged up pretty good and he could tell he would have a gimpy knee for a while—assuming he actually lived to see another day, that is—but nothing seemed broken.

The darkness into which he'd fallen was gone, banished by a brilliant light emanating from somewhere in the cellar. The light was so bright he had to squint as he began to get to his feet. Someone came over and gripped him by a hand, helping him up. Shielding his eyes against the glare, he saw that the person helping him was his deputy. Billy was squinting slightly as well, but there was an unmistakable look of stupefaction on his face. He started babbling something to Ned, but most of it went in one ear and out the other, because the sheriff of Snakebite was too stunned by what he was seeing.

Through some means Ned couldn't fathom, the interior of the cellar had expanded to twice its normal size. The gleaming, silvery walls appeared formed from perfectly smooth metal. There was no trace of the rotting clay-brick walls Ned had seen every time he'd ever ventured into the saloon's cellar, including this morning. How such a radical change had occurred in so short a time, Ned couldn't imagine and figured it was beyond his understanding anyway.

A thrumming noise commenced as the back wall—silvery metallic like the others—began to retract, sliding into some hidden recess. As the wall rolled away, the cellar began to fill with an even brighter light, the source of which was something that had been hidden behind the wall.

Shielding his eyes with a hand, Ned moved a few steps closer. He glimpsed Raven in his peripheral vision, standing off to the side and watching him with a blank expression. There were some choice words he wanted to spew at her, but for the moment he was too entranced by the simultaneously wondrous and terrifying things happening in the cellar. Quentin was standing next to her, the oversized gun he'd produced from seemingly nowhere holstered at his hip. Ned had so many questions for the son of a bitch, but they would have to wait for another time, assuming any of them were still alive later.

What the wall revealed as it retracted was a bank of inexplicable machines packed tightly against each other, standing floor to ceiling. Parts of the strange machinery moved, rotating in one direction for a while before reversing in the other direction. Lights of various colors blinked in a series of ever-changing patterns. All of the machinery was bathed in a golden glow of light from some unseen source. Once the wall was fully retracted, another thrumming noise commenced, a gap forming between two of the machines in the middle. The gap widened until it was approximately four feet across. Within this new space was only a deep blackness. A blackness that looked . . . sticky. Just looking at it made Ned feel queasy.

He looked at Raven. "What is this?"

She moved closer to him, almost to within touching range. "I know I've put you through a lot already, Ned, but there's one more thing I need from you."

He sneered, shaking his head. "I'm not doing shit for you, lady, not after killing the whole damn town."

Billy, who was standing nearby, tore his gaze away from the bank of golden-hued machinery and looked at them. "What's this about killing the town? Ain't Doyle the one responsible for this mess?"

Ned sighed. "Turns out things are a damn sight more complicated than that. You see, this lady right here." He nodded at Raven. "And that mysterious sumbitch outside somewhere are in cahoots together to some extent."

Raven frowned. "That's not true. *Doyle's*, evil. I'm—"

Ned waved off her protest with a flip of his hand. "Yeah, yeah, I'm not interested in your justifications. Might all be lies and bullshit for all I know." His gaze shifted to Quentin Brown, who was observing with a look of intent expectancy. "And what's *your* story, Mr. Overseer? This whole damn day we've been dealing with crazy shit we didn't understand, except that's not really completely true, is it? Seems you knew exactly what was happening all along and never saw fit to clue us in."

Quentin shook his head. "Only partly true, Ned. I didn't understand the full import of what was happening until Raven showed up. Even afterward, there's only so much I'm allowed to say or do without breaking protocol."

Ned scoffed at this, shaking his head in disgust. "Says who?"

Quentin shrugged. "The previous Overseer. The one who recruited me and brought me here from my world."

Billy did a double-take as he turned toward Quentin. "Hold on. You're from some other damn world? Not this one we live in right here?"

"Nope."

Billy scowled. "So all those stories you told me about your childhood in New York City were pure bullshit?"

Quentin grunted as he shrugged again. "Only partly bullshit. The stories were largely true, but I, uh, changed some details."

Billy laughed, a sound fraught with derision and more than a little bitterness. "'Changed some details,' the man says." Billy glanced at Ned, nostrils flaring as he snorted laughter again. "Can you believe the lying horseshit coming out of this man's mouth?"

Raven interjected before Ned could respond, moving closer again, until they were only about two feet apart. "You two need to stifle your indignation and shut the fuck up. We don't have time for this. Doyle might decide to jump to another reality any second now."

She took out her gun and jammed the muzzle of it under his chin.

Billy reached for Big Boomer but found his holster empty, grimacing as he realized the pistol had gone missing again. Though he was unarmed, Quentin drew his weapon and pointed it at Billy's head.

"Careful, son. I don't want to have to hurt you."

Billy leveled a lethal, slit-eyed stare at him. "Got-damn sumbitch."

Raven ignored them as she grabbed Ned by the front of his shirt and began steering him toward the freshly open deep black space between the banks of glowing machinery. He resisted at first, his heart beating harder at the prospect of entering that sticky blackness, which almost seemed to be reaching for him the closer they got to it, tendrils of darkness stretching outward into the cellar. In another second or two, he realized this was no optical illusion fueled by a brain overridden with terror. The darkness really was reaching for them, the tendrils stretching farther and farther into the room. He tried planting his feet to halt their progress toward the blackness, but Raven just jammed the muzzle of the big gun harder against his chin and kept pushing.

He had tears in his eyes when he met her gaze. "Don't put me in there. Please."

Her expression remained grim as the darkness began to envelop them. "We're both going in, Ned. Don't be afraid. This will be over soon."

Then the smothering darkness took them and the world went away for a while.

An indeterminate time later, they came out of the darkness and back into the bright light of the cellar. Ned recalled nothing of what transpired while they were in the darkness, but he was all-too-cognizant of the end result.

Raven's warm body hung limp in his arms, but he was no longer controlling those arms, having become a powerless passenger inside his own shell of flesh and blood. Another consciousness was at the helm now, directing every physical action that occurred. The terror he'd experienced prior to being enveloped by the sticky blackness was dwarfed by what he felt now. He feared some demon had seized control until that other consciousness communicated with him for the first time.

It was Raven.

The revelation came as only a slight relief. He was glad a demon hadn't taken up residence in his head, but the reality wasn't much better as far as he was concerned. The communication between Ned and Raven did not occur in the form of a conventional conversation. There was no back and forth exchange of questions and answers. She instead fed him information through a limited access neural link between their minds. Awareness of the basic facts of the situation entered his mind abruptly, arriving like a set of forgotten memories surging to the surface. Raven was in control.

The transfer of her consciousness into his brain had indeed been facilitated by their time inside that black space, which was no empty void but was instead the powerful core of the Infinity Engine. The sticky blackness inside the core was the fuel of creation in its rawest form. Immersion in the core for any length of time was extremely dangerous, but for those with the necessary knowledge it provided a means of accomplishing things that would otherwise not be possible. Things, for instance, like the transfer of a consciousness from one body to another.

There was method to the madness.

She'd performed the transfer in an effort to dupe Doyle into thinking she was dead. Because of the palpable link that existed between them when they were so near each other, he would immediately know should the spark of life inside her physical form be snuffed out.

There was one crucial fact Raven held in reserve until after gingerly laying her unconscious body on the floor. She only allowed him awareness of it after she used his hand to remove the oversized pistol from the holster strapped to her hip. A deep sense of horror engulfed him as she made his body stand and then used his hand to aim the gun at her face, the relaxed features of which displayed an illusory appearance of relaxed calmness.

Billy started yelling again, alarmed by what his eyes told him was happening. He appeared on the verge of interfering, but Quentin pointed his gun at him again and he stayed where he was.

In a state of panic, Ned tried hard to reassert control of his body, an effort that didn't amount to much more than concentrating as hard as he could. He experienced despair as Raven used his finger to begin exerting pressure on the trigger of her gun. Despite having used the people of his town as sacrificial pawns, he didn't want her to die. He didn't know why. He should hate her for the terrible things she'd done. Regardless, the desire to save her was real.

For the first time since the transference, she sent a direct thought into his mind: *Relax, Ned. This is the only way. Besides, I'll still be in here with you.*

The big gun boomed and the top of Raven's head blew open.

Her body twitched and expired.

Raven looked at Quentin through Ned's eyes. "Unlock the hatch. Let the bastard in."

As expected, the protective bubble of magic dissolved within seconds of Doyle entering the Last Chance Saloon. At some point the wind had blown the saloon's boarded-up inner door off its hinges. The door had splintered into pieces as it was thrown across the room, with some of those pieces becoming embedded in bodies. Interestingly, however, the wind's power felt dampened inside the saloon, robbed of its hurricane force and reduced to little more than a strong gust. He assumed the damping effect was something to do with the Infinity Engine, though he found it amusing that the engine's creators would build in some means of protecting this structure's interior while apparently not caring one whit for any destruction caused outside its walls once started.

He swept open his duster and put a hand on the butt of the gun holstered to his hip, ready to draw the weapon and start firing at the first sign of trouble. Doyle wasn't in love with firearms despite their crude destructive power, but on occasion a gun was a faster way of responding to threats than magic, especially when they popped up suddenly and without warning. After standing just inside the doorway for almost a full minute, however, he took his hand away from the gun and relaxed.

No one was alive in here.

No humans and none of his transmogrified minions. Losing all the minions was unfortunate, but at some point after he was finished here he would be able to reconstitute some of them through ritual magic. Perhaps even all of them should he manage to properly harness the power of the Infinity Engine.

The scene inside the saloon was one of spectacular carnage. Bodies and pieces of bodies—human and minion alike—were strewn everywhere. Doyle saw piles of them in some places. There were great swaths of red and blue blood all over the place, as well as pools of blood on the floor. A saloon girl's head was on the floor at his feet. He picked it up and peered into the dead, unseeing eyes for a moment. Nothing there. Sometimes he could look into the eyes of the recently dead and detect some lingering, fading spark, but not this time. The lady's soul energy had been sucked into the revving heart of the Infinity Engine. Doyle kissed the head's dead lips and laughed as he tossed it away.

Stepping over limbs and bodies, he moved into the center of the room and spent a few moments trying to discern the engine's likeliest point of access. To his left was a badly damaged staircase, presumably leading to a second floor where the working girls plied their wares. He doubted he'd find the access point anywhere up there. An underground location struck him as far more likely. His gaze settled on the bar and in a moment he began to smile again. He stepped over more bodies as he made his way over there, excitement growing inside him as he continued to detect no lingering traces of Raven Decker.

Behind the bar he spied the outline of a cellar door cut into the floor. The excitement consuming him became overwhelming. He rushed to the door, grasped the iron ring, and hauled it upright, peering into the brightly lit space below. It was so bright he realized the source of the illumination couldn't possibly be anything like a lantern or gas lamp. This was electric light from some source not of this primitive era. He became almost giddy. There could be no doubt he'd found what he was looking for.

Before descending into the cellar, however, he drew his weapon from its holster. With Raven removed from the equation, there was no one left in all of existence even close to as powerful as he was. Still, with this ultimate, long-coveted prize almost within his grasp, remaining cautious just a short while longer would be wise.

He let out a breath and went down to the cellar.

Even before arriving at the bottom of the staircase, it was evident no one was down here lying in wait to attack him. Along the back wall was the golden-hued ancient machinery he assumed directed the Infinity Engine's more mundane mechanical processes. The real power here lay somewhere within that wide black space in the middle. He could feel that power reaching out to him, making his flesh tingle as he took a few more cautious steps toward it.

A woman's body lay on the floor only a few feet away from that black space. Not a living person, but a corpse. That much was clear from the massive wound to the top of the person's head, which was surrounded by a halo of blood and brain matter. Doyle believed the dead woman was Raven, but he wasn't certain until he was standing directly over her. So much time had passed since he'd last set eyes on her, but not so much time that he failed to recognize her.

There could be no doubt now.

This was her.

Raven.

The bane of his existence for what seemed like forever. The diabolical bitch who'd hunted him across galaxies and centuries, across so many countless realities. Mostly he'd managed to stay well ahead of her, but there'd been times when she'd come uncomfortably close to catching up to him. He never liked to admit weakness, even to himself, but on a few of those occasions he avoided death at her hands by the narrowest of margins.

And it was *terrifying* every time.

Well, no more.

She was *dead* and would hunt him no longer. Haunt him no longer. He began to laugh heartily as a rush of exhilaration surged through him. He was free now. Finally, really free. He could indulge in all his darkest impulses to his heart's content with no fear of ever facing a reckoning for any of it. The feeling gripping him now was the closest thing he'd felt to true happiness since the Ravagers were at the height of their power and influence. Those had been the best days of his life and she'd taken that from him.

Taken it from all of them. All his dead friends.

A savage notion seized him then, one that felt so decadently righteous he immediately knew he would have to act on it. He removed the duster and cast it aside. The hat followed. He groaned in anticipation as he drooled over her unmoving body, which was still so beautiful even in death. Raping her corpse would serve as an act of catharsis, as well as a form of post-mortem revenge, the only kind available to him now. He would do it for himself and in the name of all his dead colleagues, the ones she'd personally killed and the ones she'd forced him to kill just to keep up with her.

He was pulling his shirt off over his head when he felt something begin to coil around his midsection. A shock of terror ripped through him the instant he felt the touch. It felt alien and insidious, as if it wanted to possess and absorb him. Hurriedly ripping the shirt away, he flung it aside and looked down, screeching when he saw the strange black tendril wrapping around him. He screeched again when more tendrils suddenly appeared, holding him in place when he tried to tear himself loose. Becoming desperate, he reached for the gun he'd holstered just minutes ago, but another tendril curled around his wrist and stopped him. He tried focusing his will to summon magic, but the damping effect of the Infinity Engine prevented that. It wasn't until he saw that Raven's body was farther away that he realized he was being pulled into that black space behind him.

Doyle screamed.

He was terrified, but he was also furious. The bitch had tricked him. He didn't know precisely how she'd managed it, but he had no doubt of it now. The body on the floor was no illusion. His own abilities shielded him from ever being deceived by that particular form of trickery. No, she'd hatched some far more devious scheme, one that involved sacrificing herself to ensure its success. He'd never anticipated her taking such a drastic step, believing one so powerful must be interested in self-preservation above all other things.

Apparently, however, he'd been wrong.

About that and so much else.

He screamed one last time before the thickening tendrils pulled him all the way into the black place.

Consciousness went away for a while, just as it had the first time Raven forced him into the dark place. This time, however, his conscious mind did not stay submerged the entire time they were in there. Cognizance returned as yet another presence was drawn into the darkness. Terror tinged his awareness as he realized this new arrival was the creature called Doyle.

Ned couldn't see Doyle. Couldn't see anything, in fact. Nor did he experience anything like physical sensation, but the awareness of Doyle was there nonetheless. He felt the Ravager edging up against his thoughts like a dark malignancy, trying hard to get in and take control, but Raven was there and she was ready for him. Unlike the doomed Necromancer, she could work her magic inside the core of the Infinity Engine, although it was slightly weaker than normal. She was able to call on enough of it, however, to drag Doyle even deeper into the core and anchor him in place, beyond any hope of escape. Psychic waves of terror emanated from him endlessly.

Until, that is, the Infinity Engine began to do the work Raven intended.

Golden light displaced the darkness, enveloping them all.

Ned saw Doyle hanging inside the seemingly limitless golden-hued space, his flailing limbs tangled in sticky tendrils of light. A sense of terrible awe filled Ned as he watched the Ravager's shimmery form vibrate and distend. Without being told, he knew Doyle was in the process of being unmade.

As the light grew even brighter, Ned felt his own perceptions of reality shift and twist, sending his consciousness on a disorienting high-speed ride through some of reality's endlessly branching alternate levels and possibilities. He was himself as he traveled through all of them, the same consciousness or some permutation of it, but in some of those other places he had different names. He spent a few deliriously terrifying seconds behind the controls of an impossibly advanced machine that flew through the sky. In another place, he was a uniformed man patrolling the corridors of some nightmarishly massive prison. In still another place, he was a woman lying in a bed with a female lover. That version of him was contemplating killing her lover. He was gone from there before he could know why. For another few seconds, he was a black man running through a wooded area at night

LAST OF THE RAVAGERS

while hunting dogs and men in white hoods gave chase. Then he was a housewife making dinner for her family. The year was 1969. In this reality, his name was Claire. Claire was worried about her eldest daughter possibly turning into a hippie. After that, he was a young boy named Tom. Tom was reading something called a comic book about someone called Captain America.

Just when he felt certain the tour of alternate realities would obliterate what was his left of his rapidly fraying sanity, it stopped.

Everything went black again.

Some while later, consciousness once again returned.

Ned opened his eyes and stared at a white ceiling above him. His gaze shifted to a glowing rectangle in the middle of the ceiling. The rectangle was the main source of light in this new place. He held his breath a moment, waiting to be whisked away from it again, but that did not happen.

After more than a full minute passed, he sat up on the plush white sofa and looked around. He was in a strangely furnished space of modest size. On the opposite side of the room was a large wooden contraption of some sort, one comprised of sections of varying sizes. The largest section was right in the middle and occupying that part of the contraption was a box displaying moving images. From somewhere outside the confines of this space, he perceived an array of discordant noises, various bleatings and rumbles. He turned his head and saw a large sliding window overlooking a balcony.

Getting up, he started toward the window to take a look outside, but came to an abrupt stop when it hit him that he was again in full control of his body. He held out his hands and examined his clothes, heaving a sigh of relief upon discovering he was Ned again and not Claire or Tom or one of those others. He frowned as he reflected on that dizzying experience, questioning now whether any of it had been real at all.

He jumped a little when a woman came out of a short hallway to his left and said, "Hey there."

Ned gasped when he turned and looked at her. The woman was the spitting image of Raven Decker, only without a blown open head. Thank God. Also, her hair was styled in a vastly different way and she was wearing a dress of many colors with a hem that barely reached the mid-point of her thighs.

"Um . . . "

He had no idea how to process any of this.

The woman sighed. "It's me, Ned. Raven Decker."

He frowned. "But . . . you're dead."

She smirked. "Obviously not."

Ned opened his mouth and spent a few moments fumbling for something to say. There was so much he wanted to ask her. Eventually he settled for, "How is this possible?"

"The Infinity Engine, of course."

Lack of understanding was writ large on his face as he shook his head and waited for her to elaborate.

She sighed again. "You already know how it's possible. You're just refusing to accept it for some obstinate reason. Okay, look. There are countless alternate realities. In some of these realities are different versions of you. You know that already, I'm sure. Some of the other yous are so different you'd never objectively recognize them as being you. But somewhere out there are other versions of Ned Kilmister that are virtually indistinguishable from what we'll just go ahead and call the real thing. Do you begin to get the picture?"

Ned's brow creased. "So . . . this is another you?"

She shrugged. "I'm me, Ned. Raven goddamn Decker. But I've taken over the body of another Raven from a different reality, one that's an exact match of the one I regrettably had to sacrifice back in your world."

"So you killed this other Raven? Or no . . . no . . . " The crease in his brow deepened, his mouth beginning to twist in a sneer. "She's a prisoner in her own head, just like I was."

She shook her head. "No. Not like that at all. This other Raven was essentially me, okay? Another version of me. I didn't kill or imprison her. Not exactly."

"What *did* you do?"

Another shrug. "I absorbed her into my own consciousness. Made her a part of me, essentially. Really, Ned, she's better off this way. This Raven was really kind of shallow. I mean, seriously, check out this fucking dress."

She swept her hands in a downward motion along the front of the dress.

Ned sighed.

He was tired of the argument and knew she would never see anything wrong in anything she'd done. She'd defeated a great evil. That much was true. But she was willfully blind to her own capacity for evil.

He glanced toward the window. "Where are we?"

"New York City. 1995. On a version of Earth where World War II never happened."

Ned stared blankly at her a moment before saying, "World *what?*"

She explained in great detail.

Ned rubbed his brow, feeling even wearier now. "Can you please just put me back in my world?"

"Nope." She laughed. "I mean, I *can*, but I don't want to. Not yet anyway. Look, I'm not saying let's stay here forever, but we've been through some shit, haven't we? So let's take a break from all that and chill here a while. Okay?"

He gave up upon hearing the unexpected note of plaintiveness in her voice.

"Okay."

She pulled him into an embrace and leaned into him. "We'll go somewhere more interesting before long, Ned, I promise. Maybe even have a bunch of crazy adventures together. If you want, of course. I won't force you. We could even go our separate ways if you'd rather. But I was thinking maybe I could talk you into one more wild time with me first."

She kissed him.

It lasted a while.

Breaking the clinch, she jerked her head in the direction of the hallway. "There's a bed back there that's far more comfortable than the cot in that nasty holding cell. Want to try it out?"

Ned still wasn't sure about her. He had a lot of thinking to do about some things. A *lot* of things, really.

But not about this.

He followed her down the hallway to the bedroom.

The last thing Billy Conway remembered was being down in the cellar under the Last Chance Saloon. Only the cellar wasn't really the cellar. It'd changed somehow. Through some kind of devil magic, maybe. He remembered Ned pointing the big gun at Raven's head. Something about the man seemed off in a way Billy couldn't quite put his finger on. More goddamn devil magic, he supposed. Then that turncoat sumbitch Quentin Brown conked him on the head and knocked his ass out. Now he was waking up, but he wasn't in the cellar anymore.

Billy sat up with a groan and took a look around

Quite a bit of time had passed since the confrontation in the cellar because it was daylight again. It was only early in the morning, though. He could tell because his face wasn't blistered red yet from the sun. He was sitting in the middle of the street outside the saloon, which from the look of things was the only building still standing in the vicinity. After getting creakily to his feet, he realized it might be the only building still standing in the entire town.

Surrounding him was a scene of utter devastation. The town was flattened, every building as far as the eye could see reduced to a pile of rubble. Debris filled the streets. There weren't really even streets anymore, when you got down to it. Then there were the piles of what he needed a minute to recognize as human remains. Not really bodies, because they'd all been torn to pieces. Just lumpy piles of random flesh with stray limbs strewn all about. It was a scene straight out of hell. Like something from one of Satan's wet dreams.

Billy went into the saloon and saw more of the same.

By this point, he didn't really expect to find Ned or anyone else still alive, but he went down to the cellar to check just the same. The cellar was back to being a regular old cellar again. He couldn't figure it out, but realizing no answers would be presenting themselves at any point soon, he climbed back out of the cellar. On a shelf behind the bar was one unopened and intact bottle of whiskey, the apparent lone survivor of last night's melee.

It was like a damn miracle.

He grabbed the bottle, uncorked it, and took a deep, refreshing swig. The liquor was of a rare quality for the Last Chance and tasted like God's own elixir as it slid down his gullet. Before taking the bottle away from his mouth, he heard an unexpected sound from the street.

The whinnying of a horse.

He went out of the saloon and saw a fine black stallion standing right outside, almost as if waiting specifically for him. Not only that, but it was fully kitted out, sporting what looked like a new saddle with multiple canteens, a rifle, and a bedroll. Where it had come from all of a sudden, he had no idea.

It was like magic or something.

He stepped off the porch and took another slug of whiskey as he scanned the area for any signs of someone missing a horse.

Nothing.

Just as he'd expected.

He approached the gift horse and looked it in the eye. "I'm gonna call you Abe. After ol' Honest Abe. That all right with you?"

The horse lifted its head and whinnied softly.

"Okay then."

Billy corked the whiskey bottle and climbed up into the saddle. He tucked the bottle away in a saddle bag and took hold of Abe's reins. "Come on, Abe. Let's get far away from this godforsaken pit of hell."

So that's what they did.

A little over a month later, Billy was back home in Georgia, where he remained for the rest of his days. Now and then in the years that followed his departure from Snakebite, he would think about that horse and wonder how it'd come to be outside the saloon that day. Mostly, though, he just let it slide. His was a peaceful life. A simple life of working the land.

No use troubling himself over things that shouldn't be.

ACKNOWLEDGEMENTS

A book like this one is the culmination of a lot of years of exposure to a wide range of weird and wild influences. It might not exist at all without seeing *The Good, The Bad and the Ugly* on TV as a kid in the 70's, or without reading Stephen King's *The Gunslinger* a few years later. Or without devouring the pulp novels Edgar Rice Burroughs. And then later having my innocent little mind utterly corrupted by Edward Lee, the forever reigning king of extreme horror. The later influence of Quentin Tarantino is also important. Throw all that formative stuff and a thousand other things in a blender and you just might wind up with something as deranged as *Last of the Ravagers.*

Thanks to cover artist extraordinaire Justin T. Coons for the awesome cover art, and to everyone at Death's Head Press for granting me the opportunity to wade into their playground and finally write a book like this. Patrick C. Harrison III, Jarod Barbee, and everyone else involved. Shout-outs to long-time loyal reader and friend Tod Clark, my brothers Jeff and Eric, Kristopher Triana, Ryan Harding, and C.V. Hunt and Andersen Prunty at Grindhouse Press, and my mom, Cherie Smith. I appreciate you all.

ABOUT THE AUTHOR

Bryan Smith is the Splatterpunk Award-winning author of more than thirty horror and crime novels and novellas, including *68 Kill*, the cult classic *Depraved* and its sequels, *The Killing Kind, Slowly We Rot, The Freakshow*, and many more. Bestselling horror author Brian Keene called *Slowly We Rot*, "The best zombie novel I've ever read." *68 Kill* was adapted into a motion picture directed by Trent Haaga and starring Matthew Gray Gubler of the long-running CBS series *Criminal Minds. 68 Kill* won the Midnighters Award at the SXSW film festival in 2017 and was released to wide acclaim, including positive reviews in *The New York Times* and Bloody Disgusting. Bryan also co-scripted an original Harley Quinn story for the *House of Horrors* anthology from DC Comics. In 2019, he won a Splatterpunk Award under the best novella category for *Kill For Satan!*